You Send Me

You Send Me

A Compass Cove Novel

Jeannie Moon

TULE
PUBLISHING

Dedication

To all the good men in the world. Thank you.

Dear Reader,

What makes a family? If you really think about it, it's so much more than a blood relation. It's a sense of belonging, and the security of knowing you're with your people—the ones who love you most of all. Throughout the course of *You Send Me*, Jordan learns that family is more than just a word. The bonds go much deeper. Because of this epiphany, when she's feeling most alone, Jordan comes to understand that her friends, neighbors and one very special doctor, are there for her no matter what.

Compass Cove is a place that embodies the idea of family, and to bring that concept to life, I pull from my own experiences. I'm fortunate to know that kind of love and support first hand, and I hope the story helped each of you feel a little bit closer to the people who love you best.

Jordan and Nick gave me fits from day one. I've never written a more stubborn couple, and many people need to be thanked for their part in this story. The Tule Publishing team is, without a doubt, the best in the publishing world. I am forever grateful to be part of such a wonderful family. Lisa Stone Hardt helped me see past the nose on my face, so I could really dig deep into this story. Thank you, my friend. I had a wonderful beta reader on this project, and I can't thank her enough. Alycia Corcoran, your input was wonderfully insightful. You have a storyteller's soul, and I have no doubt I'll be beta reading your book one day. Jennifer

Gracen polished my words to a spit shine, as she always does. Thanks, Jen! Finally, I have to thank reader Julie Fetter for giving Jordan's little Peagle, Gertie, her name. It's perfect, Julie…thanks!

I hope you all enjoy your visit to Compass Cove and that Jordan and Nick's love story will stay with you for a very long time.

xo
Jeannie

Compass Cove, Long Island, New York
f. 1667

In the year 1750, on the North Shore of Long Island, a young woman named Lucy Velsor mourned her beloved husband, who had been lost at sea. Not long after his death, his shipmates— hoping to comfort the young widow—brought her his compass. It was a finely crafted instrument, made by the local com- passsmith, whose family had settled the town of Compass Cove generations before. Lucy cherished the memento, taking care to kiss its face every day. One day, two years after her husband's death, the compass needle began to quiver and spin, never settling on a direction.

Desperate to have it fixed, Lucy brought it to the com- passsmith's shop. The shop's proprietor, Caleb Jennings, had loved Lucy from afar, never knowing if he should pay a call on the beautiful widow. But when Lucy set the compass in Caleb's hand, it stopped spinning and the needle pointed at him, stunning them both. Taking the compass' strange behavior as a sign, Caleb put aside his fears and began to court Lucy. It didn't take long for the couple to fall in love and marry. They spent many wonderful years together, making a home and family, living into their eighties, and dying just a few days apart. Before he left this world, Caleb credited the ghost of Lucy's first hus- band for setting the compass spinning and helping them find their way to each other.

To this day, Jennings Fine Compasses and Watches still re- sides on Main Street and is owned by one of Caleb's and Lucy's descendants. Many families in Compass Cove keep a compass in their home as a symbol of selfless love and as a reminder that hearts meant to love will always find each other.

Prologue

JORDAN VELSOR EXPECTED her last night as a single woman to be spent dreaming about her fairy tale wedding. Instead, she was sitting on the beach behind her cottage, drinking expensive champagne straight from the bottle, and wondering how she could have been so stupid.

Wearing a pair of threadbare yoga pants and gray hoodie, she dug her perfectly polished pink toes into the cool, wet sand and shivered. If it was a normal night, Jordan would have thought the chill was from the cool breeze coming off Jennings Bay. But tonight, was anything but normal.

Tonight, Jordan had been played for a fool. She'd become a cliché.

Her whole life—the future she'd had planned, everything she thought she'd wanted—fell apart before she could process how it all happened.

"Jesus. There you are." Jordan recognized her friend Lilly's voice right away. "I've been searching everywhere for you."

"Maybe I didn't want to be found," Jordan griped.

With a flick of her wrists, the old plaid beach blanket Lilly was carrying floated up and then slowly dropped to the sand next to Jordan. "Get up and sit on this. Your ass is going to get all wet."

So what? was all Jordan thought. Who cared if her ninety-dollar thong got salty and sandy? No one was going to see it. "Please tell me you brought more alcohol."

"Yep. And food. I brought cheese and bread from brunch today. Oh, and I stole some cupcakes from the rehearsal dinner."

It all sounded good, but Jordan had no appetite. "They're probably going to sue me for calling it all off. I just couldn't..."

Lilly looped her arm around Jordan's shoulder. "You owe me no explanation. As far as I'm concerned, you did the right thing."

The sound of the waves crashing on the beach matched the rushing in Jordan's head. It was an endless thundering noise that rattled her nerves, and it was all caused by the scene she'd walked in on that day at Chase's office.

Her perfect fiancé—the tall, blond, and handsome lawyer, the millionaire and favorite son of a prominent family—was caught with his pants down, grinding against his secretary. Her blouse was open, her pencil skirt hiked up to her waist, and she had one long leg snaked around his hip.

Jordan's voice caught in her throat at the sight of her future husband with another woman, and she started backing out of the office. Chase never would have known she was there if she hadn't bumped into a desk chair, knocking it into a wire cart, which then tipped over.

That foiled her plan of running, because once Chase turned and saw her, the truth of her life as it could be became clear. *Things like this happened*, Chase explained. And it was time she understood that.

His secretary never came out of the office, and when her fiancé closed the door to shield the woman inside, Jordan's heart slammed shut.

Things like this might happen in other marriages, but not in hers. It was over.

"Want to talk about it?" Lilly wouldn't press, but since she was the one who ran interference when Jordan told Chase and his family that the wedding was off, she figured she had a right to know.

"He's been cheating."

"I got that much," Lilly snarled—loyal to the core. "The rat bastard."

"His family told me I was overreacting. You know, 'I'm naïve. He's a red-blooded man.'"

"That's such bullshit."

"That's pretty much what I said." Jordan took a long pull on the bottle of champagne and realized she'd drained it. "Jeez. Cristal sure goes down easy."

"So, it's over."

"Yep. My dream wedding, my marriage, my life, all went

'poof!'"

"I never liked him."

That brought a smile to her lips. "I know."

"Now what?"

"I come back to reality. I stop living in my dreams, and face my life going forward. That's it. No more romantic fantasies for me. They just aren't worth it."

NICK RINALDI STOOD on the back porch of his grandparents' house and watched the two women on the beach slugging back something from a bottle. He shifted his stance, shuffling his weight between his leg and his cane, and wondered what they were doing out there on an unusually damp and cool August night. One of the women was Nona's tenant, Jordan Velsor. Pretty girl. She was a teacher, like all the occupants of the family cottage before her, and he thought he heard Nona say something about her being engaged to that tool, Chase Stanley.

He'd gotten a look at her the other day. Tall and blonde, with legs up to her neck, she was coming in from a run on the beach. He was envious. Running was always his way to decompress, and he'd like nothing better than to be able to run his way down the beach, through town and out to Gulls Point.

Jordan didn't see him sitting on the porch, which was

probably a good thing.

"Nicky? What are you doing out here?" His grandmother, Lina Rinaldi, had been fussing over him since he arrived home the week before. Following his eyes out to the beach, she spotted Jordan and her friend. "From what I hear, I'm not losing my tenant. The wedding is off."

"Yeah? I'd say it's too bad, but if it's true she's better off. Stanley is an asshole."

"Still, can't be easy. The wedding was tomorrow. I wonder what happened."

"I'm sure you'll find out at the café in the morning." Rinaldi's Café was the hub of their small town of Compass Cove. If there was gossip, Nona would hear about it.

"True enough." She paused and gave him a good once-over. "How are you feeling?"

"The weather isn't helping my hip any." Two months out of recovery from his latest surgery and his damn hip still wasn't right. Rain was the worst. He could tell if a storm was coming two days out. Nothing like a couple of bullets from an AK-47 to ruin your day.

His next surgery was at the end of the summer, and that was going to set him back before it helped.

Nick watched as Jordan's head dropped onto Lilly's shoulder. She was definitely hurting. Poor kid. It was too bad she didn't know she'd dodged her own bullet.

Chapter One

T HE DEEP RATTLING cough woke her from a restless
sleep. This cold was kicking her ass, but even though all
she wanted to do was burrow under the covers, she was out
of tissues, and the dog needed to go outside.

Glancing out her window, the weather had worsened.
She almost would have been content putting out a pad for
Gertie to go inside, but her tissues and cough medicine were
in the back seat of her car. She had to go out regardless.

"Come on, Gertie, time to pee."

With a whimper and a moan from her spot at the other
end of the couch, her little rescue buried her face in the
corner. Gertie was no dummy.

"Look, if I have to go out, so do you. Your bladder is the
size of a thimble, and it's going to get even worse later."

The dog sighed—*sighed* her annoyance at Jordan. A dog
with an attitude. Didn't it figure? Gertie practically rolled off
the plush cushion and settled on her back on the blue
patterned rug. Her short little legs were straight up in the air,
feigning death.

Jordan felt pretty dead herself, but they still had to go

outside.

The wind howled, and all the windows in the cottage shook like it was going to lift up and fly away. Gust after gust provided a not-so-subtle reminder that the nor'easter currently blowing across Long Island was going to make all their lives miserable. This storm was brutal. It had been wreaking havoc for the last twelve hours and based on the latest weather report it had slowed down to a crawl, meaning it was going to stick around for a while.

Grabbing the dog's leash, Jordan gently nudged the little furry blob on the floor. Nothing. She didn't budge. "Gertie! Come on!"

Ninety-nine percent of the time, she loved the little mutt. This moment definitely fell into the one percent.

After she broke her engagement, Jordan had the sudden urge to have a pet. A lot of people told her it would pass, but she knew that wasn't the case. Jordan needed unconditional love in her home, so she kept her eyes open for the right opportunity. She couldn't handle a puppy or a kitten, so when she wandered around a rescue fair one Sunday this past September, she found herself completely enamored with Gertie. A stubby-legged little mutt, Gertie was a tube of golden fur with a pointy snout and big, soulful brown eyes. She was about five years old, and her owner had just died, leaving the little dog all alone.

Jordan felt a kinship with the pooch, and took her home that day.

Lina Rinaldi, who usually frowned on her cottage tenants having pets, took to the dog right away, and Gertie loved the older woman right back.

As Jordan stared at the lump still upside down on the floor, she was about ready to offer Mrs. Rinaldi full custody. Then a deep, rasping cough shook Jordan to the core. It racked her body violently, and pain shot around her chest. God, she felt awful.

"Come on," she said firmly to the pooch. "We'll skip the leash this time. Out and in. Let's get this over with."

Gertie rolled over and trotted to the front door, giving Jordan the side eye as she waited. Donning her parka and a pair of lined wellies that she pulled over her pajama pants, Jordan grabbed the remote and unlocked her car. When she opened the front door, she was hit by a blast of wind, rain, and sleet that stung her cheeks and chilled her to the bone. "Lord, it's miserable." Looking down at Gertie, she nodded. "Okay, let's make this quick."

The two of them bolted outside, with Gertie heading for her favorite patch of grass and Jordan heading for her car. She stopped when she coughed so hard she could barely breathe. It hurt. She'd never had a chest cold that hurt so much. Finally, yanking open the door, she heard her pooch barking from the small covered porch. Jordan grabbed the bag that was filled with some basic food provisions, juice, tea, tissues, and a selection of over-the-counter cold remedies. She slammed the car door shut, and on her way back inside she noticed the whitecaps on Jennings Bay. The wind was forcing massive amounts of water into the coves and harbors around town, and she hoped it didn't breach the seawall surrounding the property. Jordan's cottage was closer to Cove Road, but the Rinaldis' big house was at risk.

Without any further delay, Jordan made it back to the porch, feeling chilled and soaked to the bone despite all the foul weather gear she'd put on. Gertie was barking frantically, having positioned herself under the old wooden swing, and Jordan was starting to lose her patience.

"Gertie, what the hell is the problem?"

That's when she heard the groan and crack. Jordan looked up just as a large section of an old oak tree, about fifty feet from the house, gave way. Throwing her body against the wall to avoid any debris, Jordan watched as the massive tree split in half and came crashing down, crushing her car in the process.

If she had waited ten more seconds to head outside, Jordan would have been killed.

Frozen in place for—she didn't know how long—Jordan startled when a large, strong arm wrapped around her.

She looked away from the wreckage in the front yard and into the gorgeous face of Nick Rinaldi.

"Damn. Are you alright?"

Was she? She wasn't sure. Jordan tried to answer, but she had trouble catching her breath. Sucking in air, he kept her steady when they walked into the house.

Waiting for the dog before he closed the door, Nick sat her on the bench in the entryway. Glancing in the canvas tote from the market, his brow furrowed.

"You're sick? What's wrong?"

With a low rattling cough that had him pressing the back of his hand to her forehead, she muttered, "Chest cold."

Shaking his head, he helped her off with her boots and jacket. "Let's get you settled in bed, and I'll go get my bag. You've got a lot more than a chest cold."

"My car…"

"We can't do anything about your car until the storm passes, so put it out of your head. It's the last thing you need to worry about."

"Are you kidding? Not worry about it?" How was she supposed to get to work or see her dad? How was she supposed to do anything if she didn't have a car? The pain in her chest wasn't just from her cough at that moment, but at the wave of dread—helplessness—that rushed through her.

"One thing at a time." Nick, a former Navy doctor, was single-minded. And as much as Jordan didn't want to admit it, he was right. In this weather, there was nothing she could do.

"Come on," he said. "Lead the way."

"I'll be fine," she said, stopping in her tracks. Those few words taxed her already strained system. She coughed painfully into her arm while Nick guided her into her room. The coughing spell was so violent, ripping at her tender lungs, she couldn't even object as he tucked her into bed.

Sick as she was, Jordan wasn't blind. Nick Rinaldi had been on her radar since he landed back in Compass Cove the previous fall. The guy was gorgeous, smart, and a gentleman to the core. But he'd settled back in with his grandparents almost six months ago, and other than a token hello, or a polite smile, he rarely spoke to her.

Still, with his lean frame, dark hair, and kind eyes, he checked a lot of boxes.

She thought she heard him mutter something about being stubborn, but her lack of breath didn't allow a response. If anyone was stubborn, he was. The man of mystery was a well-known do-gooder, and obviously she was his next project. There was only one problem with that. She didn't want his help. Needing people was a slippery slope, and Jordan had no intention of heading down that way again.

COLD, HIS ASS. The girl had full blown bronchitis, if not pneumonia. The cough he heard wrack her body could crack a rib. He had no idea why she hadn't seen a doctor.

Because she was stubborn. That's why.

Nick didn't know Jordan well, just what he'd picked up about her from his grandparents and some mutual friends. There was a common theme though. They all said she was tough. Resilient.

So, while he expected she was going to be a pain in the ass as a patient, he admired her strength of will. It would help her recover.

Nona was standing at the back door with a towel for him as soon as he entered the house. "Is she okay? That poor thing. Tell her we'll replace the car. She shouldn't worry about anything."

"I told you we should cut down that tree." His grandfather, still strong as an ox at eighty-two years old, sat at the kitchen table, ready to spout more I-told-you-so's.

"That's doesn't matter. The tree coming down may have been her lucky day because it got me over there." Nick took the towel his grandmother handed to him. He was soaked from the short walk across the yard. "She's pretty sick. I'm going to get my bag and head back."

"Sick? What's wrong?" Nona was wringing her hands, and when she reached in her pocket, Nick thought she might break out her rosary. Whenever someone was sick, Lina hit the beads.

"Best case scenario, she has bad bronchitis. Worst case, she has pneumonia."

"Oh, no. Poor Jordan. She told me she had a cold."

"She told me the same thing."

"I made soup. Let me get some food together." Not knowing what else to do, his grandmother launched into what she did best, feeding people. In her mind, there was nothing a good meal couldn't fix.

Nick, however, knew better. If his hunch was right, Jordan was going to need more than soup. Heading upstairs, he went to his room on the far side of the large farmhouse and grabbed his medical pack from the bottom of the closet. He'd done some local outreach when he was based at the hospital in Kandahar, going into the small villages, and manning poorly staffed clinics. Those treks to help people who had so little was some of the most rewarding work he'd done when he was in country, and it had given Nick some of his best memories. And some of his worst. That's what he'd been doing when he was shot.

Going through a mental checklist, like he always did, he wondered if that was all he needed.

He hesitated.

Finally, after some quick deliberation, Nick stuffed a change of clothes in a backpack, along with his tablet and a charging block. There was no way he was leaving a sick woman alone during a storm, so if that meant he had to camp out on her couch, so be it.

Nick drew a breath and looked at himself in the mirror above his bureau. This was what he was meant to do, and he had to get cleared so he could start working again.

Heading back to the kitchen, Nona had gathered provisions in a small cooler. That was his grandmother. Strong, decisive, and very good at taking care of people; nothing much spooked her. She'd lived in Compass Cove her whole life, having been born there after her family came to the town from their apartment in Little Italy. Nona's father was a baker, and bought the family a small house on the corner of Cove and Compass just a few blocks from the heart of the village. With money he'd been saving for years, he opened his Italian bakeshop in the heart of town.

The cottage Jordan lived in was the house where Nona grew up. Five rooms and a bathroom, he couldn't imagine raising three kids there, but they did. Happily.

Quickly gaining a reputation for the best pastries, bread, and espresso on the North Shore, Lina learned to bake at her grandfather's side. When she married Angelo Rinaldi, they turned the little bakeshop into much more.

Pops was a force of nature. His family had come to Compass Cove from the coal mining region of Pennsylvania, settling there around the same time as Nona's. The two of them had known each other since they first went to Saint Ann's Catholic School. They married at eighteen, had three sons, and built a successful business that served the town well. Above all, they loved each other.

"You two will be okay here on your own?" Nick was leaving his elderly grandparents to take care of Jordan.

"We've been in worse storms than this, Nicky. If the power goes out, the generator kicks on automatically." His grandfather was constantly yearning for the old days, but the man had added every modern convenience to his home.

"Right. Okay. I'll check in later." Throwing the cooler over his free shoulder, Nick kissed his grandmother on the cheek, patted his grandfather on the shoulder and headed out in the deluge to get back to Jordan's.

As soon as he stepped outside, a strong gust forced him to turn into the wind to keep his balance, all while buckets of rain pelted him in the face. God, the weather was foul. Before his injury, he'd been in the Navy for over ten years and he'd seen his share of bad storms while on base and at sea. This nor'easter was one of the worst.

He entered the cottage through the front door, but before going in he took a good look at Jordan's car. A large piece of the tree had broken off and slammed down on the roof, cutting the small SUV almost in two.

The scary part was that the limb extended well past the car on each side. If Jordan had been any closer than she was, it would have killed her.

Jesus Christ, the woman was lucky.

He expected that little dog of hers would be barking up a storm as soon as he walked in, but the place was quiet. Making his way through the house, he glanced at the framed photos dotting the living room, before dropping the cooler in the kitchen.

Ever since he'd laid eyes on her, Nick had been intrigued by the leggy blonde. She was beautiful, no denying that, but there was something about her—a deep, quiet dignity that was a powerful attractor. He'd seen her around town with friends singing bad karaoke at the pub, sipping tea with his grandma at the café, and heading into the Maritime Museum with a bunch of kids he later found out were her students. Something in her eyes, her smile—it caught him right in the gut. The woman was all heart.

When he reached her bedroom, the dog was laying with her head on Jordan's legs. The pup's eyes were locked on Nick, and based on her posture, there was a good chance he was going to get bitten if he wasn't careful.

Stepping closer, he heard a small growl come from the dog's throat. It was barely there, but he wasn't taking any chances.

"Jordan?" If she was awake, maybe the dog wouldn't pounce. "Jordan, how are you feeling?"

"Crappy." Her voice was low and hoarse. She opened her eyes and it was evident how sick she was. Rolling on her back and pushing herself up, the hacking began immediately. This time, it was bad. Endless, deep. Her dog inched up next to her, ears pinned back and worried, and Nick couldn't blame her. He was worried too.

Sitting on the edge of the bed, his pack on the floor, he held her steady as she tried to catch her breath.

Finally, when she stopped, Nick picked up her arm, gently gripping her wrist so he could take her pulse. Jordan yanked it back like his fingers were on fire.

"What are you doing?" she snapped.

He stood, realizing he'd overstepped. Knowing all too well what it was like to deal with skittish patients, Nick backtracked. "I'm sorry. I have to examine you. Mind if I continue?"

It took a second, but finally she nodded while extending her arm toward him. Her pulse was strong, but rapid. Reaching down, he pulled out his stethoscope, blood pressure cuff, and the small portable ultrasound, just in case he needed to confirm his diagnosis.

"My back hurts."

"I bet. The strain on your lungs and your rib cage is pretty intense."

"The coughing?"

"Yep." Her blood pressure checked in as normal. "I'm going to listen to your heart and lungs, okay?" Placing the stethoscope in his ears, he pressed it first to her chest. Her heart was beating rapidly, but that was to be expected after what she'd just gone through. Then he shifted her slightly and placed the diaphragm on her back, where he could hear the rattles deep in her chest. When she coughed, he got the answer he was looking for. The episode went on for a good thirty seconds, with her gasping for breath when it was over. "Yeah. You don't have a chest cold; you have pneumonia. Tell me how this all started."

"Pneumonia? Um... I came down with a cold last week. I thought it was going away, but a couple of days ago the cough came back. It's been getting worse since."

"March is pneumonia season around here, and you have a classic case. Let's get a little food in your stomach, and then I can give you an antibiotic. Are you allergic to anything?"

"No, nothing," she murmured. "This really sucks."

"Yes, but fortunately you know a doctor who makes house calls." He smiled as he fished a vacuum sealed package of pills from his pack, and put them in a tray on her night table.

"Oh. Ah." She paused. "Do we know each other?"

Her blunt response threw him, even if she had a point. Saying they knew each other was a bit of a stretch. Over the past six months they'd barely interacted, which was a shame, really. "That's true. But I come with good references. My grandmother thinks I'm a good guy."

Even feeling as bad as she did, Jordan had to smile. "I guess I can trust you then. What's in that little plastic package?"

"Really good antibiotics." He tilted his head toward the tray on her nightstand. "They should help. Oh, and my grandfather said not to worry about your car. They'll take care of it."

"Oh. That's… I'm sure insurance will help."

"Maybe, maybe not. They're not going to let you go without wheels."

A shiver pushed through her, and Nick watched as she burrowed under the plush quilt. Putting his hand on her forehead, he could feel the warmth from her skin. "Do you have a thermometer?"

"A meat thermometer." She smiled weakly.

"Very funny. You're not exactly what I would call meat."

As soon as he said it he clamped his mouth shut, hoping she was too sick to pick up on the double meaning.

Her mouth twitched at the corner. "That's good to know."

"Right," he mumbled. "I'll see if I still have a thermometer strip in my pack, but you definitely have a fever."

"I figured."

"Have you taken any medication recently?"

"Ibuprofen this morning."

"Are you hungry? Nona sent over some soup."

"A little."

"I'll take that as a good sign." Nick ran through a mental checklist. It felt good to have purpose. To feel like he could do some good. "I'll get you all dosed after you eat. Let me get that soup."

"You don't have to wait on me, Nick. I mean, you barely know me."

"So? I'm a doctor. This is what we do."

"Fixing a bowl of soup? Aren't you a combat doctor or something like that?" Her voice was scratchy from coughing, the register low. That's when it occurred to him, he'd never really heard Jordan speak. Other than a word here and there, he had no idea what she sounded like.

"I'm board certified in emergency medicine and pediatrics," he replied. "But you seem to be forgetting something... I'm still a Rinaldi. Feeding people is what we do."

"Cute. What kind of soup did Lina make?"

"You have a choice: Italian wedding or chicken."

"Oh, wedding soup. I love that." There was a flicker in her eyes that he hadn't seen since he'd gotten her off the front porch.

"Coming up."

"No. I can get it." Just as she was about to get out of bed, Nick gently held her shoulders and eased her back into the pillows. Seeing her pressed into the softness, her blue eyes gazing up at him, Nick's protective nature surged.

"Stay put. I'll get it for you."

"You don't have to." She tossed the covers back the second he let go, but as soon as she was on her feet, Jordan swayed, grabbing Nick's shoulder, and lowering herself back to bed. "Whoa."

"Yeah, I don't need you fainting. Stay in bed." He pointed his finger at her, and she gave up, pulling the covers back to her chin. "Don't move."

Making her best effort to smile at him, Jordan nodded. "Thank you."

Nick considered that progress.

ONCE SHE'D HAD some soup, and all her medicine, Jordan watched a little TV and then she was out. Still running a fever, she'd been asleep for two hours, not noticing that the wind was like a runaway train careening over the house. Nick was on the couch in the living room, surfing through social media and hoping the power stayed on as he listened to sleet pelt the windows. It was getting cold, and the last thing they needed was to lose the heat.

She'd been restless—coughing and tossing in her bed. Whenever he checked on her, she was in a different position: sometimes uncovered, sometimes with the covers pulled up to her chin. Her fever hadn't budged, and that had him worried.

Without any warning, the dog, who'd been staying on Jordan's bed, had planted her butt on the floor at his feet and was staring at him with those big, buggy brown eyes.

Gertie? Was that the little mutt's name?

Earlier, he'd found some kibble and fed her, and after, he managed to get her outside to do her business. It wasn't that long ago, so he couldn't imagine what was going on. The dog was not a fan of the storm, and Nick didn't think she wanted to go out. "What's the matter, pooch?"

She whined, and looked toward the bedroom, and Nick heard a crash. He was up and in there so fast he almost ran face first into a door. Jordan was on the floor, attempting to pick up a pile of stuff she'd obviously knocked off the night table. He dropped to his knees where he could see how upset she was.

And how out of it.

Laying a hand over hers, she looked up into his face. Her

eyes were watery and her breathing was coming in little hiccups. Tough Jordan was crying. "I was reaching for my phone, and I knocked it all over."

"Not the end of the world."

"Shit. It's such a mess. I'm sorry. I…"

"Stop. It was an accident. Get back in bed."

Jordan was frozen in place, her hand shaking, her body tense. Going against all his better judgment, Nick gently pulled her to her feet, lifted her into his arms and walked with her to the sofa.

"What are you doing? You don't need to carry me."

"It's fine."

"I'm heavy."

He chuckled. "Not really."

He wanted to tell her that she was a hell of a lot lighter than the marine he had to carry from just outside the hospital compound to the ER. Compared to that giant, Jordan was a feather.

To be honest, he liked the feel of her. She was long and lean, but soft in all the right places.

He deposited her on the blue-green overstuffed sofa and covered her with the knitted throw she'd left on the back of the matching armchair. The dog hopped up and snuggled in next to her.

Through it all, she hadn't said a thing. She just kept her head down, sniffling. Under normal circumstances, he would have brushed off her upset, and chalked it up to fatigue.

Instead, he tried to think about what she was going through. Between being sick, her car, and having someone who was almost a complete stranger taking control of your life, Jordan was certainly entitled to feel sorry for herself.

The problem was, he had no idea what to do with a crying woman.

"It's going to be okay. You're a little disoriented. Stay here, I'm going to go clean up."

"I'm sorry... I thought I heard my phone and then everything crashed."

"It's water; nothing to worry about. I'll be right back."

He grabbed a roll of paper towels from the kitchen before heading back to her bedroom. Whatever had been on her night table was on the floor. She'd knocked over the whole lot, except the lamp, and fortunately, her water was almost empty, so there wasn't much to do except pick up all her crap. Lip balm, tissues, and at least a half a dozen books, ranging from really dirty romances to self-help books with titles like *Going It Alone*. Talk about a contradiction in terms.

When he'd lifted her into his arms, he could feel she was still feverish, and if that didn't start coming down in a day or so, he'd get her to the urgent care for a chest X-ray and some stronger meds. But for now, he was satisfied that what he was doing would get her over the hump.

Still, Nick was seriously considering taking her over to Nona's house. It was larger, he wouldn't have to worry about losing power… he just felt he could take better care of her there. He also knew she wouldn't budge, and if he had to admit it, he'd have put up a fight if he were in her shoes. The past few hours had confirmed what he suspected… the woman had a hard head. And even thought she was a pain in the ass, her strong will was one of the things he found most attractive. She knew her own mind.

He liked that about her.

Well, that and her legs. Her legs went on for miles.

Cleanup was quick, and he wasn't surprised that she was a little out of it. Doped up on decongestants and cough syrup, and not sleeping well, Nick wasn't sure if her fever was making Jordan's brain cloudy, fatigue had exhausted her, or if she was in a little bit of shock from the tree falling so close to her house.

Whatever it was, this day had been shit for her from start to finish, and Nick had put himself smack in the middle of it. When he went back into the living room, Jordan was sitting with a box of tissues in her lap, petting her dog. Gertie barked as soon as he came into view. "Gertie, shh. Nick's trying to help." She looked up at him and shrugged. "She gets protective sometimes. I'm sorry she's being so fresh."

"She's just watching out for you." Parking himself in the armchair adjacent to the couch, Nick took her in. Even sick, she was probably the most beautiful woman he'd ever seen in his life. And he'd seen plenty. It wasn't just the long legs, the blond hair, or the electric-blue eyes, there was something in the way she carried herself. Even on her worst day, when Nick could see she'd taken a bit of a beating, there was the dignity that came shining through. For people who lived barely a hundred and fifty feet apart, he and Jordan were in oddly unfamiliar territory. They both knew things about each other because they traveled in the same circles, even though they didn't interact. A nod, a wave, a quick hello was all they'd exchanged when he'd been around the previous summer. She was still licking her wounds from her broken engagement, so he kept his distance.

Then, in September, he had his final surgery.

Recovery was a bitch and a half, but he'd still managed to make a few trips east for a change of scenery. His surgeon was based in San Diego, and rehab took months. But for the first time in over a year, Nick felt like he might be getting his life back.

The next step was to be cleared to work.

His hip was much better. The torn muscle was taking a little longer to heal, which annoyed the crap out of him, but he wasn't in bad shape. It was the mental toll of the injury that brought him to a personal reckoning. Hard as it was to admit it, Nick wasn't ready to go back into a trauma center. It ate at him, but he wasn't going to put a patient at risk while he was still wrestling with his demons.

He could still work with kids, though. It wasn't the pace he was used to, but it wasn't the worst thing that could happen. Maybe some regular hours with patients who weren't going to die on him was just what he needed.

For now, he was going to focus on his one patient, who had finally calmed down.

"Do you need anything? Some tea?"

"No, I'm fine. I've been drinking water, like you said. I think I could float away."

"The fluids are good for you."

"Right." She nodded. "You said that."

"Right."

Silence dropped between them, awkward and thick. There was only so much small talk he could handle.

Nick wondered when he lost his game. Usually, he could talk to a woman about anything. With Jordan, he was tongue-tied. That was another good reason to move to the big house. With Nona around, neither one of them would need to utter a word. She'd talk enough for both of them.

Keeping his ear out for any changes in her breathing, they sat together quietly. Nick hated the way the weather messed with his muscles and joints. Reaching down, he grabbed the heating pad he'd brought with him, and put it between the arm of the chair and his thigh.

"How is your hip?"

She spoke so quietly, he could barely hear her. Normally, he didn't talk about his injury. But the concern in her eyes compelled him to answer. "It's been a long recovery. Hard. My hip joint is in good shape, though. I worried about having a full replacement, but it was the right thing to do. Now it's just the connective tissue that has to heal. That's going to take time."

"You've been through a lot."

"Not as much as some, more than others. I'm not used to depending on people."

"I get that," Jordan replied. "I don't want to need anybody. Needing someone nearly destroyed my life."

There was something so sad about her declaration; about the way she'd thrown down a gauntlet against her own life.

"I was wondering," he began. "What would you think about moving to Nona's house? I know we said we'd only go if the power went out, but there's plenty of room, plenty of food, and less likelihood we would be whacked in the head by a tree."

"Always a positive, but I really think I'd like to stay here."

"My grandparents wouldn't mind," he reassured her.

"Of course they wouldn't. They live to take care of people. But I'm not going to take advantage of that."

"It's not taking advantage..."

Jordan shot him a firm look that sent a clear message she wasn't going to bend on this point. He let the suggestion drop, but had to admit he liked the fact that she was coherent, and able to have a short conversation. Nick would call that an improvement, but expending that little bit of energy had exhausted her. It took only seconds, but the next time he looked over, it appeared Jordan had dozed off. Nick could hear her breath coming out in little puffs. She was on her side, curled around a pillow and blanket, looking very comfortable right where she was.

The storm had picked up since he first arrived at the house. The old cottage had more than its share of creaks and rattles, but hearing the way the winds were buffeting the structure, Nick was thinking it could use a little reinforcement.

His own eyes were heavy, and he figured with her just falling asleep, he had a little bit of time to catch a nap of his own.

Resting his head on the back of the chair, Nick focused on the noise in his head, rather than the woman who was filling his brain with many, many inappropriate thoughts.

"Well? Are we staying or am I overruled, Doc?" she said, groggily.

Okay, so she wasn't asleep.

He chuckled and turned his eyes toward hers. "We'll stay here until we lose power. If the lights go out, we head over to the other house."

Reluctantly, she nodded. More progress. He'd take it.

"That sounds fair."

With the roar of the wind providing the background, he and Jordan settled into their respective spots. Initially, he wasn't sure if it was him she didn't trust, or men in general. What he was starting to see was that Jordan was very trusting, and that made him angry on her behalf.

"Nick?" she whispered.

"Yeah?"

"Thanks."

Chapter Two

STAYING PUT WAS starting to look like a bad idea. The windows were shaking as the wind gusted at almost hurricane force. The best he could hope for was that no more trees came down and took out any buildings on the property.

There was still power, and he had a cell signal, so that was good. His weather app was showing they were in the thick of the storm. They were also at high tide, which meant there could be flooding.

He couldn't see the bay from the front windows, and he really wanted to get a look at the surf.

Glancing at the clock he rubbed his eyes. *Three a.m.*

Rising from his spot on the sofa, he made his way to Jordan's bedroom; aside from wanting to check on her, she had the best view of the water.

Slipping in quietly so he wouldn't wake her, Gertie's head popped up from the mess of covers on the bed. Jordan was out cold. On her stomach, head turned to the side, one leg was hooked over the edge of the comforter and she was purring like a mountain lion.

He felt himself smile. If they knew each other better,

he'd be tempted to take out his phone and record the noise she was making. But as amusing as it was, he was also glad she'd finally crashed, because it meant she was getting some rest.

That was the thing he liked most about Jordan. She was real. From the first time he saw her coming in sweaty from a run, to eating a loaded burger at the café, he realized this woman didn't have an ounce of pretense, and she didn't do anything halfway.

She ate, she laughed out loud, she snored, and swore. He found it all majorly attractive.

She'd been shaky after knocking everything off her night table. It wasn't a big deal, but she wasn't handling being sick very well. It was obvious Jordan was used to having control, and right now she had very little. But her breathing was steadier, and she'd gone a good stretch without any coughing fits.

Thank God for antibiotics.

From the end of her bed he could see the water on the bay churning, the white caps visible even at a distance. Waves were crashing into the bulkhead, but so far, the water was a safe distance from both houses. This storm was all about the wind. He'd been listening to the sleet and rain, but the wind was where this storm got dangerous.

Without any warning, there was a thunderous crack and roar. Jordan popped up, her eyes wide, and Gertie started barking frantically before diving under the bed. Then it happened again. And again.

Jordan was trembling, probably because she was flashing back to when the tree came down on her car earlier. When Nick's phone rang, he saw it was his grandmother.

"Nona, are you alright?"

"We're fine, but you need to take cover. Trees are falling all over the place. Poppy and I are heading into the powder room."

"You go. I've got it here."

Right. He didn't know what he was going to do. The cottage bathroom was tiny and facing the area of the property with the most trees. Looking outside, he checked the wind direction, and that got him thinking.

The cottage had a substantial back porch, as well as an attic. Additionally, the back of the building had far fewer trees than the front. With the curtains drawn, it might be best to stay put in the bedroom. Grabbing blankets and pillows from the bed, he threw them in the corner farthest from the windows. She watched him, confused.

"What are you doing?"

Next, he gently pulled Jordan to her feet.

"You'll see. Go sit on the blankets, I'll be right there. Can you do that? Or do you need my help?"

She shook her head and did as he asked, while Nick blocked the area with an armchair and her desk. Then, he took the comforter, and the top sheet from the bed. The comforter went on the floor with Jordan, but the top and bottom sheets were attached to a picture hanging on the wall. After that, he draped it over the furniture, creating a makeshift tent.

"Not bad," he said. Looking in at her, he smiled. "What do you think?"

"A blanket fort?"

"Yep. It will keep glass off of us if the windows break. Hang on. I'll be right back."

He gathered his phone, a couple bottles of water, and the emergency lantern from the living room. Then he went into the shelter with her. The space was tight, but he knew, short of a whole tree cutting the house in half, they'd be safe.

"Scoot over toward the wall. Let me take the outside."

Jordan was too tired to argue, and Nick was actually relieved. He sat next to her, propping a pillow behind her, then covering her with the comforter and tucking it down around her.

"I'm fine. Thanks," she said.

"How do you feel?"

She took a breath and nodded. "My chest doesn't hurt as much."

"Good. That means the antibiotics are getting after the infection. You'll be amazed how much better you feel forty-eight hours from now."

"As long as we don't drown, or get crushed, I'll look forward to it."

"We won't," he assured her. "But, I can flip your mattress against the outside of the fort if it will make you feel better."

Nick got a smile out of her. Two points for him.

"I don't think that's necessary. We're pretty safe. The sheets are top quality. I'm sure they're hurricane rated."

A laugh broke from his chest. "Good to know. I've obviously been skimping on my sheets."

He watched her eyes travel around the inside of their shelter. "This is actually kind of cool. It makes me think of when I was a kid. My dad used to build blanket forts with me. We'd hide out and read and eat junk food."

"Sounds like a lot of fun."

"It was. After my mother died, my dad spent a lot of extra time with me. He's the best. I talked to him this morning. He has no idea what's happened."

"Hopefully you can check in with him tomorrow."

There was another loud crash, and she flinched. "Jeez. That was close."

It was. Nick could hear the trees cracking outside the house. It might well have been projection, but Nick was fairly sure when they looked outside tomorrow, there wouldn't be one tree left.

It was the next clap of thunder that did her in. It was so loud and so close that the whole house shook. Jordan sucked in air and closed her eyes, trying to steady herself.

Nick hesitated for a second, not wanting to cross any lines... but in the end, there wasn't anything else he could do. Jordan was terrified; she needed comfort and he could provide it. He reached out and pulled her in. There was zero resistance and Jordan curled into him like a lost puppy.

There were worse things. At least she seemed to trust him.

"It's okay. I won't let anything happen to you."

The only response was a simple nod. She coughed twice, and where his hand was settled on her back he could feel the congestion in her lungs, but it wasn't like it was earlier. That was a relief. Another day or two, and she'd be out of the woods.

"Your cough is improving." Maybe he could distract her with some good news. God knew the girl needed it. She'd had a shit day.

"I'm not going to die?" she asked, her voice gravelly.

She hadn't lost her sarcasm. A good sign, to be sure. "Not today."

Her body had relaxed some, but she was still pressed against his side. Nick wasn't looking to let go as long as she was happy where she was. He'd always been pretty good at maintaining detachment from his patients, but Jordan wasn't just a patient, she was more like a neighbor.

The shooting and his injury had messed with his head in a big way. He was done in the Navy. He'd never be able to keep up physically, but taking care of Jordan was the first sign he was mentally ready to get back to medicine, and nothing had ever been a bigger relief.

There was a huge crash that made them both jump, but best Nick could tell, it came from the front yard. If he were a betting man, he'd lay odds that Jordan's car was now flat as a pancake.

It also brought Gertie out from her hiding spot. It was comical to watch the little dog skid across the wood floor and right into Jordan's lap. Grateful she had something else to distract her, Nick focused on the mutt.

"She's so *interesting* looking." The dog's round yes were a little buggy, but very expressive. Her legs were short and stumpy. Gertie was an odd looking little dog. In a cute way, but odd. "Do you know what she is?"

Jordan stroked Gertie's head. "She's called a Peagle. Part Pekinese, part beagle. She's a little chubby, and a bit neurotic, but I love her to pieces."

"A Peagle? Is she one of those designer dogs?" In Nick's mind, a mutt was a mutt, but he knew a lot of people would disagree with him. Strongly.

"I guess you could say that. It doesn't matter to me. She's goofy and sweet. And she needed a home."

"How long have you had her?"

Jordan thought. "About six months. Her owner died, and she had no one. We kind of bonded because of that. Two girls on their own."

Six months would have put the adoption not too long after Jordan broke her engagement. "That was a bit after I came home the first time. I remember Nona bellyaching about the dog, but she never would have told you no."

Jordan grinned conspiratorially. "I think I knew that." Gertie was asleep in Jordan's lap, content and snoring. "We needed each other. People pat me on the back for rescuing her, but honestly, she rescued me."

"I think they often do. Animals are so intuitive. People could take a few lessons."

He didn't mean to do that. His comment was tinged with bitterness, and the expression on Jordan's face told him she'd picked up on it right away. Reintegrating wasn't easy. He was foolish to think it would be.

"Something bothering you, Doc?"

"No." Shifting his body, he pressed her head into his chest. "Go to sleep. You need rest."

"Uh, huh. Okay." Jordan was petting the dog in long, slow strokes.

"Really. I'm fine."

When she looked up, Nick saw the skepticism in her gaze, but she didn't push any more. Thank God. He didn't want to talk about his own wounds. He was more comfortable when he could help other people.

Of course, Jordan was a teacher, and the best of them were intuitive—sharp—and he wasn't going to be able to keep dodging questions if they spent much more time together. Even sick, he could see Jordan's brain working, always making assessments and decisions. He had to admit, that brain was mighty attractive.

Nick took a breath and did his best to shake off the response he was having to her. Beautiful, smart, and curled against him, Nick hadn't been this interested in a woman in a very long time. Too long.

Fighting a powerfully physical response, Nick said a silent prayer for the storm to end. The situation they were in was too intense and he wasn't thinking straight, so the sooner he could extricate himself from Jordan's orbit, the better.

Then, without any warning, the dog got up and crawled in his lap. She looked up at him with her big round eyes, nudged his hand with her nose and then plopped down. Gertie stretched on her side, letting out a heavy sigh for good measure. The dog was obviously a drama queen.

But the Gertie was only the half of it. Just as he was about to say something, Jordan, with her mussed hair and droopy eyes, smiled up at him. It was wide and warm, and her whole face lit up.

It was at that moment Nick realized he was toast.

When Jordan woke up, she was no longer in a blanket fort on the floor. She was tucked in her bed. And she had no idea how she got there.

That wasn't true. Of course, Nick had put her back in bed, but she didn't know when. Jordan had no recollection of being walked or carried anywhere. Which was proof she was still pretty sick.

She felt it too. Her chest wasn't as tight, but she was so tired. And her entire body still hurt. Looking at the clock on her dresser, she could see it was past nine in the morning, but outside it was still gray and dark. It was like the end of days.

When was the storm going to end?

Jordan had been through her share of storms. Long Island was not immune to blizzards and hurricanes. However, it was the coastal storms, like this one, that tended to cause trouble every March.

But the last two days felt different. It was like the rain and wind had swallowed them whole. Moving to turn on her bedside light, she clicked the switch, and nothing happened.

She tried the other lamp. Nothing.

The power had gone out.

"It's not going to work." Nick was standing in her bedroom doorway.

"When did this happen?"

"Couple of hours ago. After all the trees had come down. It was dead quiet outside, and then pop. No power."

"That figures. Why didn't you wake me?" Jordan noticed Nick had donned a heavy blue sweatshirt.

"I figured you'd be fine under the covers, but it's getting cold. We have to head over to the big house while there's a break in the storm."

A break? What was he saying? "It's not over?"

"Not yet. Another system formed and we're going to get hit again. It's gotten cold though, so we're probably looking at snow."

Jordan pulled the covers over her head. "Ugh. Mother Nature hates us."

Feeling the tug at the bedclothes, Nick yanked them down and pulled Jordan to her feet. "Come on. Even if she does, we have to go. The dog is packed up. Bowls, bed, toys, and kibble. I found a tote in your closet and packed your meds, hair goop, those elastic things... what else do you need?"

It took a second for what he said to sink in. "You went in my closet? And my bathroom cabinet?"

He was moving around the room at a good clip, unplugging chargers and collecting electronics. Jordan would have said something, but her brain was fuzzy, and Nick was a man on a mission. Until he opened her panty drawer. That got her attention.

"Whoa. Okay. Stop now."

Nick closed the drawer and turned to face her. "Sorry. I want to get you settled in the big house, with heat, before the weather turns. Do you want me to grab a couple of those books?"

"I know, but slow down for a second. Let me grab my underwear. You can go in the other dresser and pull some pajamas, T-shirts and yoga pants. And socks. Thick ones."

"Got it." He opened a drawer and grabbed three pairs of pants and two hoodies. "How are you feeling?"

"Crappy. I'm so tired." Climbing from bed was the last thing she wanted to do. The thought of going outside was almost driving her to tears. But he was right. She couldn't stay, especially if it was going to snow.

"How much snow are they forecasting?"

"It's vague right now, but I have a buddy from the Navy who works for the National Weather Service. He's saying one to two feet."

Jordan froze. "Feet?"

"Feet. Which means the power company won't be able to get anyone out to fix the lines." He stopped and thought. "I'd better take more clothes."

Jordan was going to be there for a week. Jesus. She grabbed three more pairs of panties, thankful she'd done laundry two days ago.

Once her tote was packed, she sat on the edge of her bed and thought about how many things had gone wrong in the last year. With her father in hospice care, her broken engagement, her car, being so sick she could barely function, she had to wonder why the fates had it out for her.

She was lucky in so many ways. She had a job she loved, great friends, a wonderful place to live... but the other things were starting to pile up and wear on her. Jordan was just about at her breaking point.

Nick returned with her big parka, a hat, a scarf and her

boots.

Crouching in front of her, he leveled his gaze. God, this man was gorgeous. From his strong body, to the gorgeous planes of his face, to his slightly crooked nose, he was the epitome of handsome. His hazel eyes were bright and knowing, but there was a little bit of sadness laced through the depths.

"I'm going to walk you and Gertie over first. Nona has a room all ready. Then I'll come back, get all the bags, and once I get the house closed up, I'll be there."

"Okay." She smiled weakly as Nick pulled the knit hat onto her head. "Thanks. I'm sure I look fantastic."

He grinned, and her stomach quivered. "You look fine."

He helped her on with her boots and coat, made sure she was totally bundled up, and then attached Gertie's leash.

"You're still weak, so lean on me, okay? It's slippery."

Jordan nodded and wondered how she was ever going to thank the Rinaldis for taking care of her like this. They'd been wonderful when her wedding was called off. Lina had brought her food for a week and let her know she could stay as a tenant for as long as she wanted, even though she'd given her notice. They hadn't rented the cottage, and they were happy to have her stay. Just knowing she wouldn't have to move was a relief. Now their grandson, who was movie star gorgeous, was her personal physician.

Stepping outside, with Nick's arm securely around her waist, she took her first deep breath in days. She coughed, but it wasn't crippling like the day before. It had gotten colder, though. There was a layer of ice forming on the wet ground, and she wondered how the few remaining trees would hold up under the weight of the snow.

Looking out toward the road, all she saw were uprooted or broken trees. "If I didn't know better, I'd think a tornado tore through here."

"That's been floated as a possibility. There's a house on the other side of my grandparents' that was hit by a big maple. The family isn't hurt, but the garage is trashed."

A shiver ran through her body and Nick pulled his arm around her a little tighter.

"Almost there," he said. "There's a bed and warm comforter with your name on it."

Listening to him talk about beds made Jordan's poor sick insides tingle just a little bit. Was she so in need of a good tumble that nothing mattered? Not even pneumonia?

She had, indeed, hit rock bottom.

But she didn't respond, only nodded, because she was terrified of what would come out of her mouth. Jordan could be snarky, and sometimes she was a little inappropriate. The last thing she needed to do was sass the guy who had pretty much saved her life.

Jesus. He'd saved her life.

That blew her mind more than a little bit.

Guiding her up the porch steps, Nick opened the door that led to the big mudroom. Lina rushed in from the kitchen to greet her. "You poor thing. Let me take your things." Without much ceremony, Lina nudged Jordan onto a bench. While she wrestled off her coat and hat, Nick took off her boots. It was an odd scene—no, scratch odd—it was weird. The grandmother and grandson undressing her like a toddler was weird, but Jordan was just too tired to fight.

Lina Rinaldi was a true Italian matriarch. Just past eighty, she was as spry and active as women half her age. Maybe five-two, she was what Jordan would call comfortably curvy. Her long, jet black hair was streaked with silver, and twisted into a loose bun. But it was her eyes that told you all you needed to know about Lina—she was formidable.

Once her coat and boots had been stored, Lina took her by the hand and led her into the kitchen, where her husband, Angelo, was already making friends with Gertie.

"Lina, would you look at this little mooch of a dog? She already knows how to beg for biscotti." Leaning over, he cooed. "You're a funny looking little thing, but you're smart." He looked up and gave Jordan a good once-over. "Wow, you look like hell, kid."

"Angelo," Lina snapped. "Be nice. Can't you see how sick she is?"

"Yes. I just said that."

"No, you insulted her. Have some manners."

"Jordan, were you insulted?" The older man grinned, his eyes crinkling at the corners.

Before she could answer, Lina went to her husband and

the bickering continued. They didn't give one thought to the fact that she was standing in their kitchen in her rattiest pajamas, feeling like she was going to keel over. Nick came to the rescue again, putting his hands on her shoulders and guiding her toward the stairs.

"I love them both, but they're insufferable," Nick grumbled.

"Most of the time, I think it's cute. But not today."

"I get that. Let's get you settled and I'll go back and get your things."

Gertie followed them through the house and up the stairs.

She loved the Rinaldis' house. It was beautifully decorated, but it also held a special warmth you only found in family homes. The original frame house was built at the turn of the last century, and had been expanded over the years, adding wings and extensions. As the story went, Mrs. Rinaldi was so angry about their last son moving away ten years before, she had the house gutted and redone. She hired everyone herself, from the architect, the contractor, the plumber...everyone. One day, Angelo came home and found his house under construction.

Without missing a beat, she'd moved the two of them into the small cottage, and that's where they stayed for nine months while the renovation went on.

The woman got shit done. At least, when she wasn't arguing with her husband.

At the end of the hall, Nick opened a heavy paneled door and let Jordan walk into the guest suite.

It was beautiful. The walls were painted a soft gray green with bright white trim. Three large windows faced Jennings Bay, giving her spectacular views. With high ceilings, a stunning metal chandelier, and weathered wood furniture, Jordan couldn't believe this wasn't the master suite.

A large bed with an upholstered headboard dominated the room, and it was covered with an elegant paisley coverlet that coordinated with the color on the wall.

The final piece was the plush chaise sitting next to the windows. It was draped with a soft throw, and Jordan could have happily curled up right there. The room was beautiful.

Nick smiled. "Your bathroom is over here, if you want to… well, whatever. Um, the dresser is empty, so your clothes can go in there."

Jordan fixed her eyes on his. "This is a beautiful room."

"It's all yours. I'm right down the hall."

"I'm so tired," she croaked. "Why am I so tired?"

"Pneumonia is debilitating, and deceiving. You'll feel fine for a while, then you want to pass out. Give it time."

Wanting to say more, Jordan found herself frozen in place. That's when Nick took her by the shoulders and directed her to the bed.

All she could think was that if she weren't sick, this scenario—Nick, her, and a big bed—would end with a lot of tangled body parts and heavy breathing. She could imagine it all too clearly. And that was why it was a good thing she was a hot mess of germs.

Her pneumonia was the only thing that kept her from doing something really stupid, like kissing him.

Nick tossed back the covers and when Jordan climbed in, she made the mistake of looking at him. God help her. When his hand brushed against hers, when she picked up his fresh scent, heat shot through her body, and Jordan knew it wasn't her fever.

Chapter Three

WHEN JORDAN WOKE, the only thing she could see outside the window was white. The rain had been replaced by snow and based on the color of the sky and the way it was coming down, there was going to be a lot of it.

Acclimating herself to her surroundings, she sat up in the king-sized bed and wondered how long she'd been out. It was daylight, but she had no sense of time, or date. It felt like she'd been asleep for days.

Someone had plugged in her phone and tablet, and both sat on the nightstand fully charged. There was also a glass of water, and two new meds from the local pharmacy.

It seemed Dr. Rinaldi had called in a few prescriptions for her.

And picked them up.

Grabbing her phone, she looked at the time.

Eight thirty *a.m.*

That couldn't have been right. They'd walked over about ten this morning.

She looked again.

Eight thirty-one *a.m.* No. That was impossible. Combing her memory, she had little flashes of awareness, most of them involving Nick. His hand warm on her back as he helped her sip some water. Taking her temperature. Reading in the chair by the window.

Oh, God. Reality seeped in. Twenty-two hours. She'd been asleep for over twenty-two hours.

Damn.

There were a dozen text messages, most of them from Lilly and Mia, some of them growing frantic when they didn't hear from her.

The most recent one from Lilly, however, let Jordan know that Nick had filled in her friend. Filled her in about what exactly, she didn't know.

The man was too good to be true. Kind and gentle to a fault, he was also way up in her business.

Easing herself into the pillows, Jordan couldn't imagine how she would have managed if Nick hadn't muscled his way into her house two days ago. Granted, the Rinaldis wouldn't have let her freeze once the power went out, but she'd have been so much sicker.

Now, even though her chest still rattled when she coughed, she was able to catch her breath. After feeling like she was going to faint after making the short walk from the cottage, Jordan was relieved.

The other bit of good news was that her fever had broken. She'd been sweating under the blankets, soaking her T-shirt, which made this a good time to take a shower. Knowing she had to take it slow, Jordan threw back the covers and planted her feet on the lamb-soft area rug that covered the wood floor. She sat for a minute to make sure she had her bearings. After being prone for so many hours, she was surprised she wasn't dizzy.

No, Jordan was happy to find she actually felt like a human being for the first time in almost a week.

The amount of snow coming down was crazy. Going to the window, she looked out and was shocked at the accumulation. Obviously, it had gotten cold overnight. The snow was so light it was being blown around, causing huge drifts. Looking down, Jordan could see spots of lawn that were almost bare compared to walls of white that almost obscured the garage doors. "Damn," she muttered to herself. "What a mess."

"Mess is an understatement."

Jordan turned, and Lina approached from the door.

"You look a little better." Her landlady smiled softly. "How do you feel?"

"Like my fever broke. I was thinking about taking a shower."

"Good idea! There's plenty of hot water and fresh towels in the bathroom. Nicky put your toiletries on the counter."

"Thank you, Lina. I appreciate this."

"Aw, honey. You don't need to say thank you. You're like family, and I feel horrible about the car. Whatever happens, we'll cover it." As she spoke, Lina pulled the covers off the bed and tossed the pillows on the chaise. "I'll freshen this up for you."

Fairly sure her insurance would cover the car, Jordan nodded. She didn't doubt the Rinaldis felt terrible about everything that had happened, but who could have known?

Freshen up meant stripping the bed right down to the mattress pad, which Lina then flipped over like a professional wrestler-in-training. Jordan stepped out of the way as Lina tossed all the linens in a basket.

"You shower, and I'll finish up in here. Oh, Nicky put your clothes in the dresser. He brought your slippers over, too." Lina pointed and grinned at the bunny slippers staring at her from below the night table. They were a gift from one of last year's students, and Jordan adored them, even though they were silly. "Oh, there's a terry robe in the bathroom."

"Thanks," she said. Opening a drawer, Jordan saw her yoga pants, pajamas and shirts neatly organized. In another drawer were her unmentionables, in another her socks. It appeared the doctor was a neat freak.

Yoga pants were looking good, so she chose a pair along with a soft, long-sleeved T-shirt. With any luck, the shower would be the first step in feeling like herself again. She needed to shake off the sick and start moving around. Jordan needed to take her life back.

If she thought about it, it wasn't the way Nick took control that bothered her; it was the way she'd let him. After everything she'd gone through with Chase, almost abdicating her life in favor of his, Jordan had vowed never to give up her independence. If she were ever to get involved with anyone again, they would have to be equal partners and there could be no secrets.

Jordan was grateful to Nick and the Rinaldis for everything they'd done. There was no way she could ever repay their kindness. But the sooner she was back in her own place and taking care of herself, the better it would be.

Taking a shower was a start.

The bathroom was to die for. Jordan thought she had it good in the cottage, but this guest bath was straight out of a designer magazine. The soothing coastal palette from the bedroom continued in here, giving it a spa-like feel. It had a six-head shower and a whirlpool tub, both lined with glass tile. High-end fixtures, coupled with wood and a selection of soft linens made her sigh. The final piece: the floor was heated. If bathrooms could be boyfriends, this one would be hers—no detail was ignored.

Another deep cough reminded her that she wasn't done with the pneumonia just yet, but Jordan was happy she was able to stay standing. One day at a time. That's what she had to keep telling herself.

The water was warm right out of the jets. Stepping in, she could see Nick had left her 'hair goop' where she could find it, and Mrs. Rinaldi had left some delicious smelling mint and eucalyptus body wash for her. The scent, mixed with the steam, relaxed her whole body.

It felt good. Just getting clean was a step in the right direction. Being so sick, she hadn't done much in the way of personal care. She had to give Nick credit, he didn't flinch. She knew she looked like a neglected stray, but he'd never said a word.

She soaped up, washed her hair and stood for a few minutes, letting the water calm her mind and clear her chest. Deep breaths brought steam into her tight, irritated lungs, and she gradually felt relief.

Hearing the wind blow against the large windows, Jordan thought about her students. There were several kids whose families were struggling financially, and she hoped they'd kept their lights and heat. She couldn't imagine anything worse than being scared by the cold and the dark. Jordan was incredibly lucky. Many were not.

The robe Lina left was more like a plush blanket. It enveloped her in softness… and a wave of tiredness hit her hard. Here she thought she was getting better, but it occurred to Jordan she hadn't eaten since yesterday, so she guessed her blood sugar was somewhere near the floor.

Realizing she'd left her panties on the dresser, Jordan went into the bedroom to find a half-dressed Nick standing near the chaise. Half dressed. As in, he was wearing a pair of faded jeans, and that was it. Sweet Mother Mary.

His skin, ruddy and smooth, was pulled taut over his long lean muscles. Jordan's eyes traveled from the hair curling at the nape of his neck, over his broad chiseled shoulders, and down the line of his back. Stopping at his jeans was no hardship since they rode low and gave her enough of a peek that her mind could imagine his perfect, muscled ass.

Her heart was hammering in her chest, the steady thumping echoing in her ears. He was magnificent, and her girly bits wanted him bad. "Wow," she said on a breath.

Nick turned, and her belly clenched tight at the sight of him. Her bits had obviously lost their collective mind, because Jordan immediately thought about his hands running over her skin and his body pressed into hers.

"Oh. Hey. Sorry." He smiled, and Jordan's mind blanked. Nothing. There was nothing there except Nick. In his jeans.

Sweet baby jeebus.

From the slope of his shoulders, to his well-defined chest, to the way the muscles of his midsection tapered in, he was perfection. The skin, lightly dusted with hair, had a faint bronze glow.

Speak. She needed to speak.

"Jordan? Are you alright?"

"What...what brings you in here?" God, the thoughts that man was putting in her head. She wanted to jump him.

"My phone." He held up the slim device. "I forgot it."

"Ah. You slept there last night?" She couldn't help herself anymore. Jordan moved toward him. His smell was circling around her, pulling her in. Something clean and musky. It reminded her of the woods in spring, when life was blooming and the world was waking up.

"I stayed here for a bit. I was a little worried when you wouldn't wake up. But the sleep did you good. You look a lot better."

"I feel better. My fever broke."

Laying the back of his hand on her forehead, he grinned. "I think you're right."

A slight shiver ran through her body at his touch, and Jordan knew this meant big stinking trouble for her. The man was a dream walking.

He'd been so kind to her. Lilly, who had known him since they were in grade school, had told her about him one night when they saw him sitting on the porch. Nick was a Dudley Do-Right. He'd gotten into his share of mischief as a kid, but deep down, he always had been the good guy.

He hadn't changed, apparently. He still cared for people. He tried to make things right. Even a terrorist couldn't take the goodness out of him.

As the memory from last night started to come back, Jordan debated whether she should tell him what she knew. He'd been with her a lot longer than he was going to admit.

"When did you go to the pharmacy?"

"Yesterday, before it started snowing. I wanted to get you a stronger antibiotic and something to help your cough. Come here."

He pulled her to the freshly made bed and sat down with

her next to him.

"I managed to give you this about six this morning. The next dose has to be taken an hour before, or two hours after you eat. Around dinner works."

"Okay." Jordan really hoped the instructions were on the bottle because she couldn't concentrate.

"This is prescription cough syrup. It does have a narcotic, so take it only as needed. It will make you sleepy."

"Maybe I'll just take it at night?"

"That's a good idea. There's over the counter stuff in the bathroom, but honestly, tea with honey works, too."

"Got it." She waited for him to say something else, anything else, but instead they dropped into an awkward silence. She was sitting on the bed, wet and naked under her robe with a man who looked like every fantasy she'd ever had. It was heady in some ways, but it was also weird.

As if on cue, the two of them stood, and of course, Jordan felt everything around her spin.

She swayed with the room, feeling the floor pitch and roll, and a light wave of nausea settled in her belly. Everything was spinning, and if Nick hadn't been there, she would have fallen. But before that could happen, Jordan found herself wrapped in the doctor's very strong arms.

"Hey," he said, concerned. "What was that all about?" His eyes, a deep gray green, like the churning water of the bay, were wide with concern.

"I should have expected it." Jordan was trying to shake

off the feeling that she was going to lose control of her limbs. "I haven't eaten since yesterday."

Nick didn't budge, holding her firmly against him, his body warm and strong. "I'm glad you didn't get dizzy in the shower. You could have hit your head."

There was a light tapping on the door. "Am I interrupting something?"

Lina. Her eyes were wide as she started at the two of them holding each other. Nick shook his head and helped her sit on the bed. "No, Jordan got dizzy. She needs to eat."

"Of course she does. What would you like? I can make you eggs? Pancakes? French toast?"

"Something with protein, Nona?"

"Of course. I'll run downstairs and fix you an omelet."

"Thanks, Lina."

"Come down when you're dressed."

Getting dressed was a really good idea, considering the only thing between her and Nick was her robe. She stepped back. His arms were still banded around her, but at least there was a little distance.

"Thank you," Jordan said gently pushing his arms down when Lina left. "I'm better."

She wasn't. She missed his warmth already.

"Are you sure?" Raising his index finger straight up, he held it in front of her nose and then started to move it left to right. "Follow it."

"I'm fine."

"Don't argue."

"Fine." She followed his finger and resisted the urge to roll her eyes. It was then she realized someone was missing. "Where's Gertie?"

Nick laughed and tilted his head toward the door. "She and my grandfather have become pals. For all his complaining, he loves your dog."

"Really?" Jordan loved that. "Angelo had better watch out, or I'll ruin his reputation as a grouch."

It wasn't hard to see Nick's soft spot was his grandparents. His smile was so tender when he spoke of them, it was hard not to be drawn in by the charm of it all. God knew, Jordan was affected.

She stopped herself from reaching out to stroke his cheek. It wasn't the first time, and it was that impulse she'd have to control, because things were already too familiar between them. He'd shaved. But he was one of those guys who always seemed to have a five o'clock shadow, so she guessed he'd have some stubble pushing through in about an hour.

He was all man, but inside that take-charge alpha Naval officer was a gentleman with a heart of gold. Which meant he was a really bad idea.

Rubbing her hand on her chest, she coughed and cursed the urgent care doctor who didn't listen to her. She reported her symptoms to him the same way she'd told Nick, and the jerk had told her to let the cold run its course.

More painful coughing shook her body, letting her know it wasn't over, and she watched as Nick narrowed his eyes.

"What's wrong?"

"Nothing," she held up her hand. "I'm okay. But I get the sense the coughing isn't going to stop any time soon."

Patting her knee, he grinned. "No, it's going to take a while, and the exhaustion will last for weeks."

"Great. This is just delightful. How am I going to keep up with my students?"

"You'll have to pace yourself. Take naps when you get home. Work some short weeks."

"You make it sound so easy. It's not."

"I'm sure, but you can't do anything about it now. Take another shower later. The steam will do you good." He was still trying to be professional.

"Hmm. Try telling me that with a shirt on and I might believe you, Doc."

There was a pause as he rolled his tongue around in his mouth. It was then that he grinned, and his eyes lit up with his smile. That was a sight to see—he didn't do it enough. "You're giving me shit. I'll take that as a good sign."

"Just a little. What's the news with the storm?"

"Only two feet if we're lucky, but probably more. High winds, bad surf. It's been upgraded to a blizzard."

"How is the rest of the town doing?" Jordan was still thinking about her kids. She wished there was something she could do for them.

"The village is doing okay. I mean, the market was Armageddon, but everyone is pulling together. Most people are prepared."

"Most. But not all."

With a tilt of his head, Nick took a step in her direction. "Something worrying you?"

"Some of my students. I... I just... their families don't have much. A generator is a luxury. With the storm so bad, and the power out... I'm afraid for them."

Nick's eyes softened, and he closed the distance between them again. Settling his hands on her arms, he brought his face right to hers. "The town opened a shelter at the high school. Everyone will be warm and safe. Pop and I brought over trays of pasta, so they could have a hot meal tonight. The kids are playing, and the adults are relieved. There's also a shelter for people with pets. Seniors who needed a hand were picked up and brought to family, or the firehouse. It's not ideal, but no one who has lost power will freeze or starve."

Jordan nodded, her eyes locked on his. There were so many good people in this town, and Nick was one of them.

Jordan blamed much of her breathlessness over the past few days on being sick, and that wasn't a stretch, but being so close to Nick made her wonder if he was at the root of what she was feeling in that room. He was big and powerful, a physically impressive man, and he fried every brain cell in Jordan's head.

"I'll see you downstairs." He stepped back and left her alone, probably sensing that it was time to give her back some personal space. That was something Chase had never mastered. He was all about control, and Jordan couldn't believe she'd given up so much to him.

While he hadn't ever dropped in at school, Jordan wouldn't have been surprised if Chase had eventually crossed that line. Every day, he asked her endless questions about everyone she saw, who she'd been with when they weren't together, where she'd been. At the time, Jordan told herself he was just interested in her life, that he loved her. Now, having come to her senses, she could see his behavior had nothing to do with love; he didn't trust her. Ironic, considering Chase was the one caught cheating.

As she finished dressing, Jordan's mind went back to her father. He was never far from her thoughts. The hospice house was in the town just east of Compass Cove. He was safe, she wasn't concerned about that, but his cancer was so unpredictable, he could be fine for several months, or be gone in a matter of weeks. The worry was all consuming, especially since she had so much time to think about it.

Cancer was an evil, evil disease, and it was taking away the person she loved most in the world. It upset her that for the last two days he'd barely popped in her head. The last time they spoke was right before the tree fell on her car.

Dad made the decision to go into hospice three months ago, when he was told there was nothing else to be done. He was terminal, and the cancer had metastasized, so he sold the condo in his senior community and figured if he was going to die, he'd do so peacefully, and without unnecessary intervention.

That was her dad. Independent to a fault, and always looking out for her. Once he knew there was no good outcome, he took the decision out of her hands. Jordan thought she'd resigned herself to the fact that she was going to lose him, but at that moment, her heart hurt more than it ever had before.

She felt helpless and lost. Like her, Dad was a teacher, and had spent his last ten years working as a school principal. He'd retired a few years ago and was looking forward to easier days. A bright and thoughtful man, he'd touched the lives of many. Jordan took her lead from him in so many ways.

When the initial cancer diagnosis came a year and a half ago, they didn't know how it was going to go. For a while, his condition improved, and in the weeks right before she was supposed to get married, he was in the best shape he'd been in since starting chemo. But it didn't last. Symptoms returned, he started losing weight, and then the bad news came.

The cancer was not only back, it had spread. With a vengeance.

Jordan was numb after that doctor's visit. She couldn't tell anyone, couldn't bring herself to talk about it, because even thinking about her father dying crushed her.

Then one day, she broke. It didn't take much either. Lina spotted her coming home late one afternoon at the end of January, and she asked how things were going. Jordan had no idea what was different that day as opposed to any other. People asked her how she was doing all the time, and she gave them a flat, unemotional answer. But this time, Jordan lost it. She fell apart, and Lina, in her wonderful way, picked up all the pieces.

Grabbing her phone, she hit the number for her dad's room at the hospice house. She hadn't talked to him in a couple of days, and she hoped he wasn't worried.

The phone rang six times before bouncing back to the nurses' station.

"One East. This is Sarah."

"Hi Sarah, It's Jordan Velsor. I was hoping to talk to my dad."

"Hi Jordan! He and a few of the other patients are having their breakfast. They made French toast in the kitchen. Everything smells amazing."

"I'm glad to hear it. You guys survived everything okay?" The hospice was right near the local harbor, and with the rough water over the last couple of days, anything could have happened.

"A few trees came down, but we're all fine. Do you want me to get George?"

"You know what? I'm going to call him back after I eat.

I've been sick, and I finally feel like putting some food in my stomach."

"Perfect. You do that, and I'll let him know you'll be calling in a little while."

Relieved, Jordan set an alarm on her phone to remind herself to call in an hour. She needed to hear his voice, to know he was okay.

Jordan wasn't sorry she broke her engagement, but it seemed to trigger every bad event that followed, starting with Dad. When her father thought she was going to be settled and happy, he wasn't as sick. It was as if the planning and excitement—the idea of what was to come—kept the disease at bay. Jordan knew it was a ridiculous notion, but Dad looking forward to a future with more family and grandchildren down the line seemed to work better than everything the doctors had thrown at him. The idea that she would have Chase and his family to lean on was never far from her father's thoughts. Or hers, if she was honest.

But Chase's family was never going to support her. They didn't have it in them. Jordan was just window dressing. She was from an acceptable old family, but lacked significant money or clout. Perfect for the socially conscious Stanleys without being too much of a threat.

Her stomach growled, and Jordan had to believe that was a sign she was getting better. Food was definitely a good idea. Something else to be thankful for. She might not have a car, her cottage was probably frozen solid, but she wasn't going to land in the hospital.

Jordan had gotten through most of her life trying to look at the bright side of things, and it was getting exhausting. But today, she'd take the little gifts that had come her way.

Heading back into the bathroom, she found a blow dryer and got most of the moisture out of her hair, braided it and got dressed. It felt good to be somewhat pulled together.

Time to face the day.

Unlike the day she came over, Jordan was able to take in the beauty of the Rinaldis' home. Wide plank wood floors, heavy detailed molding, simple earthy colors all came together to make the farmhouse warm and welcoming. The long hallway was the home to three bedrooms, each with a bathroom. Nick's room was closest to the front stairs. She wondered how it was for him, living with his grandparents, after being away for so many years. Jordan figured Lina and Angelo would have hunted him down if he'd tried to find his own place, and there was something to be said for having someone to dote on you when you were recovering. Even if you weren't sure it's what you wanted.

Wobbly from the lack of food, she carefully made her way down the back stairs, which brought her right to the kitchen. Just as she hit the last step, Lina called her from the kitchen.

"Jordan, your omelet is ready."

"I'm here. Thank you." Entering the kitchen, she looked around at the space with new appreciation. She imagined it filled with noisy children and grandchildren—mobs of happy people talking, laughing and cooking.

It was rare to find a space that exuded such joy, but that was the hallmark of Lina's kitchen. There was only one thing, or person, rather, who was missing. "Where's Nick?"

Lina tilted her head toward the side porch and Jordan heard him stomp his feet in the mudroom. Poking her head around the corner, Jordan saw Nick unzipping his snow-encrusted parka and Gertie giving herself a good shake.

He'd gone out in the storm with her dog.

How did you pay someone back for that?

Lina had left a couple of towels in the mudroom, knowing they were going to have to dry off. The wind was wicked, blowing the snow in sheets that pounded the house. She couldn't imagine worse weather. Giving him a good once-over, she decided he looked almost as good as he did when he was shirtless.

"You are the slowest peeing dog ever, Gertie," he said to her. "What the hell?"

She heard Gertie moan in response, and Jordan chuckled. That was her dog, always with the last word.

"Yeah? It's a little late for an apology." He was talking to her dog. Jordan couldn't count the ways she loved this. "Well, look here. Come on, get up. Nona left us towels. I'm going to dry you off."

The sight of Nick and her dog in a mutual love fest as he rubbed down her wet fur gave Jordan more joy than anything in the past six months. He was scratching her belly, and she was looking at him like he was the only person in the world. The little traitor.

Still, Jordan let that sink in—he'd bonded with her dog. Considering how fussy Gertie was, it spoke volumes about Nick.

He continued to fuss over Gertie, not realizing that she could hear the entire one-sided conversation. When he and the dog came in with towels draped over them, Jordan burst out laughing. It quickly dissolved into a coughing fit, but the look on Nick's face when he realized she heard him having a full out conversation with her little hound was worth it all.

"Yeah, serves you right for eavesdropping, doesn't it, Gertie?" he growled sarcastically. He grabbed the towel from the dog's back and tossed both in the basket in the laundry room that was perched off the kitchen.

"It's good to see you back in the land of the living. The shower was a good idea."

"I don't smell, so yes. I still feel crappy, though."

"I'm not lying when I tell you it's going to take a few weeks, maybe a month, before you feel totally like yourself."

She still couldn't get her head around that. "A month? This is not going to be fun."

"If you're lucky it will be a month. Full recovery takes a while. You'll improve quickly, but like I said, the cough will linger, and you'll be run down."

"I've got no time for that," she snapped. "I have to go to

school. What about my students? And my dad…" She trailed off. Damn, she wasn't ready to tell him, but there was no way around it.

Sitting in the chair Lina had pulled out for her, Jordan folded her hands in her lap and dropped her head.

"How is your father, sweetie?" Lina sat in the chair next to hers and rested a hand on her shoulder.

Feeling her eyes burn, Jordan looked up and took a breath. "He's been doing okay. Stable, but that could change any day. I miss him. I haven't talked to him in a couple of days, and I don't want him to worry."

"What's up with your father? Can I help?" Nick stood on the far side of the table, holding a cup of steaming coffee.

Talking was the last thing Jordan wanted to do, because the words somehow made it more real. "Lina didn't tell you?"

"I'm not following," he said. "Tell me what?"

She took another deep breath to calm herself before plowing forward. "My dad is a patient at Shoreline Hospice House. He has liver cancer, it's metastasized, and he's terminal."

The expression in Nick's eyes, on his face, went from curious to concerned to compassionate. There was no need for explanation. He was a doctor. He wasn't clueless.

"I'm so sorry, Jordan. When was he diagnosed?"

Unlike everyone else in her life who danced around the question, Nick was direct. Jordan nodded. "About a year and a half ago. We had high hopes, but right after Christmas we found out it had spread. There was nothing left to do."

"I had no idea. I'm... I'm so very sorry."

"I just... I haven't seen him for a while. I didn't dare walk in there when I was so sick. I've called, but he hates the phone. And now I don't have a car."

"In a few days, I can drive you over, or if you're up to it we'll get you a rental. Try not to worry."

Of course, Nick was right. Dad was safe, but she didn't want *him* to worry. Then a thought hit her. She didn't know why, or where it came from, but in her desperation, she blurted it out. "Could you go? Check on him?"

Nick sat on the other side of her and put his hand on her knee. "I will if you want me to, but they won't tell me much."

"No, just go visit with him. I'll tell the nurses who you are, but I just don't like him being alone so much. Most of his friends either still work, or have moved away, and we don't have much family."

"Will he be okay with that?" She could see he was hesitant, and Jordan felt bad taking advantage of Nick's willingness to help, but she was desperate. "Oh, he'll love meeting you. He's a vet, like you. And he loves people. God, they called him 'the mayor' in his neighborhood. That's why I'm so worried. If he's isolated too long..."

Worried was an understatement. Jordan was frantic. She was terrified he'd die before she got to see him. Logically, she knew there was still time, but if he was lonely... anything could happen. She knew the fear was irrational. The disease would do what it was going to do, but Jordan never discounted the power of her father's emotional state. There wasn't time to waste.

Nick was the perfect person to visit him.

"Sure." He nodded slowly. "As soon as the roads are clear, I'll head over."

The wave of relief propelled her out of her chair and right to him, but she stopped just short of throwing her arms around him. As much as she liked him, as much as she appreciated what he'd done, that was a step too far. Her voice cracked as she held herself back, only reaching out to touch his hand. "Thank you. Thank you, Nick. I know we don't know each other well, but I'll never forget this."

The pull to him was primal, she felt it down to her very core. Everything about the man drew her in. It was heady, and dangerous. She was too close to him. Attraction like this was raw, visceral, and she felt vulnerable just thinking about him.

Having sworn off men was proving to be a lot more inconvenient than she thought it was going to be, especially with Nick Rinaldi in her life.

MINT.

It was swirling around him, coming off her skin and her hair. She was fresh, clean, and her body reached out to his in a way that was intoxicating, and very, very dangerous. Up close, he could see the curve of her neck, the softness of her earlobes, the pink flush of her skin. His blood heated in a way it hadn't in... jeez, longer than he could remember, and there'd barely been any contact.

"Ahem," his grandfather said while clearing his throat. "Jordan's food is getting cold."

Crap. What was he doing? Her eyes were locked on his, deep and crystal blue. She felt it too. He could see in her gaze that she was as affected as he was.

And she was not happy about it.

Stepping away, Nick had to reorganize his thoughts before he could say anything.

"He's right. You need to eat something."

He liked Jordan, but at this moment in time, she didn't need a guy with a hard-on. She needed a doctor, and a friend. Right.

"I'm sorry. I shouldn't impose on you."

"It's fine," he responded. "Come on." Hoping to coax her, Nick pushed her plate closer.

"Thank you. I mean that." She obliged him, picking up her fork. "This looks wonderful, Lina." Giving him a quick glance, she grinned. "Just what the doctor ordered."

The woman was a stunner. Sitting there, freshly showered, her hair still damp on the ends, she had a natural beauty that transcended any illness. Her eyes were a bright blue, wide and intelligent, and now that she'd started beating back the infection, he could see the life in there.

Again, he wondered about her engagement to Chase Stanley. He couldn't see the two of them together in any reality. They were so different, and Jordan didn't seem like the type who would go for money. What he did know was that the breakup left some scars.

Jordan had been babbling in her sleep, tossing and muttering things about his secretary, and letting the occasional f-bomb fly. He had to laugh; even asleep, she swore with conviction.

But it also told him the broken engagement still weighed on her, and that made him wonder exactly what had gone down. Even months later, the gossip mill was still spinning, because the Stanleys always seemed to be at the center of any town drama.

That was one thing he didn't miss while he was away. He loved his hometown. It had given him an upbringing like no other, but Nick didn't need drama, and it was one of the reasons he'd been laying low. He didn't want questions, he didn't want pity, he just wanted to find a way back to having a normal life.

Treating Jordan reminded him that he could be a doctor even if his hip never straightened out. The message couldn't have come at a better time.

He kept his focus forward and that meant he couldn't

allow Jordan to relapse. She seemed to be over the worst of the pneumonia, but that could change on a dime. If he could give her some peace of mind by going to visit her father, that's what he was going to do.

How he got himself in these situations, he had no idea.

LINA WATCHED AS Jordan and Nick sat at the kitchen table, the chemistry between them actually generating heat. She knew she shouldn't spy, but she wondered if the two of them realized they were each other's perfect match.

"What are you doing?" Lina jumped when Angelo's gravelly voice came from behind her.

"Shh. I'm watching them. I think there might be something there, Ang. I don't know, but the way those two dance around each other…"

"Oh, good grief, Michelina. You can't tell those things. Jordan is a pretty girl, and Nicky is only human."

Waving him off, she peered back into the room. They were talking now, and he was laughing at something she said. "You men don't know anything about affairs of the heart. Look at him, the way he looks at her, his eyes…"

"I knew enough to catch you, my love." Angelo's arms looped around her waist. What was left of her waist, in any case.

"I just want him happy. I think she could do it."

Her husband kissed her on the cheek. Bicker they might, but Lina knew she was lucky to find such a man as Angelo Rinaldi.

"Maybe, but she has to want to be happy herself."

Lina knew this was true. The two of them were so wounded, both carrying around scars on their battered hearts. Nick felt he failed in his duty. Jordan felt as if she wasn't good enough. If only they could see the possibilities of what they might have together.

Chapter Four

THE SNOW HAD finally stopped, but not before it left twenty-seven inches across the North Shore. Compass Cove was doing pretty well, but recovery was going to take a lot of work, and more time than anyone wanted to think about.

Jordan sat on the chaise in her room at the Rinaldis' house waiting for the verdict on the cottage. With the power out, and the frigid temperatures, pipes on the outside wall had frozen solid, and one had burst.

Lina told her Nick had done his best to protect against a freeze, but there was nothing that could have prevented what happened.

Now she just wanted to know if the place was habitable, or if she'd have to find another place to live in the meantime.

"Jordan?" Lina's voice carried through the house like it was on wires. "Lilly is here. I'm sending her up."

That brightened Jordan's mood immediately. Lilly was her best friend, and she'd missed talking to her with all the craziness of the last few days. Scratch that… the last week. She could only imagine how her friend's salon was faring since the storms.

"Well, aren't you the princess?" Lilly Vasquez entered the room with two take-away cups in her hands and a wide smile. "You are living the life, my dear."

"I wouldn't say that, but the Rinaldis have taken good care of me." Jordan adjusted the soft knitted throw covering her legs and lap. Gertie objected, but she moved and got comfortable again.

"No doubt." Lilly set the cups on the table and gave Jordan a big hug. "I'm so glad to see you. I was worried."

"I'm much better. I was lucky." She coughed twice, relieved that every day she was getting stronger.

"Hot lemon mint tea. Perfect for what ails you," Lilly said as she nudged one of the cups in Jordan's direction. Lilly grinned before she sat on the edge of the chaise. "But back to your point about luck, you were lucky to have a very hot doctor on call, I would say."

Jordan didn't respond at first, because she was looking for a way to disarm the comment. "He's been very...*kind*. I was fortunate he was able to step in when he did."

"Kind. Right." Her friend wasn't buying it, and why would she? Jordan wouldn't believe her if the roles were reversed.

"Lilly, don't turn this into anything. Okay? Tell me how the town is doing? How are you? Are your parents okay?"

"We're digging out. That's the best I can say about it. The salon has no power, which means my apartment doesn't either. Fortunately, my parents have a wood stove and a fireplace, so the house isn't freezing, but there's no hot water. I was going to head over to the firehouse to shower."

"You have clothes with you?"

"Yeah, in my truck, why?"

"Shower here. Lina won't mind."

Lilly breathed a sigh of relief, running her fingers through her silky dark hair. "Normally, I'd say no, but a hot shower sounds so good right now, and compared to the firehouse, I may take you up on it."

Focusing on Lilly, Jordan started when the deep voice came from behind her. "Hey."

Nick.

Turning her head sharply, she felt her stomach tighten when she took him in. God, it was like he got better looking every day. Jordan found herself frozen in place, but Lilly bounced right up to give him a hug.

"Hey! Thank you for rescuing my poor sick friend. I was so relieved when she told me you had been there to help."

"I'm glad I could. When she's not giving me attitude, she's a good patient."

Feigning shock at first, Jordan had to smile. The teasing grin on his face was too adorable to resist. "I do not give you attitude. I have been a model patient."

"Yes, when you were asleep, you were perfect." He stuffed his hands in the pockets of his jeans and the smile faded away. "Jordan, we have some news on the cottage."

Based on the downward cast of his expression, she was fairly sure it was not going to be good. "A pipe burst and flooded a section of the basement, including the laundry area. Additionally, some of the wallboard in the kitchen need replacing. You're not going to be able to go back for at least a few days until we can dry it out and replace the water damaged floors and walls."

"My furniture? My things?"

"All fine. Your kitchen table was sitting in a couple inches of slush, but that may be okay in the end. It's being pumped out now. Pops and I grabbed the clothes that were near the washer and dryer and I filled another tote with some personal items you might need." He put the tote bag on the floor next to the door. "Nona is sorting all the laundry. We'll send some out and she's taking care of the rest. It's just a precaution since you've been sick."

"I can send the laundry out..."

"No need. It could have been much worse. Pop has a construction crew coming tomorrow, and the insurance adjuster will also be here."

"I have renter's insurance..."

"Good. We'll keep you posted. But for now, it looks like you're going to be here until we get the mess at the cottage sorted out. Like I said, at least a few more days. The power company is hoping to have the electricity back to this street by tonight."

"So, I'll stay here?"

Nick nodded. "You can stay as long as you want."

"I understand, but this is so unexpected. I can find another place." That was a lie, she had no idea where she would go, but imposing on the Rinaldis much longer, and staying in Nick's orbit, wasn't good either. He made her think of what could be, and that wouldn't bring Jordan anything but heartache.

"It's not that long; at most, it will be a week. And it's good because I can keep an eye on you." He winked.

Mother of God.

Lilly shrugged. "You can always stay with me. My sofa pulls out."

Nick raised an eyebrow. "Didn't I hear you say something about not having heat?" he asked.

"Details, details," Lilly grinned.

"I appreciate everything, Nick. Thanks." It was nice to know she had options, but staying with the Rinaldis for a week? That could prove to be awkward. But Lilly's was out of the questions, especially without heat.

Nick nodded and left her with Lilly, who blew out a breath when he was out of sight. "Oh. My. God. He is so into you."

"There are times when I think we have moments, but then he shuts down again. He's so guarded." Jordan would like nothing more than to find out what made the man tick, but it made her nervous too. *He* made her nervous. "It's better that way, I guess. Especially if I'm going to stay here."

"Ah. I see. Who's guarded?" Lilly took a sip of her coffee and widened her eyes in the way she did when she wanted answers.

But Jordan wasn't ready to give her any. Mostly because she didn't know what she would say. Her life had been turned upside down, first by her cheating ex, then by her father's prognosis, and now the damn storm. She felt adrift. Lost.

"Okay. Yes. I am… protective of my heart. I don't want a man in my life."

Nick had been great, but she didn't think tying her line to a guy who was dealing with his own baggage was a good idea. If she was honest with herself, Jordan didn't trust herself enough to get involved with anyone.

Lilly seemed content with her response; at least it appeared so, since she didn't ask anything else. Jordan had no idea why she kept talking.

"He's going to visit with my dad later today."

"Nick? Why? I mean that's nice, but…"

"He's going because I can't—I'm still too sick. And I'm worried. So, he's going for me."

Lilly's eyes rounded again. "Ah."

Her friend and the 'ah.' "What?"

"Nothing. I just… it's very nice of him to do that for you."

"Yes, it is."

"Not typical doctor-patient stuff, though."

"I guess not." Jordan sipped her hot tea. The taste of lemon, honey and mint soothed her raw throat. "But, admittedly, it's been an odd few days."

Lilly nodded. "That it has, my friend. That it has."

THE HOSPICE FACILITY was a few miles east of Compass Cove, set just outside of a town that was born around the same time. So many of the North Shore communities had similar roots. Settled by New Englanders coming across Long Island Sound, the rich soil and protected harbors allowed for towns to spring up from the far east end all the way to Manhattan.

Jordan was recovering quickly, so leaving her on her own wasn't as much of a problem as it would have been a few days ago. She was still tired and run-down, but her lungs were clearing. Nick was glad Lilly Vasquez, who he'd known for years, stopped in with tea from Nona's café. Lilly was one of Jordan's closest friends, and probably the perfect babysitter because she wouldn't take any of Jordan's crap. In comparison, he would look like a pushover.

He pulled into a spot in the large lot that was next to a massive snowbank. From the looks of it, they got about the same amount of snow as Compass Cove, but being not quite as isolated, they'd cleaned up faster. The building itself was impressive. It had been constructed on land that was once occupied by a large marina, and Nick had to say, they did a nice job blending into the area. Just one story, and designed to look like a coastal inn, the facility couldn't have been more welcoming.

He'd done his research on the place. The nursing organization that ran the hospice house had taken great care to make it as homelike as possible. Entering through the front door, it felt more like walking into a large home than a medical facility. Depending on the progress of their disease, residents received as much or as little assistance as they needed. The goal was to abide by the patient's wishes and keep them as pain free as possible.

He signed in at the desk and must have looked lost enough that the receptionist offered help.

"I'm here to see George Velsor," he said. "I'm a friend of his daughter."

"Oh, Jordan! We haven't seen her in a while."

"She's been sick, recovering from pneumonia."

"Oh, that's right! The poor thing. She must be so worried about her dad." The woman, whose name was Nancy, was extremely nice. She warmed the facility up without even trying.

"That's why I'm here." Nick liked the feel of the place. He could see why Jordan felt her father was in good hands.

With directions to the room in hand, Nick made his way down the hallways. The building was really beautiful. Some residents were in a large sunroom, talking and playing cards.

The room itself had a wall of windows that faced the harbor, and since it was a nice day, the space was bathed in natural light. Other patients were with family. There was a woman in what looked to be a large communal kitchen, fixing a sandwich. Taking in the scene, it was the sense of normalcy that struck him. People here were terminal, they were going to die, but the environment catered to the business of living. It was calm and quiet—peaceful. There was no visible medical equipment and Nick knew that was the whole idea. It was about making the most of the time left.

Finally, he came to George's room. The door was slightly opened and there was a nice looking older woman with salt and pepper hair standing just inside the space. He tapped lightly on the door and the woman turned and smiled.

"Well, hello there, young man," she said. "Can I help you? I'm Tally, the social worker."

The way he moved, Nick felt anything but young, but he smiled and extended his hand. "I'm Nick Rinaldi, I'm a friend of Mr. Velsor's daughter."

"Oh, Jordan! We heard she has pneumonia. George is just taking care of business." She waved toward a door in the corner. "How is Jordan?"

"She's recovering. Still very tired, but getting better."

"Are you from Compass Cove? We heard the flooding was horrible and they're still digging out from the snow."

"Yes, it's been a challenge. There are a lot of narrow roads, and we had hundreds of trees come down. It's hard for repair and road crews to get around."

"It wasn't as bad here," Tally remarked. "Hard to believe since it's a stone's throw away."

"One theory is a tornado touched down. That's why so many trees were lost in one area."

"Goodness. That's terrifying."

Small talk. It was supposed to make people comfortable, but Nick sometimes found it tiresome. Tally was a nice woman, though. He couldn't fault her for trying.

When he looked around the room, he saw the TV was tuned to a pre-season baseball game. After the last few days of bad weather, pretty much everyone was wishing they could be in sunny Florida. That's when a tall man, with a shock of gray hair returned to the room. After looking Nick over, he flashed a huge smile.

It was Jordan's smile, and her father also possessed the same deep blue eyes. "Hello there," he said, stepping into the room and picking up a coffee mug. "Are you the ambassador dispatched by my offspring?"

Okay. This guy had a major personality. "Nick Rinaldi. I'm a friend of Jordan's. Nice to meet you, sir."

The elder man chuckled and shook Nick's outstretched hand. "Call me George. Please sit down. Would you like something?"

"No, thank you, sir—uh, George."

"So, how is my girl?"

The man was friendly and outgoing, but Nick could see

what they were up against. His pallor was a little gray, and there was the slightest tinge of yellow in his eyes. He was thin, and Nick guessed he wasn't always that way. If Jordan hadn't seen him in over a week, she was going to notice.

"Getting there, but it's going to take a bit. She was very sick."

"I told her to see a doctor." He shook his head. "Always worrying about everyone else. She's recovering okay? Not giving you too much trouble?"

"Yes. Every day she's improved. My grandparents are making sure she's well fed." That was the truth, but getting the woman to rest was a full-time job. "She needs to take it easy. Which is tough, because she's stubborn."

George burst out laughing. "Stubborn. Yes, she is. She gets that from her mother."

"The worst seems to be over. I'll bring her by in a couple of days."

"Good. So, Lina and Angelo must like having you under the roof again. If I remember, Lina wasn't happy unless there were ten people around her dining room table on Sundays."

"That pretty much says it all." Nick had to laugh. It was so true. "I've been home for about six months, give or take time for some surgeries. Just discharged from the Navy Medical Corps."

"I guess you'll be taking her a full report on my condition?" George's voice trembled. He wanted to protect Jordan from the truth.

"I won't have much to tell her, since I don't have access to your medical records."

"Ah." George sipped his coffee. "I'll tell you. I'm getting worse."

"What's happening?" Nick leaned forward, elbows on his knees. He couldn't treat him, but he could listen. And the more he knew, the better he'd be able to help Jordan cope.

"Restlessness—I can't seem to get away from myself. I have a fever on occasion. The jaundice. Nausea. I'm losing weight, but my belly is distended. Confusion. I'm guessing it's spreading because there's more pain."

"You're here so you can be comfortable. That's the point. There are medications—"

"I know." George cut him off.

The man may have known, but there was a level of denial in his behavior. "What do you *want* me to tell Jordan?"

"If I had my way, you wouldn't tell her anything." George glanced out the window behind him. Then he snapped his fingers. "I know. Tell her I found a girlfriend."

Nick had to laugh. "You don't really want me to tell her that, do you?"

He shifted in his seat. "I mean, she's going to figure things out soon enough. But I want her to take care of herself. Bring her when you can."

Now he understood why Jordan had been so upset. She knew her dad's condition was deteriorating, and that if she wasn't there, she would never get the whole story. Her father would deliberately keep her in the dark. So, while she was trying to protect him, he was still trying to protect her.

"You going to tell her?" George asked.

"Not unless you want me to." Nick took his confidence seriously, and if a dying man asked him to keep something to himself, he was going to do it.

"I don't. I don't want her running over here before she's ready. Understand?"

"I do. I'll take care of her."

"Between me, and itching to go back to work, she must be driving you crazy." George shook his head and smiled.

"Her fever just broke yesterday, and she has no stamina. School is a week or two off, at this point. She's a bit of a pest, but she's not impossible. Yet."

"*Yet* is key. Give her time." Jordan's dad glanced out the big window that faced the water. "Can you come with her? She hasn't seen me in over a week. She'll notice the difference, and it's going to be a tough visit."

Nick nodded. "I was planning on it. She still doesn't have a car, and I don't want her overdoing it."

"I appreciate this, Nick. I'm so worried about her. She told me about the car…"

Nick could relate to what he was feeling. Over the past few days, he'd been pretty worried about her too. The woman had gotten under his skin in a big way.

Nick wasn't easily impressed by women anymore. His uniform was like a magnet, so he could date a different woman every night if he wanted. And when he was younger, he did.

Not now. If he was going to get involved, it would have to be something steady and real, with a woman who gave him a run for his money.

If he was honest about it, a woman like Jordan.

George had turned to the TV, his attention fixed on the screen.

"Who's playing?" Nick asked.

"Oh, um, the Yankees and the Braves."

"How's it going?"

"Yankees are winning. That new outfielder can belt 'em out of the park."

"Yeah? I haven't been following too much."

"So, your grandparents had three sons, is that right?"

"Yes. My father is Marco."

"Ah. He moved west, what was it? Almost twenty years ago. Your grandmother wasn't all too happy about that."

"Not quite twenty years, but yeah, Nona likes us to stick close." He remembered the day his parents left town like it was yesterday, partly because he'd opted to stay behind to finish his senior year of high school. It was strange moving in with his grandparents, but he wasn't about to leave—not when he had a girlfriend and was set to be a starter on the football team that fall. His folks were still happily settled in California, managing operations at one of the big vineyards in the Napa Valley. He'd seen his parents a couple of months ago, and his mother was still trying to get him to settle down out there, but he had no interest. And the truth was he'd always been closer to his grandparents than his parents.

Sure, the area was beautiful, and he could find work if he really wanted, but Compass Cove kept him grounded. People here were good to him, they appreciated what he'd been through, but no one put him on a pedestal. He didn't need to be admired; he just wanted to find a way to be productive. To be normal. And to move on.

"So," George began. "How did you get hurt?"

That gave Nick a moment's pause, but he figured the last thing George wanted to do was talk about himself.

"I was based at the joint services hospital in Kandahar. I went out to a village to help at a local clinic giving kids vaccinations." He took a breath because the memory still hit hard. But being in the presence of another vet, someone who understood, made it easier to tell the story.

It was a hot day, probably close to a hundred degrees, and dust was blowing around, getting into every crack and crevice. Still, he heard local kids outside the clinic window talking and laughing. There were another half a dozen kids and parents in the small waiting area.

He'd been to this clinic nearly a dozen times, and even though it was a good hour from the base, he liked coming out. The kids had taken to calling him Dr. Nick, and he liked helping out the locals. Sure, he handled the emergency room at the hospital, but he was one of the only people deployed who was also a pediatrician.

He was talking with a new mother about keeping her six-month-old baby properly hydrated in the heat when he heard the popping from outside, followed by screaming.

He'd never forget the sound of the kids screaming.

"There was an ambush. Insurgent. He came in firing. Killed everyone in the waiting room before I could even grab my sidearm. The marine who came with me had taken two bullets, and I took three before I was finally able to get off a couple of shots and take him down."

"One guy? Wow."

"With an automatic weapon and a big clip, you only need one guy."

George let out a low whistle. "Killing kids. What has this world come to?"

"That village is filled with the nicest people. You can't imagine."

"No, son. I can't. I'm sorry you had to go through that."

This was more than he'd told anyone so far—not even his close friends or his family. Somehow, Jordan's father understood. And he knew exactly how much to push.

Nick appreciated that.

"Vietnam was a shitshow. I hated every minute, but I got through it. You'll get through this, too."

They settled into an easy silence. The kind of quiet that happened between old friends. But George was uneasy. He twisted his fingers into knots, the knuckles going white.

"Are you scared? Is there anything you need for anxiety?"

"Nah, they got me covered here," he responded. "This disease is a bitch."

Nick shook his head. "It is. Jordan told me about the prognosis."

George grinned. "Did she? That's not like her."

"She was under the influence of some pretty strong decongestants. It all kind of tumbled out."

"She's something. I'm sure glad she has you to help her through... well, you know... everything."

Everything. Nick wasn't quite sure what he was driving at, but the guy was a talker. He'd find out soon enough.

"I don't know when I'm going to slip into the next stage, when the next big failure is going to come. It could be gradual, it could happen all at once. Apparently, I could become delirious. I could go like that." He snapped his fingers. "It's going to be hard on her."

"The staff here will know how to manage it." Nick could see the fear in George's eyes. It hit him hard.

"I can't tell you how relieved I am you came to see me. At least I'll know she's not alone. That she has someone."

"Someone?"

George nodded and patted his knee like they were old buddies. "Nick, I'm not stupid. I can see in your eyes how you feel about her. I mean, why else would you come to see her old man? Do you have a date in mind?"

A date? Awareness came slowly but once it did, he was

sucker-punched. Her father thought he and Jordan were together. That maybe they were engaged? *Shit.*

"Uh. It's…"

"I shouldn't have asked. Sorry. I don't mean to push. You're a good man. You have a good family. I'll be able to rest easy knowing my girl isn't alone."

Jordan wouldn't be alone. She had a ton of good friends, and Nona and Pops would watch out for her. But they weren't a couple, and he didn't know quite how to tell George the truth.

That made him wonder if it really mattered. Did he have to tell him that Jordan wasn't his girlfriend? Was there harm in giving a dying man comfort?

"I'll watch out for her." That wasn't a lie. He would watch out for her.

"I know you will. I want her happy with a pack of kids. She's going to be a wonderful mother."

Nick had no doubt she would be.

"She always wanted to wear her mother's wedding gown, did you know that? The last guy thought it wasn't fancy enough."

"I didn't. But she looks beautiful in pretty much anything. She doesn't need anything to be overdone." Again, not lying.

"That's the truth. She looks just like my Jane." The way he said his wife's name made Nick take notice. Wistful and happy, it was the way he wanted to feel one day when he talked about his wife.

"What happened to Jordan's mother?"

"Oh, Janie died when Jordan was just six. Car accident. Wet road."

"I'm sorry."

"Me too. It broke my heart. She was the love of my life. After that, it was me and my girl. We did okay, watched out for each other, but it wasn't the same."

He didn't think it could be. He imagined that's why Jordan was so distraught. Why she was so viscerally affected about losing him. Her father was all the family she had.

"You don't have to worry."

Keep it vague and you're fine, he thought. *This will comfort him.*

George's eyes filled. "You're a good man, Nick Rinaldi. She's lucky to have you. Don't wait too long to make her your wife. If you're in love, you shouldn't wait."

"We're not rushing anything. She has a lot on her plate right now." That was the truth. "I'm planning on bringing her over the day after tomorrow. She should be well enough by then."

"Excellent."

"Right." What had he just done? And how had George jumped to this conclusion? Nick thought carefully about everything he'd said, and there was nothing that should have led the conversation in that direction.

Nick had so much explaining to do to Jordan. He was

going to be lucky if he was walking the day after tomorrow. She was going to bust his kneecaps.

He had to get her to see that a little white lie told to comfort a dying man wasn't a bad thing. They could pretend to be a couple for her father's sake. It wasn't going to hurt anyone, and he'd leave this earth with some peace of mind.

Nick believed in honesty, without a doubt, but he also believed in compassion. And letting George Velsor think his daughter wasn't going to be alone when he slipped into the most cripple stage of his disease was a compassionate thing to do.

Sure, it was old-fashioned. It was archaic, if Nick really thought about it, but George believed in love. And he wanted that for his only daughter.

Nick intended to give him exactly what he wanted.

Chapter Five

JORDAN'S EYES FLUTTERED open, and she realized she woke up to the same thing she'd fallen asleep to—an empty house. The Rinaldis had been incredibly generous and caring while she recuperated, but the truth was Jordan was lonely. Three short days out from the end of the storm, and Compass Cove was getting back in its groove. The high school was back in session, the stores in town were back to a full schedule, and everyone in her life was busy. Rubbing her chest, Jordan was relieved that she felt so much better, but she was frustrated that she wasn't able to get on with her life.

Loneliness. It was the emotion that scared her the most. It was when she felt most vulnerable, fearful, helpless. And that's how she was feeling right now. The world was going on around her, and Jordan was stuck in this room, unable to go anywhere and too tired to try.

She came up here right after Nick had left to visit her dad. She was grateful he was willing to go, even if she wanted to go herself. But there was no way she would risk getting her dad sick. He was too fragile; even a sniffle could be disastrous.

Feeling the heaviness in her body, Jordan wondered when she'd stop feeling so tired. This morning when she got up, she felt as though she might have turned a corner. Her cough was much better, her breathing was easier, she'd slept through the night. But then, in the late morning, waves of tiredness hit. She could've fallen asleep standing up. Her body was weak and achy, so she crawled back into bed, which is where she'd been for over three hours.

"Work *would* kill me," she mused. Which was what Nick told her yesterday when she hinted that she wanted to go back to school when it reopened. Just the thought of being on her feet for hours at a time exhausted her. Standing, Jordan walked to the window and gazed down at the grounds. The downed trees had been cleared, and yesterday the insurance adjuster had her car taken away. Nick and Angelo had been great. They negotiated a good price for the car, and Angelo was going to talk to a friend of his who owned a dealership about getting hers replaced.

The sound of power tools echoed in the distance. From what she'd been told, the repairs on her cottage were going well and she might actually be able to get in there in a few more days. More wallboard than expected had to be re-placed, but considering what could've happened, she was lucky. Her furniture had been spared, and the majority of the damage had been cosmetic.

Still, the Rinaldis were making sure the cottage was in perfect condition before she moved back in, and Jordan had a feeling Nick had a hand in it. After the construction was done, the cleaning crews were heading in. Lina guaranteed her she would be returning to a spotless home. Jordan was never worried that Lina and Angelo would skimp on anything, but she'd heard Nick giving them the extra push, reminding them about her recovery.

Over the drills and nail guns, Jordan heard voices below her window. Craning her neck, she saw Nick and the construction foreman by the corner of the front porch. They both assumed 'the position,' as she called it—their legs were spread wide, their arms folded and each of them nodded while the other spoke. She expected Nick wanted an update on the cottage, and the foreman was telling him all the problems they were running into. It didn't really matter, Jordan decided, but she was greatly enjoying the view of Dr. Rinaldi.

His five o'clock shadow had returned before lunchtime, the scruff making his face deliciously masculine. From where she stood, Jordan could see his broad shoulders through his bulky navy-blue parka. The wind was blowing, and his dark hair was mussed and curly. Rugged and strong, with the sun reflecting off the snow, his face was more old-time movie star than small-town doctor.

When the men shook hands, that was Jordan's cue to run a brush through her hair, check her breath, and head downstairs. She wanted to know everything. How her dad looked and sounded, if he gave any indication to Nick how he felt.

If there had been any changes. Dad had a terrible habit of keeping her in the dark about his condition. He thought he was sparing her, but not knowing only added worry to her already long list of concerns. She was hoping, with Nick's background as a doctor and a vet, Dad would open up.

He didn't turn when she came down the stairs. Nick was standing at the island flipping through the mail, his cheeks pink from the cold wind that was blowing off the water. Shaking it off, she had to get back into a good headspace, in particular, one that didn't have Nick taking up quite so much room.

Jordan took the last step into the kitchen, and Nick finally noticed her standing there. His eyes were steady, and his mouth didn't twitch into the grin she'd gotten used to over the past few days. His reaction told her one thing: she was right to be concerned about her father.

"Hey," he said as he unzipped his parka. "The contractor said you'll be back in your place in a few more days."

"That's good. There must be a dozen of them at the cottage. I didn't know that many people could fit in there."

Nick laughed and took off his coat before settling himself on a stool. He motioned for her to sit down, and Jordan's stomach drew into a knot, wondering what he was going to say. His face was serious, but not dire. His brows weren't drawn together, and his eyes were looking straight into hers. "My grandfather promised them lunch for a month if they hauled ass on the project."

That sounded like Angelo. He wheeled and dealed like a seasoned salesman.

"Well? How's my dad?"

Nick grinned, and Jordan's stomach released a little.

"He's a character. Funny, and great to talk to. He's worried about you."

"I'm worried about *him*." Jordan wasn't the one dying, and she wished Nick would stop beating around the bush. "How is he?"

"Talkative. Lucid. He did get tired after a little while, so that was my cue to leave. The disease is draining his energy."

"The fatigue has been getting worse," she acknowledged. "How did he look?"

"His pallor was a little off. He told me he's losing some weight."

"God." She rose and circled the island. "I wish I could see him."

Nick leaned into the island and folded his hands, his long fingers woven together. "I'll take you over in a couple of days. How does that sound?"

"Not tomorrow?" She coughed.

"Give yourself another day. The cold snap is supposed to break tomorrow. Super cold air could irritate your lungs."

Jordan had learned not to argue with the good doctor. Over the past five days she'd asked a million questions, and he'd answered every one; he was unfailingly respectful. But Nick wanted her to rest, and he wasn't going to clear her to see her dad before he thought she was ready. Considering how quickly she'd improved under his care, she wasn't going to fight it.

"Okay. I'll call him in a bit."

"Good idea. Let him get a little rest."

Nick stood and went to the mudroom to hang up his coat while Jordan stayed at the island. "You were gone a long time," she called to him.

"Yeah. I had a consult with my orthopedist. He said I can go back to work."

Jordan knew that was a big step for anyone coming back from an injury, but for Nick, who'd been out of commission for a long time, it had to be a relief.

"That's great! I mean, you're ready, aren't you?"

Nick opened the refrigerator and scanned the contents. "Last week I would have been less sure, but yeah. I am."

Jordan nodded, a little jealous. "That's good. Congratulations."

"Thanks." He was still in the fridge. "Are you hungry?"

"Ah, no. Not right now."

"Nona and Pops are out tonight. I'll go to the café and pick up dinner. Are you in? Whatever you want... my treat."

Jordan laughed. "Your treat. Isn't it free?"

He responded with a raised eyebrow. "Details. What do you say? Dinner and a movie?"

Jordan was surprised how she reacted to such a simple proposal. Dinner and a movie sounded like a date. But it wasn't a date. It was friendly. Just friends. Hanging out.

True to form, she was overthinking, and that had to stop. Since breaking it off with Chase, she overanalyzed everything. People were scrutinized and she only put her trust in a select few. Shaking off her hesitance, she agreed. If anyone deserved her trust, it was the man in front of her. "Sure. That sounds great. I've been spending too much time in bed." *Oy.* His mouth twitched a little and Jordan composed herself. "You know, resting. Like you said."

"I get it."

"Anyway, thanks."

"You're welcome. What do you want to eat?"

Jordan thought about it. She'd been eating lightly the last few days. Her diet had consisted of soups, omelets, and small servings of whatever Lina or Angelo had fixed for dinner. She hadn't had much of an appetite until today. This morning she woke up ravenous. Along with her eggs, she'd had a fresh scone with jam and two pancakes. She'd made herself a big sandwich for lunch. Thinking about dinner, her mind zeroed in on one thing and one thing only.

"Rinaldi's specialty burger with curly fries. Medium. Loaded. But no mustard."

Nick's face was flat. No expression, except for the amused sparkle in his eyes. "Planning for that heart attack, are you?"

"I've been eating like a bird for days," Jordan snapped. "I need sustenance. Don't judge."

Nick threw up his hands in defeat, smiling, and causing the quiver in Jordan's belly to intensify. "Specialty burger it is," he said.

"Loaded."

"No mustard."

"Thank you," she said.

"My pleasure." With that, Nick grabbed his backpack and headed upstairs, once again leaving her brain muddled, and her body wondering what she was missing.

THE RIDE BACK from the town was the most normal it had been since the storm. The snow was melting, and other than the occasional patch of ice, it was pretty easy to get around. School was back in session, and he knew that was driving Jordan nuts. She'd FaceTimed with her class and found out that about a third of the kids still didn't have power at home. Which made her worry, and question him about how much longer she'd have to stay home. Even with all her improvement, Jordan still tired easily. After their talk about her dad, she'd gone back to her room and fallen asleep for two hours. The exhaustion would linger longer than the cough, and Jordan, who lived a very busy life, would have to slow down.

When she woke, he ordered the food and left her in charge of finding a movie. Probably not his best idea, since that meant he'd probably be spending the next few hours watching a chick flick. Still, it could be worse. The company was nice.

Entering the kitchen, the under-cabinet lights cast a warm glow over the space. He liked it here. The house felt like a home, and even though he was taking advantage of not having his grandparents around, he was glad he'd come here to recover.

His grandmother seemed to know when he needed help and when he needed space. Mostly. Sometimes she overstepped, but for the most part, Nona let him heal on his own terms.

Getting a beer from the fridge, he almost whacked his head when Jordan's raised voice startled him.

"Shoot the damn puck! What are you waiting for, an invitation? Sweet Jesus! SHOOT IT!"

Okay. Not a chick flick.

Grabbing the bag and a beer, Nick found her in the den, kneeling on the couch. It looked like she was ready to lunge at the TV. Gertie was curled up on the chair nearby, watching Jordan intently. For himself, Nick stood in the doorway for a good ten seconds and she never noticed he was there. That's how intently she was focused on the game.

It was the last thing he expected.

Hockey. The girl was a hockey nut.

She coughed several times, and that was Nick's cue. "Couldn't find a movie?" he said as he set down the food.

Barely breaking from the game, she glanced over. "I never looked, once I saw this…" Turning to him, she tilted her head. "You don't mind, do you?"

"No. Not at all. I just didn't know you were a fan."

"Oh, insane. My dad and I—" Her eyes darted back to the screen and she leaned forward, almost falling into the coffee table. "HIT HIM! Don't let him do that… oh, my God!"

The coughing was worse this time, and Jordan pulled up the neck of her T-shirt to cover her mouth. She kept going, catching her breath and tipping onto the pillow at the end of the couch.

Finally, it settled. Tugging her shirt back into place, Jordan sat up and turned her eyes back to the TV.

"There was a break in play while you were bringing up a lung."

She glanced at him out of the corner of her eye. "Funny. You're going to joke about my illness? What kind of doctor are you?"

"A bad one who brought you lots of unhealthy food." He pulled the to-go containers out of the bag, along with some silverware and napkins.

"What did I say about judging?" Jordan took a sip from a glass of water on the end table.

"Uh huh." God, she was fun. She was all sass and brains, wrapped in a gorgeous package. She made Nick think about having fun again. Something he hadn't done in a long time.

"What did you get there, Doc?"

He flipped open the top of the container and there sat a specialty burger. Loaded, with fries.

Jordan gasped in faint indignation. "A burger, Doctor Healthy?"

"Don't. Judge," he snapped. "Or you won't get any of these." He raised a third to-go box in the air, just out of her reach.

"What's in there?"

"Gruel," he teased.

"Gruel," she laughed. "You're fresh. Gimme."

This was too much fun. He moved the box closer, and as soon as Jordan reached out, he pulled it away.

Folding her arms, she glanced back at the TV, content to watch the between period recap. That's what he thought, until she pounced and grabbed the box.

"Ha! Don't let your guard down around me."

"You're impossible." *She was fantastic.*

Women who were demure and agreeable were never Nick's type. No, he went for a woman who would challenge him, who would push all his buttons. Jordan was bold, and packed with attitude. He could get used to her.

When she flipped open the box, she groaned with pleasure. "Onion rings. These things are practically a religious experience and you were going to keep them from me?"

The look on her face when she took a bite was almost orgasmic, and Nick wondered what it would be like to get that look for himself. He'd pictured it more than a couple of times. Jordan, pressed into a plush mattress, little giggles and groans coming from her as he brought them both to the edge of reason.

Physically, Nick had always found her attractive. Long, lean, and model gorgeous, how could he not? But now that he'd gotten to know her? The attraction was deeper, more visceral. Even with her face scrubbed clean, and her hair pulled into a mess of a bun, she was easily the most beautiful woman he'd ever laid eyes on.

He had to get a hold of himself, refocus. "I had no idea you were such a rabid Mariners fan."

"Oh, yeah. Since I was a kid. Dad and I have had a ticket package since I was around ten, I think? We'd go to at least twenty games a year. Until this year."

He thought about their history. With Jordan being without her mother for most of her life, her dad was everything. The gravity of the loss she was facing became very real.

"I have tickets for a game in a couple of weeks. I'll have to give them away, I guess."

"Why?" Nick grabbed an onion ring from the box. "If you take it easy, and you know, don't jump over the boards during the game, you should be okay."

"Yeah?" Jordan nodded and took a healthy bite of her burger. The homemade sauce his nona put on the sandwich oozed out the sides of the bun, making it a special kind of mess. Jordan had no shame and took another bite. "Want to go with me?"

"What? To the game?"

With her mouth full of burger, she nodded, then swallowed. "Sorry." She wiped her mouth with a napkin. "I eat like a starving longshoreman. So, do you want to go? We have great seats, and you can make sure I don't overdo it. It will be fun."

Would it be fun, or would it be too hard for her since this was something she always did with her father? "If there's no one else you'd rather take…"

"Oh, well, I asked you, didn't I? Have you ever been?"

Nick was trying to figure out if she'd just asked him out on a date, or if this was a *let's-be-pals-and-go-to-the-game* kind of thing. "One time. I was a football and basketball guy. I mean, I used to play some pick-up hockey when the pond in the park froze over, but I haven't been to a game since I was eleven. It's been a while."

"Long overdue, then." She dipped a French fry in some ketchup. "I'm so going to pay for this dinner, but man is it good."

Nick took a bite and let the flavors of the meat and seasonings melt in his mouth. "I get that, but you're right. It is good."

"It's my favorite thing at the café, except for breakfast. Breakfast is all about the–"

"Banana pancakes." Nick finished her sentence.

"Yes! Oh, my God. They're decadent. I haven't had them in months."

"I'll make some tomorrow."

Jordan's eyes locked on his and her soft pink tongue darted out of her mouth. "You know how to make Lina's banana pancakes?"

Nick nodded as he popped a fry into his mouth. "Yep. It's how I get girls."

Jordan blinked. Twice. Then she burst out laughing.

"You think I'm kidding?"

She leaned back into the cushions, reaching out to pet Gertie, who snuggled into Jordan's thigh. "I don't doubt you can make them. But I don't think you need pancakes to get women. I'm sure there are other things they find more attractive."

"Eh, I don't know. The pancakes are pretty special."

"Trust me, Nick." She leaned in conspiratorially. "It's not the pancakes."

Their faces were so close he could feel the heat coming off her skin as she flushed from awareness. Frozen, they held in place for what felt like forever. Her eyes, big and blue like the waters he'd seen in the Mediterranean, stayed focused on his, a million questions in their crystal depth.

What would happen next?

Then there was a shift, her body turning slightly into his, and her eyes dropped to his mouth. She was close, so close. He barely moved. Nick just leaned in the final inch and kissed her.

Her lips were soft, warm, and melted together with his.

Electricity shot through him with each little sip, each taste. As kisses went, it wasn't long and deep. It didn't trigger lust, but it made him want. It was tender and sweet, and it made him think about growing old with this woman. He was speechless.

When they pulled back, Jordan's eyes slowly drifted open. A barely audible *"Wow"* came out on a breath.

"I didn't plan that. When I offered to buy dinner…" The last thing he wanted was for her to think he'd been planning to make a move on her all along.

"I know you didn't, but I don't think we should do that again."

Her gaze was fixed on the TV. The second period of the Mariners's game was about to start.

"Okay."

"And don't say you're sorry," she added.

He was about to apologize, but it wouldn't have been honest. He wasn't sorry for the kiss, but he did regret crossing a line with her. "Okay."

They dropped into silence, watching the game without exchanging a word. Finally, Jordan spoke.

"I didn't hate it. I mean, you're a good kisser. And I'd be lying if I said I didn't find you attractive."

"But?"

"But, my life is a shitshow, Nick. I'm not ready for… for you."

"I get it. I do. And I never wanted you to feel uncomfortable. I didn't…"

"I know. Can we go back to being friends? I think that's best."

Friends. He nodded in agreement. When they sat down to eat, Nick intended to tell Jordan about her father's confusion regarding their relationship. Now, after the kiss, and the boundary she'd just established, Nick didn't know what he was going to tell her.

Or when.

Chapter Six

"I'M SURE EVERYTHING will go well, Samara. The class can be a handful, but I love them to pieces." Jordan's sub had been a Godsend. they'd only been back a couple of days, and she made the effort to call simply to check in. Jordan appreciated it.

"Yeah, they miss you, but they're being very good. They just went to art. How are you feeling?"

Feeling? Jordan was still rattled from the kiss Nick laid on her last night. Innocent as it was, she was reeling from a wash of emotions. But she had to admit, the kiss was something pretty special. Nick was pretty damn special.

"I'm much better. Looking forward to getting out tomorrow. I haven't seen my dad in almost two weeks."

"Getting out will be good for you," Samara said. "It's got to be hard being cooped up."

She had no idea. Being this close to Nick without being able to explore the bubbling attraction was torture, even if it was just physical. Lord, who was she kidding? It wasn't just physical. There were many things she found she liked—really liked—about him.

He seemed perfect, and if Jordan had learned anything because of her debacle with Chase, it was that no one was perfect. Not even the sainted Dr. Nick.

Jordan had gone into the relationship with Chase Stanley with blinders on. He'd pursued her relentlessly, and—no doubt—it was flattering. Never one to play the boyfriend game, Jordan dated when she felt like it. She was too busy with her life to worry about a serious relationship. At twenty-eight, when she'd met Chase, she was busy teaching, as well as training to run her first marathon.

At that point, she was still living with her father in the house where she grew up. Her focus was on herself, her career, and her goals. Meeting Chase at a party threw her off her game simply because his attention was so consistent, and he was charming.

And handsome.

And well-educated.

And rich.

Most definitely too good to be true, because as she learned, the guy was also a snob and a liar who was more interested in keeping Jordan as an accessory than loving her.

They were together for over a year before Chase proposed on a romantic vacation to Fiji. He'd engineered the entire trip, whisking her off to an ultra-exclusive resort and popping the question as they watched the sunrise from their private villa.

Jordan was all in. She'd bought the romantic fantasy.

Considering how it all turned out was proof that she couldn't trust herself where her heart was concerned. As much as the attraction to Nick was pulling at her, she wasn't ready.

Every now and then, the flood of betrayal and hurt that she felt when she discovered Chase cheating the day before their wedding was more than she could handle. Sure, it was a good thing she'd found out about his affair before she'd said 'I do,' but that didn't mean it hadn't wounded her to the core.

Hurt and humiliation were only two of the feelings that still crept up without warning. Betrayal, anger, doubt... it was a smorgasbord of self-recrimination and pain.

She hadn't thought about Chase recently, but it wasn't because she'd gotten over what he'd done. It was because she'd been preoccupied with her father. Getting closer to Nick, however, was a harsh reminder of the pain she could be subjected to if she let her guard down.

Samara had been talking during Jordan's side trip, and she found herself agreeing with something her sub had said about one of her more challenging kids.

"I have to go, Jordan. The first bus just arrived, but I'll email you with the field trip details."

"Thanks, Sam. I'll talk to you soon."

Ending the call, Jordan thumped her head into the back of the chaise. Gertie jumped up, crawling across her chest so she could land a few good kisses on her chin. "What is it, silly dog?"

Gertie's little stub of a tail wagged frantically, and she turned her head toward the spot where Nick stood, shoulder pressed into the doorframe. His eyes asked for permission to enter, but he didn't say anything. Based on his tentative posture, it seemed he was affected by last night's kiss as much as she was.

"Nona had to go to the café, but she left you some breakfast," he said, not budging from his spot.

Jordan, who was feeling stronger than she had in a week, wanted to take care of herself. She couldn't wait to get back in her own space. "I wish she wouldn't do that. I can fix my own food."

Nick chuckled, and Jordan's insides curled at the way the corners of his eyes crinkled in amusement. "Have you met my grandmother?"

"I know, I know." Telling Lina not to feed her was like telling a fish not to swim.

Nick looked away, stuffing his hands in his pockets. "I'm sorry if I made you uncomfortable last night. That wasn't—"

She cut him off. "You don't have to apologize. It's been an odd few days."

Talking about the kiss would only serve to trigger another flash of memory, another swell of longing. Her chest ached when she thought of it. His lips, his warmth... it was perfect.

And it could never happen again.

Nick presented too much of a risk for Jordan's fragile heart. Just knowing how easily she surrendered to his touch was enough to throw up a red flag.

Thankfully, she'd be back in her cottage in a couple of days and she could put a little distance between them. Jordan needed time to process what Nick made her think and feel. What he made her want.

Jordan gazed out the window, unable to make eye contact. She wasn't sure if it was embarrassment, or if she was worried.

"Okay, then. I'll see you later."

"You're going out?" She turned back to see she'd thoroughly confused him. *Oh, fabulous mixed signal there, Jordan. Pfft.*

"I have an appointment in town. Do you need anything?" He was so damn polite.

"Oh, ah… no. No. Have a good day."

"You too. I know you're feeling better, but don't overdo it."

He was bossy to the end. But she knew it was because he cared. That also made him too attractive for his own good.

"Yes, boss." Jordan saluted.

"Funny." The smirk on his face was to die for. "See you later."

Listening, she heard Nick's fading footsteps as he went down the stairs, through the kitchen, and as soon as she heard the back door close, Jordan picked up the phone to call Lilly. This situation had the potential to spin out of control, and she needed her friend's advice before it did.

LILLY SAT ON a stool at the kitchen island and listened. She said nothing. She just listened, and the longer Jordan went on, the more she thought she was losing her mind. And it was all Nick's fault.

Since her engagement hit the skids, Jordan had spent months building a wall around her heart. Now Nick, with his charm and kindness, and wicked good looks... and that oh-so-sweet mouth... Jordan started wondering what could be.

What could be.

In the tiniest corner of Jordan's battered heart, she felt hope. It was just a flicker, a tiny shimmer of emotion, and she didn't know how to handle it. She didn't trust herself to make the right choice. She'd thought Chase was perfect and look how that ended up.

"He's messing with my head," she said to her stone-faced friend.

"Is he? It sounds like he's being AHHH-MAZING. And you're messing with your own head."

"Lilly, come on. You know what I went through."

"I do. And I know the pneumonia, along with worrying about your dad, has you stressed to the max. But you need to stop projecting."

Jordan wondered why she called the friend who was the least likely to give her sympathy. Lilly wasn't going to coddle her. Not even a little.

"I'm not projecting."

"No?" Lilly went to the fridge and refilled her water glass. "Yes, he kissed you. But he didn't propose marriage. It was a peck on the lips by your account."

"It was."

"So, what's the problem? Be honest. What has you so spooked? The kiss? Or how the kiss made you feel?"

Damn her.

The last thing Jordan wanted to admit was how that kiss made her feel.

It was bone-melting. Sweet, sensual. Glitter showers flashed behind her eyes. Her heart beat a little faster, her mind raced.

Chase had kissed her thousands of times, and never once had she felt the thrill she'd felt when she kissed Nick.

"This wasn't supposed to happen."

"Why?" Lilly scooted to the stool next to Jordan's. "Look. Life isn't mapped out with some perfect plan. You know this. If you're going to go on living, not just existing, you have to be ready for what comes your way."

Lilly was right, of course. Jordan had no right to expect her life would be without twists and turns. It just seemed lately she had a target on her back. She needed it to end.

"He's a nice guy," she finally admitted. "He has a good heart. I just wish I knew more about him. You know, what makes him tick."

Lilly nodded. "He's been kind of a ghost since he came home. We all know about his injury and that the recovery was a beast, but I guess the toughest wounds are the ones we can't see."

"I'm sure you're right." Jordan wished she knew what was haunting him. Behind Nick's smiling eyes was a shadow, and she wanted to help him. "Do you think I can trust him?"

"Trust him? What do you mean?"

"As a doctor, a friend... more, if it gets there. I know I have to be ready for the occasional curveball, but I can't handle deception. Duplicity."

"I don't think that's going to be an issue. The man is a straight shooter."

Lilly would know. Nick and her brother, Luca, had played football together in high school; if there was something not right about him, something she should worry about, Lilly would tell her.

Right then, her phone rang. Lilly reached over and handed it to Jordan.

"Liam Jennings? Why is he calling you?"

Jordan shrugged. The Jennings and Velsor families were longtime residents of Compass Cove. It was one of Jordan's distant cousins, Lucy, who had stolen the heart of Caleb Jennings, the local compasssmith. In the loosest and most distant way possible, they were family. But Liam never called her. Ever.

"Hi Liam."

"Hey, Jordan. How are you feeling?"

"Getting better. What's up?"

"My dad left me a cryptic message about you getting married and that I needed to get the ring ready. I want to know when you need it."

"Wait, what?" Married. What the hell? Ring?

"Dad went out to the east end to check on some trees that were downed on our property in Southold. I can't get a signal, or I'd ask him. Congrats, by the way. When did this happen?" Liam was probably the sweetest guy she knew. Big and blond, he was a few years older than Jordan and possessed a bookish, nerdy charm that made him damn near irresistible. He was an artist and had taken over the compass shop in town when his father retired, keeping it in the family for another generation.

"Uh… I'm…"

"Damn. Did I spoil the surprise? The note is really vague. It said, 'George called. The ring needs to be cleaned for Jordan.'"

Jordan's brain went bonkers trying to figure out where this crazy idea came from. It made no sense. Why would her dad think she was getting married? "Liam, I'm going to call my dad and talk to him. I'll call you back."

"Okay. Hey, glad you're better."

"Thanks."

She hung up and looked at Lucy. "That was weird. Liam thinks I'm getting married."

Lilly burst out laughing, but reined it in when she saw Jordan wasn't laughing along. "Who's the lucky guy?"

"I have no idea." With timing that was almost eerie, Nick walked in the back door. As soon as he looked up and smiled, all the pieces snapped into place.

Son of a bitch.

Somehow, Jordan had a feeling the 'lucky guy' Lilly had asked about only seconds ago was now standing less than ten feet from her, and Jordan wanted to know what in blazes was going on.

Chapter Seven

"**Y**OU TOLD HIM what?" Jordan felt her jaw tighten as her conversation with Nick progressed. It had been five minutes since he'd come back from his errands in town. Lilly had gotten out while the getting was good. Jordan was ready to commit murder, and he hadn't even said that much.

"Hear me out before you get angry."

"I'm already angry!" She stood up and circled the big kitchen to get farther away from him. Of all the outrageous things he could have done. "What were you thinking? There was no need to tell him a lie like that!"

"I never actually told him. He just assumed, and I went along with it."

"That's irrelevant."

Nick threw up his hands. "Just listen to me."

"There's nothing to talk about." Truth was everything to Jordan. Everything. She'd broken her engagement over a lie. "How could you do that?"

"I didn't lie. I was trying to keep him from worrying about you. It's on his mind."

"It's wrong. We should tell him the truth."

She loved her dad with all her heart, but why he thought she needed a man to be happy was beyond her. He raised her to be able to take care of herself. What had changed?

"Why?"

When she heard the question, she could barely believe it.

Nick was dead serious. He was also, obviously, out of his mind. "Jordan, I see your point, but how if it gives him some peace of mind, what's the harm in letting him believe what he wants?"

"Nick, I never lie to my father. Ever."

"It's harmless. A little white lie so he can have some peace."

Jordan thought about her dad, and she didn't want to cause him any kind of stress, but lying to him about a relationship wasn't what she had in mind. Nick's motives, pure as they might be, were misguided. Lying never led anywhere good.

"I don't like this whole chauvinistic 'I-need-a-man' thing. What the hell is that all about?"

"He's old-fashioned, also not a bad thing. He wants you happy. Can you blame him?"

Daddy always wanted her happy. That's what he promised her after her mother died. That he'd do his best to make sure she was always happy. But that didn't include having a fake boyfriend.

"This is going to be a disaster." Jordan folded her arms and looked out the window.

"How? He's in the next town over. No one is even going to know."

"Are you kidding? How long have you lived here? If this town was good for nothing else, it would be good for gossip. And one town isn't going to stop anyone from finding out. I know that for a fact."

He rolled his eyes. "I think you're overestimating our importance. There's much better dirt for the gossip mill."

"I think for a smart guy, you're pretty clueless."

"Clueless? I was trying to be compassionate."

Sweet Mother Mary, he did not get it. "When did we get together, Nick?"

He froze at the question. His wide eyes narrowed because she'd put him on the spot.

"What's our history? Oh, and here's one... how did you pop the question? Did I get all misty and cry?"

"What kind of questions are those?"

"The kind people are going to ask! Jeez, Nick. This is going to get around and we're going to have a lot of people to answer to."

"You're overreacting."

"No. I'm not." Jordan plopped into a chair at the big island and dropped her head on the granite countertop.

Compassionate. He was trying to be... *compassionate.* Oh, no. Looking up, Jordan locked eyes with Nick, and the truth smacked her right upside her head.

"How bad is it?" It was the question she'd been dreading

to ask. The thing was, she already knew the answer.

"Jordan..." He stopped and sat on the stool next to her before continuing. His expression softened as his hand settled between her shoulders. "He's worsening. His symptoms are getting harder to control."

Don't break. Don't break. "I see. Is he in pain?"

Nick's hand had started to move on her back in a gentle up-and-down motion. "He didn't say, specifically. Just that he was having a tougher time."

"Jaundice?"

He hesitated. "Yes."

Jordan realized at that moment that honesty might be overrated. She would have given anything for Nick to tell her that her father was stable, that there was no change.

"I knew this would happen. I mean, he's terminal. I knew it was coming. Strangely, I thought I'd be ready. I'm not."

A tear rolled down Jordan's cheek, then another, and another. Without thought, her head dropped on Nick's shoulder.

"His condition. That's what made you lie?"

"A lie of omission, but yeah. I didn't correct his assumptions. I guess he thought, you know, since I showed up there we... ah... meant something to each other."

Jordan raised her eyes and found herself drowning in Nick's gaze. His eyes, the color of the ocean, let her know she wasn't alone.

It had been a long time since Jordan had been able to take comfort in the strength someone else offered her. While she held fast to her independence, it was nice to lean on someone who you had faith wouldn't let you down.

"This is going to blow up, though."

"You don't know that."

"Come on." Jordan sat back and grinned. "You can't possibly be that obtuse."

Nick's body stiffened, and they were right back where they started.

Lina found them like that when she burst into the kitchen, unwrapping her scarf and hanging her coat on the hook by the back door. "We need to talk."

"Wow," Jordan said in mock surprise. "That didn't take long."

"Knock it off. You don't know what it's about." He was so mad. It was actually kind of fun to see Dr. Perfect all pissy.

Nick kissed his grandmother on the cheek and pulled out a chair for her. She cocked her head, shook her finger at him, and then started pacing.

"What is it, Nona?" Nick asked.

"The news that you two are an item? When did that happen?" She mumbled something in Italian as she ran her finger along the edge of a shelf. "And not just dating, apparently you're getting married? *Married?*"

Sometimes, being right was so satisfying. This was one of

those times. That was until she had to make a decision and figure out what to say to Lina. Nick was absolutely no help. He just stood there, stunned.

"Well?" she asked.

Looking down, Jordan did not want to make eye contact. Just like school, eye contact meant she would have to give an answer. The room went silent. She could hear Lina's breathing, but she and Nick were acting like two teenagers who had been caught making out. Gertie came out from under the table, her nails clicking on the floor. She plopped in front of Lina, her little stump of a tail wagging.

"Gertie?" Lina asked. "Are you going to tell me?"

The dog barked.

Slowly walking around the room, Lina thought out loud. "I guess it's possible. I mean, you've been interested in Jordan since you got home, Nicky, isn't that true?"

"I, ah…"

"Oh, you didn't tell her how you'd watch her when she came in from her runs on the beach?"

"Nona, stop."

"And Jordan," Now Lina had turned on her. "You're a lovely young woman. I imagine you're ready to get even with that snake of an ex."

"I don't do revenge, Lina."

"No?"

Jordan couldn't tell if Nick was panicked or exasperated, but she had a feeling it was a little of both. Based on his face alone, it looked like he wanted to put his beloved grandmother in a closet. "Nona, it's not that complicated," he began. "But just to clear things up," he said to Jordan, "I don't watch you."

Lina smiled. The woman was a master game player and her grandson was being beaten. "Oh, don't be shy. It was adorable the way you'd sit out on the back porch and pretend to read."

"For Pete's sake," Nick said to his grandmother. "It's not what you think."

"It doesn't matter what I think. It's what people are talking about. And if something is going on, I don't like hearing about it through channels."

"Channels?" Now Nick was annoyed. His hands were stuffed in his pockets, and his shoulder was pressed into the doorframe; he stood there looking all broody and mad. Jordan could actually see the vein in his neck pulsing.

"Yes, channels. Eileen Tufano, she's a nurse on your father's floor. She told Laura Earl, who told Tara Finn, who told Krissy DeSano."

"And Krissy told *you?*" That didn't sound right, Jordan thought, because Krissy was only sixteen years old.

Lina threw up her hands. "She did! She works for me a couple days a week after school, but she came in today because the heat at the high school conked out. Tara was in picking up an order for her son's lacrosse team and told Krissy to ask me."

"I told you." Jordan was happy to point out to Nick that she was right.

"Jesus H. Christ," Nick snarled.

Jordan rubbed her forehead. She was getting a headache.

"So? Are you two a *thing*? I don't think it's a bad idea, but *Madonna mia*! Could you keep us in the loop?"

Gossip was like wildfire in Compass Cove, and Jordan didn't want anything getting back to her father that could upset him before she had a chance to see him. Nick was about to tell his grandmother the truth when Jordan thought back to what Nick told her about her father's condition, and she made a snap decision.

"I won't deny that we've been getting closer." That wasn't a lie. She was wickedly attracted to Nick, and her emotions were all over the place where he was concerned.

"We have. Maybe George sensed that," Nick confessed, playing through on the story. "But the words 'engaged' or 'wedding' or 'marriage' were never spoken, at least not by me…"

Lina's eyes had gone soft, and she approached Nick with her hands raised. As soon as she was close enough, she reached up and took his face in her hands. "You wanted to give him some comfort."

"I didn't think it would blow up. I mean, shit. Was the nurse eavesdropping? Because I have a problem with that."

"No. I've known Eileen for years. I called her. She said George told anyone and everyone who would listen. Told her you were being pretty tight-lipped, Nicky, but he read something into your visit. Apparently, he's hoping you guys make it snappy, so he can walk Jordan down the aisle."

Considering George's condition, that was soon. "How did this happen?" Nick scrubbed his face with his hands.

Lina shook her head. "How did you get through medical school being so dumb? Honey, the town lives for stuff like this. For goodness' sake, this whole place was built on a romantic legend."

The compass legend grounded Compass Cove. Jordan felt a special closeness to the story, since Lucy Velsor, the woman whose broken compass brought her the love of her life, was one of her ancestors. "Your grandmother is right."

Nick groaned as he pushed off from the wall. "He was happy. You know, when he asked about it." He turned to her and there was almost an imperceptible note of pleading in his face. "I can't be sorry about this."

"I'm sure you're not." When was any man sorry about anything?

Jordan was so bitter and jaded from her experience with Chase, it was hard for her to wrap her head around being part of a couple again. But if she agreed to keep her father in the dark, that's exactly what was going to happen. She would become Nick Rinaldi's fiancée. It might be in name only, but they'd have to start acting like they were a couple.

And she'd be the envy of every woman in Compass Cove who had a working pair of ovaries.

But beyond that, it would give her father peace of mind. Nothing was more important than that.

"Maybe we should let him think what he wants." Shit, what did she just say?

"It's wonderful to see you two getting closer," Lina said. "But if you're stretching the truth at all, you'd better get your stories straight. Your father won't like that you lied to him, whatever the reason."

"I know. Thanks, Lina."

Once his grandmother left, Nick expressed a modicum of regret. "I had no idea he'd make these assumptions."

Shaking her head, there was nothing she could say. He didn't plan it. Who could have known how the visit with her dad was going to go? Jordan's heart ached, and she wasn't sure if it was because of her father, or the man who'd just gone down on one knee to scratch her dog's belly.

"Nick, can I ask you a question?"

"Shoot."

"Did you really watch me run?" The little truth bomb Lina dropped was one of the few bright spots in Jordan's day. It was nice to know she could still get someone's interest.

"No… yes." He paused to collect his thoughts. "It's not like you think." Rubbing his hands up and down on his trousers as he stood, Nick sat next to her. "I was jealous."

"Jealous?"

"I ran all the time. It was my way to de-stress. I haven't

been running since I was shot. I'd see you on the beach, and I don't know... I wished I could do the same thing."

"Is there any reason you can't run?"

"You mean will I hurt myself? No. But I don't know if I have any form at all."

"Poor form isn't a reason not to try. When I'm better, we'll go on a short run." Jordan let her hand drop on his knee and she noticed how warm he was. The heat from his body radiated right through the khaki fabric.

Nick raised an eyebrow. "I won't slow you down?"

"Nope. You're just going to have to keep up."

Chapter Eight

THE BUG IN her system was still kicking her ass. Jordan spent way too much time in her room, either asleep, half asleep, or thinking about sleep. The pneumonia was doing exactly what Nick said it was going to do: one day, she felt fine; the next, she was flat on her back. But thinking about this whole mess with her father was doing a job on her head.

She called Dad that morning to let him know she still couldn't come, and he told her again how much he enjoyed talking to Nick and that he was so relieved she had someone to depend on. When he'd first said it a couple of days ago, Jordan didn't think much about it. Nick had been unbelievably supportive during her illness. Now that she knew what transpired between him and her father, the comments had added meaning. In Dad's eyes, she was going to marry Nick Rinaldi, and he wanted specifics.

She'd have spent the day giving Nick a hard time about the trouble he'd caused, but he had accepted a trial position with the pediatric practice in town, so he'd been out of the house since breakfast. Not wanting to start his day out on the wrong foot, she didn't say anything.

Lina had insisted on fixing her a plate of eggs and break-fast potatoes, which she ate while sitting across the table from her fake fiancé. He ate his waffles and sipped his coffee, glancing up occasionally, his face telling her nothing of how he was feeling. If she had to guess, the scope of the lie, and how fast it had spun out of control, had Nick worried about how they would keep from getting caught.

He'd checked on her last night, coming into her room and setting off Jordan's very dirty imagination. It had become his habit over the last week to give her a quick examination before she went to sleep. They'd talk a little as he checked her pulse and temperature, and she'd gleaned little tidbits about him. It wasn't much—his favorite snacks. Where he'd like to take a vacation.

But last night, he was quiet. Listening to her lungs and offering his relief that she was improving, but still had a way to go. She'd tried to make small talk, but he just nodded, and as soon as he was done, he put as much distance between them as possible.

This morning wasn't much better, and she had no idea why he was in such a snit.

Once he left the table, Lina shook her head. "He's stubborn, that one. You're going to have your hands full."

"If he doesn't talk to me about what's bothering him, we're going to have a big nothing burger."

"He will. Be patient with him." Lina kissed her on the

forehead and patted her cheek. "There're cold cuts and soup in the refrigerator, but take it easy. Call the café if you don't feel like making anything, and I'll send someone over with whatever you want. Angelo is going to be directing the workmen all day, and if everything goes as planned, you could be back in the cottage in a day or so."

"Thanks, Lina." Jordan couldn't get over the way the Rinaldis had just jumped in to take care of her. "I can't believe how fast he got things done."

"Well, the basement is dry now, and that's where most of the water was. Since it's not finished, there was nothing to do except get the water out and clean it."

"Thank goodness for small favors. I'm lucky I didn't lose anything."

"Amen to that. You rest, missy. I'll see you later."

Rest. That was all she was doing. She'd read three books in the last two days, and she was starting to go a little stir crazy. This was the second day school was back in session and she missed her kids.

Looking out her window, the grounds were buzzing with workmen. There was a small swarm around the cottage, as well as a full crew to take care of all the fallen trees on the property. Snow was mounded wherever there was room, and in the spots where it had melted there was nothing but thick, goopy mud. Once everything melted, it was going to be a mess.

The day crawled by, and by the time lunch hit, Jordan

was convinced she was going to eat herself out of all her clothes. The Rinaldis' house was stocked. With everything. There was enough food in the pantries to feed a family of fifteen for three weeks, and Jordan never needed to call the café. There was plenty to choose from right here.

The house was so big and so empty. Her footsteps echoed on the wood floors, and the only other sound was the ticking of Gertie's feet behind her. It was a look into her future.

Crawling onto the big bed, Jordan suddenly felt overwhelmed. She was so tired of being brave. Her last conversation with her dad brought back too many memories. She remembered how lost he was after her mother died. How she would hear him pray to her mother at night when he thought Jordan was asleep.

"Janie," he'd say. *"I don't know how I'm going to do this without you, but I promise Jordan will never want for anything. I'll make you proud, my love. I will."*

He'd been everything while she was growing up. Her coach, her teacher, her cheerleader. He was mother and father rolled into one.

Suddenly, the reality of his disease hit hard. She'd known for a few weeks that the cancer was taking over his body, but she didn't want to face it. It wasn't going to be long before he couldn't fight any longer, and he would die.

And then she'd be all alone. Just like she was now.

Curling onto her side, Jordan clutched the pillow, trying

to hold onto the control that had been fraying for the last several days. A throbbing drifted through her chest, stealing her breath in a way that had nothing to do with the pneumonia. Finally, feeling a hot tear track down her cheek, Jordan broke.

Turning her face into the pillow, she tried to muffle her sobs, but it was no use. Everything—the grief, the fear, the frustration—came pouring out of her in great gulps. There was no attempt to stop it, no shame in letting her feelings control her for once. Jordan didn't want to swallow her feelings anymore.

There was no slow build. No trickles of tears on her cheeks, no burning sensation in her eyes. Jordan just lost it.

Crying like she never had before, even on the night she called off her wedding, Jordan's body went cold and it caused her to shiver. Pulling the blanket tighter, she jumped when she felt a hand drop on her leg.

"Jordan, come here." It was Nick. She felt his weight settle next to her on the bed, and without any hesitation, he pulled her into his arms.

Holding her tightly against him, Nick pressed her head into his chest. The embrace was warm, safe, and it gave her permission to let go of all the grief and pain that had been building up for months. "Let it out," he whispered into her hair. "You don't have to be tough. Let it out."

The tears now were as much from relief as from sadness. Allowing herself to give in, she let Nick comfort her. For just this once, she didn't have to be strong.

He stayed with her through the whole thing. Never letting go, keeping her trembling body tight against his, he protected her. And when he said he wouldn't let anything happen to her, Jordan believed him.

What a man this was. He was doing everything for her with no thought for himself, and she'd done nothing but question his motives. What was wrong with her? Was she so bitter, so angry, that she couldn't accept simple kindnesses?

Nick's hand shifted and made gentle circles on her back. It was soothing in the most unexpected way, but there was something different about the gesture. Something more intimate.

Her breathing steadied, and only the occasional shudder had him pulling her in. Loving how safe she felt pressed into him, Jordan didn't want to move. This had to be what heaven felt like.

"How are you doing down there?" She could hear the smile in his voice.

"I'm okay."

Easing her away from his body, Nick kept hold of her arms and examined her face. His eyes went deep, and in a move that felt natural and protective, he leaned in and kissed her on top of the head.

"That was an impressive meltdown."

"I can't remember ever losing it like that. I'm sorry you had to see it."

"Sorry? I'm glad you weren't alone."

Jordan looked away and felt the tears threaten again. "God, Nick."

"What? What did I say?"

"Nothing. I'm just overwhelmed. Cabin fever can't be helping."

"That's..." He stopped, thinking before he continued. Taking hold of her hand, his smile lit up the room. "Let's go out."

"What? Can I? We put off seeing my dad..."

"For a little while. It's not that cold and there's no wind. A walk in town will help clear your head."

"Okay," she agreed. "That sounds good."

Going for a walk never thrilled her quite so much. Jordan was practically giddy.

Standing at the same time, Jordan grabbed Nick by the hand and gave him a shove out of the bedroom.

If they were going out in public, Jordan needed to make herself presentable.

"I'D LOVE A hot chocolate?" She looked at him expectantly as they walked together down Main Street. The snow had melted off the sidewalks and roads, but there were still mounds of it piled up near the water and in parking lots.

"It will probably exacerbate your cough."

"Oh, right. Tea then?"

"Sure. We'll stop in at the café and get tea." Nick was glad she'd relaxed around him again; considering she was still annoyed with him over what happened with her dad, this was a marked improvement.

"And a chocolate tart."

"That would be worse than the hot chocolate."

"Bite your tongue," Jordan snapped. "I love those tarts."

"As you should. They're one of Nona's specialties, but they aren't good for someone getting over pneumonia."

He thought he saw Jordan roll her eyes, but didn't say anything. It wasn't worth the fight. They were at the intersection of Main Street and Cove Road, the heart of town. A mosaic compass adorned the intersection, making it clear to visitors where they were and how they could get to where they were going. Nick was hoping to figure that out himself.

It was one of the reasons he'd come home. Dealing with his injury was only one part of his recovery; what was going on inside his headspace was something else entirely. Being back among the familiar had helped. Little by little he could see a future for himself.

He could have easily gone to his parents' house in Northern California after leaving the hospital, but his grandparents provided him with the grounding that he craved.

Nick looked over and thought if he had gone to his folks, he never would have met Jordan. The tug at his heart from that thought made him take notice.

Currently, she was keeping pace with him as they walked toward the café. Her breathing seemed steady, and she wasn't flushed. In fact, her face was tilted up slightly, and the afternoon sunlight made her glow like a goddess.

They continued in silence, a light breeze blowing off the cove. It was chilly, but not cold, and in the distance, he could make out a stray fishing boat. What surprised him was the sight of a dozen harbor seals hauled out on the rocks along the shore.

Dropping his hand on her arm, Nick pointed to the sight. "Look over there."

Jordan's eyes went wide, and a smile bloomed across her face. "I've never seen them this close to shore. Usually, they're out in the water, bottling. All I can see are their heads bobbing up and down." With her hand gripping his arm, Jordan pulled Nick across the street so they could get a better view. "Let's look."

Going right up to the gray stone sea wall, Jordan leaned over and scanned the scene below. The seals were like big dogs with flippers, catching some rays. Some were lying on their sides, while others were on their bellies, flippers out. The whole group was basking in the early spring sun, their gray-and-white spotted fur shiny and smooth.

"I love this," she said, her eyes fixed on the animals. "They're such cool creatures."

Nick had always thought so too. While he'd been deployed on different ships, he'd seen some amazing marine life, but there was something loveable about seals. And something very loveable about the woman so enamored with them.

It was clear that getting her out of the house was the right thing to do. For someone like Jordan, who was constantly on the go, being cooped up—even if she was sick—was going to mess with her head. But he didn't want to keep her out too long.

"Are you ready for that tea? We can head back toward the café before I take you home."

She nodded, coughed, and took a breath. "That sounds like a plan."

Nick took her gloved hand and tucked it in the crook of his arm as they crossed the street. To his surprise, Jordan leaned into him. "Tired?"

"Yeah. It snuck up on me." She coughed again, this time a little deeper.

"The exhaustion is the hardest part of the recovery. Listen to your body's signals."

As they walked up Main Street, Nick noticed a lot of heads turning. Word had definitely gotten out about them being together. People who passed them smiled, and a few offered congratulations. She'd been dead-on about how fast the news had spread. And she hadn't let him forget it.

"Thank you for getting me out of the house."

"You're welcome." He was happy to be spending time

with her, especially considering the past two days. He'd fucked up in ten different ways.

Pulling the large brass handle on the door of the café, Nick held it wide open so Jordan could enter. It was after the lunchtime rush, so only a handful of tables were occupied, but a few regulars were sitting at the counter chatting with his grandmother, who enjoyed this time of day more than any other. She waved as soon as she spotted them.

"Nicky! Jordan! Speak of the devil," Nona called out. "The group here was just talking about you two."

"Really," he said as he felt Jordan's hand slide off his arm. "What about?"

"They were asking about your engagement." Nona's eyes were wide, her smile fixed. She didn't know what to say and was looking to him to take the lead. *Shit.* All he wanted was to give Jordan a break and give her brain a rest, and now they'd walked into the fire.

Nick surveyed the counter. Two men and two women, one of whom was named Judy Hoyle, the worst gossip in town.

"Our engagement." He glanced at Jordan, whose eyes were on him. Great. "It's been... great. Um. We're happy."

"Details are forthcoming," she jumped in. "No firm plans yet. It's still very new."

He liked that. It was succinct. Diplomatic.

"How is your dad, dearie?" Judy asked. "We've all been thinking about him."

"I haven't seen him since I've been sick, but I have talked to him and Nick tells me he's in good spirits."

"That's good. He must be happy you hooked yourself a man after the mess you made of your last wedding. That must have been hard for him, worrying about you."

Ouch.

Nick reached over and took Jordan's hand in his, and she squeezed it tight in response. The café had quieted, waiting for Jordan's reply to Judy's bitchy comment, but she took her time. No one was going to rush her. Nick admired her restraint, because she had to be fuming. Nick had learned the hard way, that Jordan made up her own mind.

"My father wants me to be happy." Her eyes were blazing. "He knows why I cancelled the wedding, and he understood."

"Oh, honey," Judy said. "Of course, he'd say that. But you gave up a lot of security. That must have worried poor George, don't you all think so?" The question was asked of anyone who was still listening.

No one at the counter replied to Judy's blabbering, but Jordan finally did.

"Mrs. Hoyle, my father raised me to take care of myself." Jordan pulled to her full height, and God, she was impressive. "If I'm with Nick, it's because I want to be, not because I need to be." She turned her head and coughed into her sleeve.

"Judy," Hank Johnson said firmly. "Leave the girl alone.

Everyone knows the Stanleys tell the story that best suits them. I've known George for thirty years, and he never questioned Jordan's decision." Hank was a math teacher, and if Nick crunched his numbers right, the gentleman had probably taught half the population of Compass Cove how to do differential equations before he retired.

Judy started to say something, and Jordan shushed her. "No, Mrs. Hoyle. We're done with this." Without missing a beat, she turned to his grandmother. "Lina, can I get a mint green tea with some honey and lemon?"

Yeah, impressive was a good word for Jordan Velsor. She'd shot down Judy Hoyle in fine fashion. Once again, she displayed a composure and poise that Nick could only admire. She would have been completely justified to lash out at Judy, but Jordan's calm and deliberate resolve was far more effective. The woman had class.

Nona smiled at her, and then at him before turning to make the tea. Nick stepped back to watch as Jordan talked to her dad's old friends. The epiphany hit him so hard right between the eyes, it nearly knocked him over. He might be pretending to be Jordan's fiancé, but his feelings for her were becoming very real.

WITH A PIZZA box between them on the big bed in her room, and Gertie asleep and snoring on the chaise in the corner, Nick couldn't believe he'd agreed to play twenty questions. Jordan's reasoning was sound: they had to know each other, but things were going to get dicey. So far, they were on their third round, which meant they'd moved past favorite colors and foods to questions that probed a little more deeply, and he was afraid he'd spill his guts.

"What scares you?" she asked.

"Like horror-movie-scares me? Or real life?"

"Real life." Sitting cross-legged and gobbling down the extra cheese and sausage pizza against his advice, Jordan had never looked prettier. With her long blonde hair loose and wavy, she'd changed when they'd gotten back from town, and no one worked a pair of pink flannel pajama pants and a T-shirt like the woman in front of him.

"Well, while I'm always preparing for the zombie apocalypse, my biggest fear is letting people down. I worry about that all the time."

She shook her head. "I find that so hard to wrap my head around. You're Mr. Dependable."

"Not always." Dropping his head, all he could see were the bodies of the kids in the clinic. "I've made a lot of mistakes."

"We all have. That's life."

"It's just…" He stopped and got a hold of himself. "It's not important." Jesus, what was she doing to him? He never talked about his guilt. Never. Before he could say anything else, Jordan pushed the pizza box aside and reached for him, taking his hand in hers and closing the distance between them.

The feel of her, hip to hip, as she settled next to him, was close and intimate. More than a friend, but not yet something more.

What scared him? she'd asked.

This. This scared him.

"I don't know what's going through your head right now, but you know you can talk to me, don't you? I want to help if I can."

He hesitated. "I know, but there are things I find better left in the past. I can't do anything about what happened when I was deployed, but I do know there are people who have sustained far worse injuries than I have."

Jordan's face set and she let go of his hand. "Typical guy. Seems to me talking might be the only way to fight those demons you're carrying around."

"Who said I have demons?"

"Don't you?"

"No." Another person who wanted to analyze him.

"Right. You keep telling yourself that."

How did he make her understand? He didn't have the right to his pain. "A lot of people went through shit over there. It wasn't just me. Soldiers and marines are getting blown to hell by IEDs. Trust me, I got lucky."

"Lucky? How many surgeries have you had?" Jordan leaned forward and pushed every button. "I think talking is what scares you. If you keep everyone out, no one can see where you're hurt."

This was Jordan's flaw. She didn't know when to back off. She had no idea what he'd gone through and if he didn't want to talk about it, he wasn't going to.

She was also so close, he could have kissed her and made them both forget what they'd been talking about. And he wanted to. He wanted to touch every bit of her smooth skin, to kiss that lush mouth. He wanted to sink into the soft bed and make love to her until she cried.

But she'd probably want to talk after.

"Jordan, we're in dangerous territory here." Putting some distance between them would be a very good idea, yet neither of them moved. "It could spiral out of control so quickly. That's not what you want, is it? The other night didn't end so well."

"Okay," she whispered as she scooted away. "Better?"

"You know I'm right."

"Maybe, but I haven't had sex in months."

Did she just say that out loud? Way to stoke the fire. How did he even respond to that?

"I get it. I feel like a monk, but that doesn't mean we should jump into anything."

"Right. Of course. Says the man who kissed me."

"I remember." He could still feel her lips. "What are you saying, exactly?" Nick had never been so torn in his life. The battle raging between his head and his libido was furious.

"On one level, you're absolutely right." It appeared Jordan was as conflicted as he was. "It's a line we shouldn't cross. I think I said something like that. But, I mean… I *am* attracted to you. And the kiss…"

Quiet surrounded them as he reached out and cupped her velvet-soft cheek. Jordan leaned into his hand, her eyes steady and clear.

"Same," he responded.

"It could be fun."

"What?"

"You know…" Blushing, Jordan hesitated. *Jesus Christ, she blushed.* "Sex."

The soft purr that came out of her throat just about killed him.

Nick considered the idea of that with her, he was in over his head. Everything about the woman—the brains, the beauty, the compassion—were muddling his brain.

Getting them back on track was the only way to save his sanity. "I think it's my turn to ask a question." He pulled his hand back and picked a card from the pile. "Okay. Is there something you feel you've missed out on?"

"Hmm." She laid flat on her back, her hair fanned out around her, her chest rising and falling with a slow steady rhythm. Her eyes drifted closed as she thought. He couldn't stop staring at her. Then she answered.

"I've never made love outside."

Damn. She was a wicked, wicked woman.

Drawing a breath, Nick levered himself over her, hovering just far enough away that their bodies didn't touch. The energy between them was electric, throwing all his good sense into a tailspin. Seeing her like this beneath him, hair loose and wild, her breath catching...

"You're playing with fire, Jordan."

"Why is that?"

Brushing a strand of hair off her face, Nick felt a wave of protectiveness surge through him. "You're vulnerable. You've been sick. I have to draw the line."

"You have to draw a line? Why don't I get to decide if it's okay?"

"It's not that..."

"What?" Her eyes were issuing a challenge. He'd pissed her off by trying to do the right thing and he didn't even know how it had happened. Seeing her steady, steely gaze, Nick quickly figured there was no way to win this argument.

"Yeah." With a push, he removed himself from the bed and walked toward the hallway.

"Running away?"

"No." It was bullshit. That was exactly what he was doing. Growling, he glanced back over his shoulder. She was going to kill him. No doubt about it. "I'm going to take a cold shower. A really long one."

Chapter Nine

"WHY DO YOU need to stop at the compass shop?"

"You'll see. There's something I need to get from Liam."

Waking up this morning, Jordan's close encounter with Nick weighed heavily. She had no idea what had gotten into her, but her emotions were pinging around her head like a pinball. He was brutally handsome. Intelligent. Honorable. Brave. How was she supposed to resist him? The bigger question was: why did she have to?

For the first time since she'd walked out on her engagement, Jordan felt like she could feel love again. Nick was everything she'd ever wanted.

He was flirty and sweet, affectionate and attentive. But he also shut down when she started to get too close to what made him tick. Chase kept her at a distance too, which was why she couldn't see him for the snake he was. Nick was a different animal, no doubt, but she wasn't going to be shut out again.

They weren't engaged, not really. Which was all the more reason for her to see Liam about a family heirloom her father had put in his care.

"You're related, aren't you? You and Liam?"

"Yes... distantly. Lucy Velsor, who married Caleb Jennings, was my great aunt, ten times removed, I think. I'll ask Liam. He'll know. He and Ed, his dad, are the keepers of all family history."

"But it goes back hundreds of years. That's amazing. We're trying to get past a roadblock in the Rinaldi ancestry because a fire destroyed the church in Siena that held the records."

"You'll have to go visit with your grandfather. You can drive each other crazy for a couple of weeks."

"That's not a bad idea." Nick smiled, and Jordan's heart did a little flip. He was all about his family. She did know that.

Jordan loved the bond Nick had with his grandparents. It was sweet, and she loved that a thirty-six-year-old, jaded war hero could be sweet with his grandma.

Back for the second time in two days, more snow had melted, so parking wasn't bad on Main Street. Jordan found herself happy that there was a little bit of a walk involved to get to the shop. The fresh air and the movement were a special kind of medicine.

Jordan used to be fascinated with the history behind the family, and the legend of the compass. But after she'd been betrayed, she'd lost her belief in the magic, and that she'd ever find a soulmate.

Which was another reason to keep Nick at a distance; at least for now. She didn't trust her own heart enough to make a decision that involved any man, but especially one that tied her in knots.

Entering the shop still brought a smile to her face. An antique bell tinkled overhead, and Liam Jennings, who was just finishing up with another customer, looked up and waved.

Jordan adored Liam. They were only related by the loosest connections, but he held tight to the fact that they were cousins, and he and his parents always treated Jordan and her father like they were close family.

It helped her feel more connected to the town, and that feeling of belonging was precious to her. After her mother died, when everything was at loose ends, she and her father found a small place in the town where he was teaching, just a little west of Compass Cove, and settled down there. It wasn't far away, and they ended up moving back when Jordan was in high school. But two years ago, he sold the house and moved into a senior living community. Jordan moved into the Rinaldis' cottage, thinking she'd wouldn't be there very long. She'd already started to date Chase, and it was obvious he wanted the relationship to be more.

Chase never understood her connection to the town. If she was honest with herself, her ex didn't get her at all. Jordan wasn't a debutante. She wasn't a socialite. And she certainly wasn't going to defer to him just because he was the man. But that's what he'd expected, and it was Jordan's fault for not seeing him for who he was sooner.

He'd blinded her with his charm and good looks, and she wasn't going to let that happen again. She deserved better.

Jennings Fine Compasses and Watches had been in the same spot on Main Street in Compass Cove for better than three hundred years. Granted, it wasn't the same as the store founded by William Jennings, a compasssmith, when the family helped settle the town in the mid 1600s, but it provided the village with an anchor and a connection to its seafaring past.

The shop that was once filled with sextants, charts, spyglasses, and the finest compasses on the East Coast, now housed estate jewelry, fine watches, artisan glass, and crystal, along with the finest compasses on the East Coast. Only now, most of those compasses were bought when a new couple set up house to remember that their hearts had found each other.

Nick looked into the locked case that held the compass that was at the root of Lucy Velsor and Caleb Jennings's romance.

"My grandmother used to love coming in to look at the compass. She said when she and my grandfather first got married, she'd be here every other day." Nick had his hand flat on the glass. Jordan walked over and looked in. A plaque was attached to the velvet base on which the compass sat.

Lucy and Caleb ~ m. 1750

"It draws people in." Liam walked over and gave her a big hug. "So good to see you, Cuz. How are you feeling?"

"You too. How did you know I was sick?"

"Lina stopped by." He turned to Nick and shook his hand. "Been a long time, man. Glad you're back."

"Thanks. Good to be back." Jordan noticed him glance in her direction, but he turned his attention back to the compass. "Nona still stops in?"

"Yep." Liam, who was a good three inches taller than Nick, pushed his too-long blond hair off his forehead. "She comes by when she's angry with your grandfather."

"Really? Still?"

He nodded. "My grandpa told me that when they were first married, she was here all the time. She'd look at the compass and remind herself that she chose Angelo, and that they would find their way. They were adjusting."

Nick laughed. It boomed from his chest in a way that filled the shop. It was the most wonderful sound. "I heard something about that. And now?"

"She comes in once in a while. Not too often, but she was pretty angry with him after the storm."

That was true. They'd had a couple of good arguments when they were deciding what to fix and when. Jordan made a point to stay out of their way.

"So, Jordan wouldn't tell me why we had to stop here." Nick folded his arms. "You gonna fill me in, buddy?"

Liam raised an eyebrow in Jordan's direction. "You didn't tell him?"

"No."

"But you're engaged." Like a cartoon, Liam looked back and forth between them. Back and forth.

"Yessss..." Nick said with hesitation.

"It's a long story." Jordan waved her cousin off. "Why don't you get what I came in for, and then I'll tell him."

"Right." Shaking his head, Liam disappeared into the back room.

"Okay. What's going on?" Nick pulled her toward him, busting to find out. Settled against him, Jordan felt her insides go warm as his hand slipped around her waist, securing her body to his. "Jordan?"

Just as she was about to answer, Liam came from the back room and held out a black velvet box. Recognizing that this was a jewelry box, Nick's eyes opened wide.

"This feels strange." Jordan went toward Liam and took the box from his hand. "Like I'm taking something I shouldn't."

"Would you show me, already?" Poor Nick, he was so annoyed.

"Fine. Calm down." Jordan opened the clamshell and showed him what was inside.

Set on a bed of black velvet was an antique diamond ring. It had three stones, a rose-cut diamond at the center, and two smaller stones, set one on each side. The ring, fashioned from yellow gold, formed into an intricate scroll pattern. It was lovely, but it wasn't flashy.

"That's a beautiful ring." Nick reached out, taking the box in his hand. "It's so different."

Jordan smiled. "It's Lucy's ring."

He didn't say anything immediately; too stunned to speak, he just stared. "That's... wow. That's amazing."

"It's over two hundred and fifty years old, and it's *Jordan's* ring now." Liam's explanation seemed to drop Nick out of his trance.

"I still feel funny claiming it as mine." Jordan never felt comfortable taking anything from the Jennings family, but they never thought twice about her right to claim her heritage.

"It's yours, Jordan. You're the only living female relative on Lucy's side."

Taking the ring from the box, Jordan held it up to the light to see the diamonds sparkle. Then she slipped it on the ring finger of her left hand. It fit perfectly. "Wow."

A tingle ran up her arm. It felt... well, it felt strange. And incredibly right.

"So, this is going to be your engagement ring?" Nick wasn't staring at the ring anymore, but at her. He wanted an explanation, a reason for taking something important away from him. Jordan didn't think it would matter, but apparently, it did.

Liam must have sensed the tension, because he stepped

away. *The coward.*

"Yes," she said softly. "It's a family heirloom. And that takes off the pressure to buy one."

"I don't mind getting you a ring."

Seeing him tamp down his pride, Jordan took his hand in hers. "I know, but I need this, too. I'd wanted to wear it when I was engaged to Chase, but he bought me a big, flashy ring. I hated it. It wasn't about me, it was about him. This ring represents endless love. It's important to me, and it will make my dad happy."

Hesitating, Nick lifted her hand and examined the ring. He gazed at it a long time, examining it from all sides.

"It's an amazing piece. I can see why you'd want to wear it."

He might have understood, but something in his bearing said otherwise. This was more than Nick's wounded pride, and his reaction both touched and baffled her. Their engagement wasn't the real thing, so why should he care?

"If that's what you want, you should wear it. It's a piece of your history."

You. Your. Two words indicating that Nick was making the engagement, fake or not, all about her. Something her real fiancé never did.

"Thank you for understanding. It means a lot to me."

"Okay." Nick nodded, and Jordan's heart twitched for the second time that day. He respected her decision. That meant the world to her, too.

Her hand was still clasped in his, and new feelings started to push their way through the bitterness and the pain. But Jordan knew better than to trust her heart. As much as she appreciated Nick, and felt real affection for him, she knew that was as far as it would go.

Jordan wandered over to the compass case and looked in. There was a small painting of Lucy and Caleb with their children at their home on the water. Ironically, the house wasn't far from the Rinaldis', just a few doors down.

The compass itself was typical for the time. Not too big, it would have fit neatly into a sailor's pocket.

"Can I see the compass, Liam?"

"Really? That's a first."

It was the truth. Jordan had never held this piece of her history, even though she'd always been curious. Would it know she was searching for the kind of love her parents had? The kind of love that dreams were made of?

Nick's mouth dropped open in surprise. "A first? You've never held it?"

"No. I love the story, don't get me wrong, but the idea of it leading you to your true north? I don't know."

"So why now?" Nick asked, completely serious.

She thought about the question. It was a good one. Once upon a time, Jordan embraced the legend as her very own, but now—jaded and disillusioned—she didn't have much faith in affairs of the heart. Why did she want to hold something she didn't believe in? Jordan didn't really have an answer. "I'm not sure."

Maybe it was that she was feeling so lost, so at loose ends. Maybe she thought the compass could help her find some direction. Maybe she wanted to see if the little voice in her head knew something she didn't. Liam picked up the instrument, almost holding his breath, and gently set it in Jordan's hand.

It was heavier than she expected, warm, and it settled neatly in the cup of her palm. It was brightly polished and the tiny, hinged sundial was still securely attached. It was, indeed, a work of art.

But as she watched the needle, it did exactly what she expected.

Nothing.

No wobbling. No wild spinning. Just nothing.

Nick must have sensed her discomfort and he moved away, taking in a shelf filled with nautical collectibles.

"It's pointing north," Jordan said. "Other than a little wiggle, it hasn't moved."

"Hmm." Liam looked at the compass. Then at her. And finally, at Nick. "I'm not so sure about that."

"What? Yes, it is. Look." She nodded toward her hand. How could he deny what was right there?

"Jordan," he whispered. "North is *that* way." And his finger shot to the left.

"Are you sure?" She raised an eyebrow at her cousin. "It's not broken?"

Nodding his head in that annoying way he did when he knew he was right, Liam grinned. "I'm sure."

They stood in silence, watching the compass for any change, and glancing up at Nick, who was now flipping through a photo book about the history of Compass Cove.

"Liam?" Jordan stated firmly. "You will say *nothing*."

"I don't know what you mean..."

Jordan focused in to his stormy-gray eyes. "Nothing."

Shrugging his shoulders, Liam didn't respond and stepped over to her pretend fiancé while Jordan took a breath. Once again, when she looked at the compass, nothing had changed. But one thing was clear: the needle was pointing at Nick.

Jordan heard the little voice in her head utter the words it had been saying for the better part of a week: *true north.*

True north, it said again.

Shut up, she thought.

"NERVOUS?"

Jordan was twisting her fingers into a knot, and Nick's heart was pounding just watching her. It had been three full days since she agreed to go along with what he told her dad. But she still wasn't convinced it was the right thing to do.

"I shouldn't be nervous to see my own father. God, I hate lying."

Reaching out, he took her hand. Touching her was risky considering the strong physical attraction, but he couldn't shy away from it. Not now, when she needed a friend as much as anything. She looked at their joined hands and sighed.

"Every time I go, I wonder if this will be his last good day." She uttered a quiet oath, cursing the disease that would eventually steal her dad from her. "I wonder if the cancer will finally win."

"I wish I could give you an answer." He'd never heard her swear, and it clued him in to how scared she was. She also hadn't let go of his hand. In fact, she was holding it even tighter.

The time they'd spent together over the past week had given Nick a new appreciation for Jordan. He never knew a lot about her. She was his nona's tenant. She'd been engaged. She was a teacher.

She was so beautiful it hurt.

But that was pretty much it. Now, he'd spent hours with her, first when she was sick, and then when they figured they had to get to know each other.

Their round of twenty questions had gone on for hours the other night; it was enlightening. Sure, he'd found out all the basics like her birthday, favorite food, and favorite color. But there was so much more to her than what was on the surface—Jordan had secrets.

He'd told her nothing about his experiences, still unable

to lay himself bare, and he knew it had to annoy her. Only a few people knew how the deaths at the clinic haunted him, and that was out of necessity—his doctor, his shrink, a buddy from his unit. Intellectually, he knew he'd done everything he could to save lives, but it still didn't matter. There were days he was consumed by guilt. He wondered how Jordan would react if she knew everything. If she knew about the people he'd failed.

God, what did this all mean?

Now examining the ring on her left hand, Nick thought about what he could say that might help.

"It's all going to work out," he reassured her. "Even if he finds us out, he's going to understand."

"I know. And I don't want you to think I'm not grateful. I am. You've done so much for me. This is really... I don't know."

"Crazy? Misguided? Stupid?"

She smiled, and that was worth every minute he spent with her. "Maybe a little crazy."

"Can I ask you a question?" he began. "About your family?"

"Sure. What do you want to know?"

"You've said a couple of times when your father dies, you'd be alone. That you have no family. It seems to me the Jennings clan sees you as family."

Jordan glanced out the window at the tree-lined streets leading to the harbor.

"My father always felt this reverence about our connection to the town, but I don't know. I guess I'm more... realistic. I don't want to be let down again."

"Just because Chase and his family can't be trusted, that doesn't mean everyone is that way."

"I suppose you're right. And I do love Liam. He's always treated me like a little sister. The whole family has."

"Don't think for a second you'll have to handle life alone, Jordan. I couldn't count how many people will be there to support you."

What he'd learned about Jordan was that she tended to be cautious. She only did things after carefully considering every option. From planning lessons for her sub to deliver to her six-year-old students to making a purchase, she took her time, learned as much as possible, and then made a move. He had no idea how she'd ended up in such a shitty engagement, except that maybe Chase had fooled her the same way he'd fooled a lot of people. And now she was second-guessing everyone, herself most of all.

They pulled into the hospice parking lot and as they walked toward the door, Jordan reached out. The trust she placed in him with that simple gesture made his heart twitch. He was in such trouble with her.

Nick didn't get involved. He'd seen too many marriages go south because of long hours and long deployments. It wasn't that he didn't want a wife and kids, he did, but the Navy was his first wife and she hadn't let go easily. He'd found purpose as a military doctor. Something bigger and beyond what he would do as a civilian.

But now that the military wasn't part of the picture, Nick could think beyond his next few months to the rest of his life... and who might be part of it.

They walked down the hall and Nick heard her father's big belly laugh. Immediately, Jordan smiled. The charge nurse waved from her desk, her blue eyes twinkling when she called out a greeting and congratulations. There was no halfway with the engagement story, they were in it up to their necks.

As they got closer, Jordan couldn't hold back; dashing into the room, she hugged her dad and he held on as tight as he could.

"There's my girl. You look pretty as ever. How are you feeling?"

"Feeling much better. Thankfully."

Suddenly, her dad's face dropped. "I wish I could have been some kind of help." His Adam's apple bobbed up and down, and his eyes opened wide. "You're really okay?"

Nick could see the strong bond between father and daughter. Whether it was the eye contact or a movement, it was palpable. Jordan crouched before him and took his hand.

"Yes, I'm much better. I still need to take it easy, but I'm really fine."

"That's good. I'm glad you could come back."

"Me too."

"So, how is your life of leisure? Are you going crazy?"

Satisfied George had settled, Nick was startled when he looked to his right. He didn't expect to see Adam and Jack Miller rise from the couch.

"George, we're going to go now that you've got your daughter here." Adam, who was the football coach at Jennings College, was an old friend, as was his brother Jack, an FBI agent. Seeing them visiting Jordan's father was unexpected, but it shouldn't have been if he thought about it.

The Miller brothers were part of the circle of founding families in Compass Cove. Like the Velsors and the Jennings families, the Miller, Perry, and Sammis families also traced their roots back to the beginning of the town. Still, it never occurred to Nick he'd see his old friends. Jack had served in Army Intelligence before joining the FBI, and Adam had been a standout pro football player until an injury sidelined him for good. They'd been his teammates, classmates, and friends for the better part of his life.

"Surprised to see you guys. How are you?" They all shook hands, but something felt off.

"Gran wanted us to come and check in with George. She usually stops by every week, but she has a bit of a cold, so she stayed home."

Nick nodded, suspicious of the looks passing between the men. He followed as they moved to the hallway, saying goodbye to George and Jordan.

"So, ah… heard about the tree that took out Jordan's car." Jack eased into the subject like a trained investigator. If Nick were a betting man, he'd lay money Jack was going to start fishing for information about their relationship. "And that she was pretty sick."

"Yeah, she was. Much improvement there." He refused to give too much. Jack was going to have to work for the information or ask straight out. It was a game, and Nick wasn't going to play.

"Mia's been worried," Adam added. He and one of Jordan's friends were engaged. It was a match Compass Cove was still trying to figure out because the shy librarian and the high-octane jock seemed like polar opposites, but they'd clicked and were going to be married in a few months.

Nick nodded. "Mia should stop by to see her. Jordan's not going back to work for a few more days." He almost laughed because Jack was getting frustrated.

Silence dropped between them, and Nick could see in their eyes that their brains were turning over trying to figure out what to do or say next. Inside, he was laughing at their sorry asses.

"You're not going to tell us, are you?" Jack mumbled.

Nick grinned. "Tell you what?"

"About you and Jordan," Jack snapped.

"You could have opened the conversation with 'Congratulations' if you wanted to talk about it." Nick leaned into the wall, glad he'd had the opportunity to face down some of the gossip. Even friends were talking.

"What the hell? Last I heard, she'd vowed never to get involved in a relationship again."

"Don't believe everything you hear," Nick reminded him. "Especially around this town."

"So, you're not together?" Adam asked.

"No, we are." It felt good to say that, for some reason. The more he got to know Jordan, the more he wanted to know. "It evolved slowly," he lied. "We didn't draw a lot of attention to it because we wanted to avoid being gossip fodder. You know how it is."

Adam nodded. If anyone understood how information traveled in Compass Cove, he did. His celebrity life came crashing to earth when he played fast and loose with rules.

The brothers looked at each other. There were no questions they could ask that wouldn't make them look like nosy old women. If they got personal, Nick might have to hurt one of them. And that was fine. The less he said, the less he had to remember. This was what Jordan warned him about.

After a couple of minutes, they gave up.

Patting him on the shoulder as they made their way out, Jack looked back and called to him. "Good luck, man. Congratulations. I hear she's a handful. But let's get a beer soon, okay?"

Nick had no doubt that Jordan could be a challenge, although he didn't know if he liked the way Jack said it. That was the kind of shit the Stanleys had been telling people about her, and even though the Velsors were well-known in town, it seemed people always listened to petty gossip.

Nick wanted to know a lot more about her, and most of it had nothing to do with questions and answers. He'd love to know what it felt like to kiss her deep. To have her in a big bed so he could make love to her for hours. The woman had him tied up in knots. Stepping into George's room, he found her seated in a chair next to her father, looking over a piece of paper.

She popped up when she saw him. "They changed his medication. Can you tell me why?"

Handing over the paper, Nick could see the anxiousness in her face, in her bearing. Every change triggered dread, and he understood. With a terminal patient, changes could mean they were coming up on the time everyone had been fearing.

Looking it over, the dosages on most of his medications were the same, except one. They'd increased his pain medication. Which meant George was having more trouble than he was letting on.

"Changes are to be expected at this stage," Nick said gently. "It's not unusual."

She might have known, but Jordan was terrified what the next stage would bring. The end was going to be horrible for her.

Nodding, she sat next to her father. "You make sure you ask lots of questions. Or I'll ask. I can get Nick to help, too. Are you eating enough? You seem thinner than the last time

I saw you."

"Honey, I'm aware of the medications. You can't let every change cause you this much upset."

This was where George wasn't being completely honest. He was thinner. He'd mentioned that he was losing weight when Nick saw him a couple of days ago, but Jordan hadn't seen him in almost two weeks, so the drop in weight was more obvious. He guessed George wasn't eating as much, or he was having trouble eating, especially if he had nausea or vomiting.

These were things he and Jordan could talk about later, depending on what she wanted to know. He bet that Jordan was pretty well versed about what was going to happen next. She was a smart woman, not much was going to slip by her.

Which made the whole ordeal that much more difficult.

"How's your place?" Her father was turning the tables, changing her focus.

Jordan breathed a sigh. "I moved back in this morning. It's good as new."

"Good, good," he said. "Are you getting enough sleep? You have dark circles around your eyes."

"Thanks, Dad. That's nice."

Her father laughed, and Nick had to say, the father-daughter pair was something special. His parents loved him and they were proud of him—at least, his mother was—but they operated with their own set of rules. That wasn't bad, but it wasn't something he understood. When they took his sister and moved across the country, their concern was pretty singular. They didn't like that he wouldn't go with them, but they didn't look back when an opportunity to manage a major vineyard popped up.

The thing was, neither did he. He didn't want to leave his town, his friends. Not yet. Nick was used to being a free agent. Now he had to think about someone else, even if it was just for a little while.

After about an hour, Jordan kissed her father goodbye. "Behave, Daddy."

"Never." He chuckled as Jordan rolled her eyes.

"You're impossible," she called out. As she and Nick left the room, her father was still laughing.

Stuffing his hands in his pockets, they walked down the hall side by side. Barely touching, but not. Relaxed, but not. Jordan stopped to speak to one of the nurses, who admired her ring and wished her luck. If she was uncomfortable, it didn't show. Oddly, her dad hadn't brought up anything about their being together except to acknowledge the ring on her finger.

Once they cleared the building, Jordan linked her arm with his. It was familiar, comfortable. Nick didn't know if she was still playing a role, or if it was just a nice show of affection. Whichever it was, he'd take it.

"How are you?" he asked.

"Worried. Part of me wishes I knew what to expect, and part of me doesn't. I'm so torn."

"I wish I could tell you what happens next, but there's no way to know."

She nodded and leaned her head on his shoulder.

"Are you hungry?"

Looking up at him, she nodded. "I am. What do you have in mind?"

"I don't know. Let's see what we can find."

JORDAN SAT IN a gorgeous Tuscan Italian restaurant across from possibly the sweetest man on the planet. He was also a complete mystery. She still hadn't figured out what drove the do-gooder inside Nick Rinaldi.

Looking around at the frescos painted on the walls, the twinkling lights and the roughhewn tables, she might think this was a date. But they weren't dating, they were pretending.

"How is your pasta?" he asked.

She'd ordered an amazing fresh linguini with shrimp, spinach, and tomatoes. Everything was cooked to perfection. The shrimp had a sweet, savory flavor, and a little snap to let her know it was fresh. The pasta was perfectly done, and it was all tossed in garlic and oil. Nothing had tasted this good in a long time. It was the first real meal she'd had since she was sick.

"Delicious. Your lasagna looks good."

"It is good. I was thinking about something else, but I went for comfort food."

Jordan laughed. "Isn't that always the way? For me it's brownies. Really dark chocolate and fudgy."

"Ahh. There's a bakery nearby that makes brownies just like that. We could get some before heading home."

Jordan's mouth watered. "Could we? The chocolate won't be a problem?"

"I'll feed you small bites." As soon as he said it, her heart picked up its pace. The suggestion was seductive, intimate. Sexy. And Nick knew it. His eyes had darkened, smoldering with suggestion. She'd love it if he fed her chocolate. Or anything else, for that matter.

Dropping her eyes, Jordan caught her breath and changed the subject, floundering for something safe. "Does your nona hate when you eat out?" She knew how Lina reacted when she brought home takeout. It was like she had some kind of radar—she always knew. Before Jordan could get the take-out bag in the house, her landlady would yell across the yard that there was no need for her to carry food in, and eating that crap was going to kill her.

"You mean do I get 'That crap is going to kill you' every time I bring home takeout? You bet. Everyone does."

Jordan thought about Lina. She put her nose into everyone's business, but no one was sweeter or more well-meaning than that lovely lady. It always overwhelmed Jordan to think how Lina came by every day after she called off her wedding to bring her food. Some days, it was a sandwich. Other days, it was sweets. On one of her days off, she made them root beer floats to have on the back porch.

She could see from where Nick got his heart.

"She's been so good to me. All of you have. I don't know how I'm ever going to repay your kindness."

Reaching out, Nick laced his fingers with hers. The warmth wiggled inside her, just like it did the other night, and inched its way right to her heart. Jordan wondered if something real could be happening. If the compass might be right.

"You don't owe us anything. This is what friends and neighbors do. We take care of each other."

Her thumb drifted over his knuckles in lazy circles. Touching him was becoming second nature, and that could end up being very dangerous. "I hope someday I can do the same."

Jordan looked up and her eyes met his once again. She should be used to seeing him by now, but taking him in like this still made her breathless. The man didn't have a flaw, but his eyes were the door to his heart, and it was there that Jordan knew she could be lost.

A soft gray green, they were deep and the same color as the water around Compass Cove in the winter—sometimes turbulent, sometimes calm, but always deep. Jordan could drown in them. Then, without any warning, his face dropped. "Give me your other hand," he demanded.

"What? Is everything okay?" Just about to turn around, Nick hissed at her.

"No. Look at me. Your ex is here with some redhead, and his parents." He glanced toward the bar. "Damn if those people don't look as hard and cold as all the marble in their McPalace."

Jordan smiled at the description. "There's probably a nice big piece stuck..."

Nick laughed before she could finish the thought. "Probably."

"I have no idea what I ever saw in him. I wonder who the redhead is?"

"She's not a local, but looks like a nice enough woman," Nick observed. "I wonder if you should tell her to escape while she can."

It was sad, really. Jordan knew there was nothing she could say to change the woman's mind. Chase was that good at fooling people.

"He's coming over," he said softly, then his eyes flashed with mischief. "You're totally into me, okay?"

Jordan nodded, not telling him that really wouldn't be a stretch.

"Well, look who's here." Chase Stanley glared at her like she'd slipped into the grand ballroom from her place in the kitchen. The guy was a first-class tool who used people and then threw them away. How had she not seen it?

"Chase." Jordan didn't want to give him the time of day.

Even asking him how he was was more than he deserved.

"So, I hear congratulations are in order. Didn't take you long, Jordan," he sneered.

Jordan tilted her head. "A dig about moving on from a man who cheated on me the day *before* the wedding? Did you really go there, Chase?"

Boom. If Jordan had a mic, she would have dropped it. Heads turned at the surrounding tables, and Chase was none too pleased about being called out so publicly. Trying to regroup, he continued. "Right. Do you have a date for this wedding?"

Nick squeezed her hand and again, a mischievous look came to his eyes. "Not yet. We're going to enjoy the engagement."

"Well, be careful," Chase warned. "She's not too stable. Doesn't stick."

That bastard. Not stable? She didn't stick? Screw him.

Rising, Nick approached Chase, and placing one large hand on Chase's back, he grinned as he leaned in. "You're such a stupid fuck, Stanley." Nick's voice was deep and menacing. "You don't even know what you lost. But here's some advice—don't insult my fiancée again, or I will bring down a world of hurt on your sorry ass."

"Are you threatening me?"

Nick turned his eyes to Jordan, and then to Chase. With two quick pats on the back, Nick said simply, "Yes."

Without responding, Chase made a quick retreat, nose in

the air like he smelled something rank. And all Jordan wanted to do was stick his face in a bowlful of pesto. "I have no idea what I ever saw in him."

The feel of Nick's fingers stroking the back of her hand was heady. "I don't either," he said. "I never did."

"He really fooled me."

"He fooled a lot of people. I saw the two of you together, and I couldn't get my head around it. I mean, I never liked the guy. I've known him since high school. He's always looking for an advantage. He never did anything or talked to anyone without calculating the value."

"The anti-Nick?" Jordan wondered aloud.

"I guess. Thanks. Are you ready to head home?"

Jordan found herself staring as he paid the check and made small talk with the waiter. He was so kind, extending simple courtesies to every person he met. Couple that with the realization that she really liked him, and Jordan found herself up against wicked desire.

Sure, the guy was a dream walking, but gorgeous men were easy enough to find. Men who were genuinely kind and honest? Decent? Not so much. As hormones flooded her brain and all her nether regions, Jordan found her attraction to him overpowering her good reason.

The revelation was nothing Jordan ever expected. After having her heart broken in a dozen ways, and her trust shattered, she didn't know if she could put herself through that again. But the pull toward the handsome doctor was proving too much. She either had to get him off her radar, or she had to stay off his.

Or, she had to take a chance and see what happened.

Once they left the restaurant, it was a short walk to the car, but her brain was a jumble of thoughts and emotions, everything rushing in and out like the ocean. The streets echoed with quiet, and she expected it was because so many people were still recovering from the storms that had hit only a week ago.

A week. Everything had changed, and it was only a week.

With her hand tucked into Nick's elbow, Jordan drew in the scent of his leather jacket and the salt air. This was the longest she'd been up and out of bed for five days, and she'd grown used to him being there. Simply leaning into him for support was like second nature, and that was dangerous. Yet, knowing all that, it didn't stop her.

The taillights of his car flashed when he hit the remote, and Nick, being ever the gentleman, opened the door. That's when Jordan did something she never expected to do.

She kissed him.

Chapter Ten

NICK WASN'T AN idiot. He realized the chemistry between him and Jordan was off the charts, and that they were getting closer. They'd spent a lot of time together, and the idea that they were a couple, even if it was only for her father's benefit, was starting to take root.

He liked her, and he wanted her.

But Nick never expected to find himself with the woman pressing her body into his, and teasing kisses out of him. Especially since she'd been keeping him at an appropriate distance since their close call the other night.

One second he was opening the car door, and the next she had his face in her hands and her lips against his.

Naturally, he responded like it had been his idea.

Wrapping his arms around Jordan, one hand settled on the small of her back and the other tangled in her hair. Her scent, the mint body wash that had become so familiar, circled around them and made him a little drunk.

Their mouths tangled in a rhythm that was perfect and familiar. Everything felt natural, like they'd been together forever, and that alone should have had every alarm bell going off.

Instead, Nick went in like a starving man.

Holding her tight, his mouth came down and captured Jordan's in the kind of possession he usually kept in the bedroom. These were intense, hungry, possessive kisses, the kind that lovers shared, the kind that were meant to heat the blood and drive a man crazy.

Jordan drove him crazy. As his tongue swept through her mouth, he tasted the sharp sweetness of the cannoli she had for dessert. Just like her, it was a contradiction, and Nick wanted to understand what drove her, what moved her. She was kinetic and edgy... she was everything. And Nick wanted her to feel his need, to know he wanted to make love to her until they were both too exhausted to move.

Hearing a high-pitched wolf whistle from behind them, Nick crashed to earth. He pulled back, examining her face. Jordan's cheeks were flushed and dewy, and her eyes had drifted shut. When she finally looked up through the smoky haze of her lashes, realization hit her full on.

Nick held her gently by the shoulders, touching his forehead to hers. Both were breathing heavy, but Jordan was putting in extra effort trying to hold it together.

"I can't believe I did that. You must think I'm a horrible person. I didn't mean to lead you on, Nick. Jesus. I don't know what came over me."

He didn't think anything except that it was the greatest kiss of his life. "Don't beat yourself up. It's been an emotional day."

"I had no right. I'm very sorry."

"Jordan, don't apologize."

"No, I shouldn't have…"

He stopped her, pressing his finger to her lips.

"Get in the car," he finally said.

"What?" She was really out of it.

"The car. I'm taking you home."

Turning and looking behind her, she nodded before lowering herself into his low-slung sports car. Nick watched as she pulled in a very long, shapely leg, and immediately he imagined those legs wrapped around him.

Fuck, he was in a lot of trouble.

Just looking at the woman set him on fire. It didn't help that he hadn't been with anyone since before he was shot. Not that he slept around, but he wasn't a monk. If he thought much about it, he was probably relieved. Hard-ons had been few and far between over the past couple of years.

So, while he was driving home with a raging case of blue balls, he was thankful to know everything was still in working order.

Once they were on their way, he glanced to his right to see Jordan practically pinned to the passenger side window. If she thought she could get away with it, she would have ridden on the roof.

"It's okay."

"That was not okay," she hissed. "It was like the other

night."

"Jordan—"

"Nick, stop. I shouldn't have kissed you, especially like *that*. What's got into me?"

Like that was pretty spectacular. He was still feeling *like that* in his twitching dick. "I don't know. But you can't deny we've been headed this way."

"Yes… no. Ugh. I don't know anything anymore."

"We've been spending a lot of time together. I'm familiar, emotions were running high, that's all." His emotions were so jacked up he was going to need days to come down. "And there's no denying the chemistry."

"You're right. It's the fake engagement. It's a mess, and it's going to fail, and I'm going to look desperate and pathetic. We should come clean now."

That wasn't what he expected, and for some reason, it was the last thing Nick wanted. "Think it through."

"I have. Everything we're doing goes against my moral compass. That's ironic, isn't it? I don't want to lie to anyone. I don't want to be attached to anyone, even for my father's benefit. It's wrong."

Nick should be impressed with a woman who was so independent, who was so sure of what she needed, who didn't need a man… but instead, he felt like he could be losing the best thing that ever happened to him. He was tied in knots over Jordan, and for the first time in his life, he wanted to see if what was going on between them could be something.

Still, he didn't respond.

"You understand, right? You don't need me with all my baggage dragging you down. It's always better to be honest."

"Sure. Of course." The problem was, he liked her, and helping her carry the load she was given was something he was more than willing to take on. She was worth every bit of effort.

Making the turn onto Compass Road, his eyes adjusted to the lack of streetlights, and he turned on his high beams. The thick silence lingering in the car was like a humid summer day in the city. There wasn't anything left to do. This was all Jordan's call.

Making a quick right, he pulled into the driveway of his grandmother's house, which sat on the corner of Compass Road and Cove Lane.

The tree that had crushed Jordan's car had been cleared and the wreckage of her SUV had been hauled away by her insurance company. Pulling to the front of her cottage, Nick killed the engine of his car and hoped he could think of something to say.

There was no small talk, however, and Jordan let herself out before he could utter a word. Taking her lead, Nick followed so he could walk her to the door of her cleaned and repaired cottage.

"I enjoyed dinner," he said.

"I did too."

"I like spending time with you, you know? This isn't only about what we've told your dad." He meant that, but he also knew he shouldn't push.

"You've been so great, Nick. Thank you for everything. I mean that, but I don't know what I should do. I'm very confused. And obviously crazy."

He chuckled and took her hand securely in his. "You're not crazy, but here's an idea. If you want to tell your dad the truth, do it. I'll take all the blame."

"Really? Thank you. You don't have to, but I appreciate it."

"You're welcome. Think about it." This was so fucking awkward. He wanted to kiss Jordan until she couldn't breathe, not make pleasant conversation. He wanted her in bed, under him, reeling from pleasure, but he also wanted her quiet, curled against him, and safe from the rest of the world, like she'd been the night of the storm.

He could find a bed partner. That wasn't a problem. But Jordan was the first woman he wanted to be more. Their kiss had unleashed powerful proprietary feelings where Jordan was concerned. The way they connected emotionally, the way their bodies meshed together... this was his woman. And he didn't know how in God's name he was going to get her to give him a chance, because she was hiding behind a pretty big wall.

She didn't make a move to kiss him, but she didn't let go of his hand either.

"I, ah..." She was stammering. "I wish things could be

different."

"I'm not sure what you mean by that." Now he was confused. "Different how?"

"Between us. You know…"

Maybe the wall wasn't as big as he thought.

"Jordan, this is your decision. If you want your life to be different, let it be different. Whatever you decide about your dad, I still want to see you."

"I'm kind of a basket case." Her voice cracked. It was times like these that Nick wanted to run Chase into the ground. He hated seeing Jordan doubting herself so much, so afraid to take a chance. "I hide it well, but I am."

"I get it." Without thinking, he leaned in and kissed her forehead. It was a friendly peck more than anything else, but he sensed she needed it. He needed it, too. "But basket case or not, I like you. Good night."

WHY DID HE have to be so damn philosophical?

"*Let it be different…*" she repeated. "Is he out of his mind? Can you believe him, Gertie?" Now she was talking to the dog. "I want to be happy, but just because I don't want to lie to myself about our relationship doesn't mean I'm afraid."

Gertie sat and stared. Not a bark, a moan, nothing. She just stared, which was about as helpful as Nick's comment.

And the truth was, she *was* afraid. She was a damn coward.

Nick. She kissed *him*. Right on Green Street. In front of the whole world, she just laid one on him.

And it was magic.

Jordan had been in love before. She'd felt the thrill of attraction, the tingle of awareness. But her reaction to Nick was like nothing she'd ever experienced. If she needed proof that she and Chase were totally wrong for each other, it was the way Nick made her body hum, her heart pound, and her mind race.

Nick Rinaldi made her think about the future in a way she hadn't before. In his arms, with his mouth against hers, she didn't think about a future spent being the dutiful wife—she thought about how he made her feel. How they connected deep down; that if she'd let him, he'd know exactly how to touch her, or what to whisper in her ear.

Nick would make her feel that way every day for the rest of her life, and it would never be routine. It would always be new and exciting.

His kiss brought her heart to life. It was terrifying, because unlike Chase who, in the long run had only made her feel like a fool, Nick could break her heart, and that was a far scarier proposition.

When she walked into her living room, she gazed at her couch and imagined him asleep. He'd stayed there while she was sick, and the vision of him—arm draped across his eyes, snoring like a bear—made her smile. With all the jerks in the world, Nick was one of the good ones. He was smart, kind, and funny, but he took no crap. That he was gorgeous was the cherry on top, as her dad would say.

As all the reasons to say yes to him stacked up, Jordan had to admit that there was only one reason she didn't want to try: he had secrets. Pieces of himself he wouldn't share.

And while she might have been anxious to let him in completely, he wasn't any different.

A little ping came from inside her purse. Retrieving her phone, she had a text from Lilly. *How are you feeling? Are you back in your place?*

Better, and yes, she typed. *Saw my dad, had dinner out.*

Dinner, huh? Good offer?

You could say that. Do you want to come over?

It was only eight o'clock, and Jordan could use someone to talk to.

Immediately her phone rang. *Lilly.*

"Do you need anything? Ice cream? Wine?"

"Nah, ice cream still makes me cough and I can't have wine with my meds."

"Well, that's no fun," Lilly joked. "You're still really hoarse. Where did you go to dinner?"

Jordan cleared her throat, aware that her voice had dropped a gravelly octave. "Lambrusco's. It was good."

"It always is. Were you with Nick?"

"Yes. But I need you to come over, okay?"

"Fine, fine," she giggled. "Oh, Mia and Fiona are with me. We'll be there soon." The call ended before Jordan could respond.

"Great," she tossed her coat on the window seat. "It's going to be an inquisition."

Pulling back the curtain from her big front window, she could see the lights on in the main house. Nick was in there, probably filling in Lina and Angelo about the visit to her father and about the ring. She wondered what he was thinking. Had he decided she was crazy, or was he as fixated on the kiss as she was?

It didn't matter either way. Jordan had used up her courage in the relationship department.

Before she flipped on the light in her room, she went to the tall windows that faced Jennings Bay. This time, she wasn't thinking about Nick as she gazed out, but she wondered about the future. The moon was casting a blue glow across the beach and she could see the gentle waves ripple on the water. In the distance, lights from waterfront homes caught her attention.

There were stories connected to all those lights. Family stories. Love stories. Stories that would make her cry, and stories that would make her smile. Whatever was going on in those homes, people had made a choice. For better or worse, they had committed to something.

Jordan's future was like the water—calm for the moment, but there was always the possibility of a storm. Nick was a Category 5 storm and he had the potential to turn her life upside down. She couldn't deny the attraction between them, but did she have it in her to try?

With her friends coming over, she exchanged her sweater dress and boots for soft pajama pants and a big warm hoodie. Rifling through her drawers, she found her favorite pair of soft socks.

Glancing around the room, it was like nothing had ever happened here. No storm, no burst pipes, no pneumonia. Everything had been put back in its place. But not really. Jordan had never felt so adrift in her life.

Gertie followed her to the kitchen, and Jordan loved that she could open the door and let the dog out into the newly fenced space right next to the cottage.

Nick had braved rain, snow, and wind to take the dog out, and even in the worst weather, Gertie had taken her sweet time. It had bugged Nick to no end. So, yesterday a fencing company showed up and created a nice little yard in the open space between the houses.

Jordan was already thinking about planting flowers along the outside of the fence when the weather warmed up. For the foreseeable future, it didn't look like she was going anywhere. Popping a pod into her brewer, she pressed the button and the aroma of the herbal tea filled her little kitchen.

The rapping on her front door cued Gertie's yowling bark and signaled to Jordan the questions were about to commence. Once she was inside, Gertie raced to the front door, slipping and sliding on the wood floors. She got there just as Lilly, Mia, and Fiona entered the cottage.

Lilly and Jordan had been friends for years, but in a very short amount of time, Mia and Fiona had become very important to Jordan as well, and if she needed good advice, she knew any one of them would be ready and willing. All three had offered to go out in the storm and get her food and medicine. Each of them had checked in on her and spent time with her as she recovered. She was lucky to have such good friends.

She also knew she'd be relying on them in a big way when her father died.

When he died.

It was the first time the words were real. Nick had explained what the changes in his medication probably meant. And when they talked to the nurse practitioner on staff, she confirmed Nick's suspicions. Not only had the medication made her father nauseous and unable to eat, he was more confused.

Adding a dollop of honey, she grabbed her mug and went to face the tribe. The scene that greeted her in the living room made her laugh. Gertie was rolled on her back, her stub of a tail wagging away, as Lilly, Mia, and Fiona cooed over her and rubbed her belly.

Who's a pretty girl. Aw, pretty Gertie. Who's a sweet puppy?

The dog was so spoiled.

It was a few more seconds before any of her friends realized she was standing there. When they did, each one rose to give her a hug. Lilly, having seen her the other day when she was still pretty wiped out, gave her a good once over.

Mia DeAngelis was engaged to Adam Miller, the head football coach at Jennings College. New to Compass Cove, Mia found herself in a whirlwind relationship with Adam, a native son and ex-NFL superstar. The two of them were adorable together. Mia was a beautiful, brainy librarian, and Adam was just gaga over her. Once she came to town, the confirmed bachelor was a goner.

Fiona Gallagher worked with Mia at the college library and she was a bit more of an enigma. She was smart and bold, and Jordan really liked her, but she still had to figure her out.

The four of them couldn't be more different, but inside, they just clicked. There was an understanding and a bond. None of them had sisters, but together they were sisters of the heart.

"You look better today," Lilly said. "Your color is back."

"I feel so much better. Now that school has reopened, I want to go back to work, but Nick conspired with my regular doctor and I'm clear to go back next Tuesday."

"I bet your class will be thrilled." Mia was cross-legged on the floor with Gertie in her lap.

"I miss them. My principal came by with a card the whole class signed. They're so cute."

"But you saw your dad, and went out to dinner?" Lilly asked.

"Yes," Fiona plopped on the couch and crossed one long leg over the other. "I want to hear about your dad."

"My dad is fine. There are some changes to his meds, but he's in good spirits. He was chatty, but you know, that's him."

"Chatty is good." Fiona was wiggling her food. "I hear he really likes Nick. Wants a date for the wedding."

"He does. They get on great." Jordan didn't know which one was going to ask the question, but she knew it was only a matter of time. "It's awkward."

"Awkward," Mia said. "How awkward? I see a ring on that finger, so it must not be that awkward. I think it's exciting. And a mystery."

"A ring? You didn't tell me he bought you a ring?" Lilly lunged and grabbed her left hand. "Oh, my God. It's beautiful. It's..." Lilly froze. "Holy crap, is this what I think it is?"

Mia and Fiona looked at Jordan's hand, which Lilly was holding up for them to see.

"That is a beautiful ring," Mia said quietly. "It's stunning. Is it an antique?"

"Yes." Jordan knew Mia believed in the compass myth like little kids believed in Santa Claus, so the word on the ring would blow her mind.

Lilly looked at the two librarians. "It's Lucy's ring." She smiled at Jordan. "I remember seeing it years ago. Mr. Jennings had it on display for some reason."

Mia gasped. "Oh, that's... that's incredible. Really? I mean... how?"

Jordan took a sip of her tea and let the hot liquid soothe her throat. "Lucy is my tenth or twelfth great-aunt. Because I'm the only living female relative, the ring, which has been in possession of the compass shop, came to me."

Lilly was still beaming. "So, you're engaged? To Nick? That's amazing!"

Mia clapped her hands together. "This is wonderful! I'm so happy for you."

"I, ahh..." Jordan felt her will crumbling. She just couldn't do it. "Not... exactly."

"Not *exactly?*" Fiona asked. Immediately, Mia and Lilly stopped talking, waiting for Jordan to explain.

"We're not really engaged, Fiona. My father jumped to conclusions when Nick went to visit him, and Nick didn't say it wasn't true. It snowballed from there. I don't like pretending I'm something I'm not. I don't want anyone to think I have to have a man in my life." She took a deep breath. "I know Nick meant well when he let my father to believe we were together, but... God, this is such a mess."

"That's not what I expected you to say," Lilly said quietly.

"I know. And I'm so torn. I see how happy it makes my dad, but I hate lying. And Nick..."

Jordan dropped her eyes, staring straight into her teacup, but she knew everyone was looking at her, waiting for more information. She wasn't going to tell them about the kiss. She wasn't...

"I kind of kissed him." *Shit.*

"Really?" Mia leaned in. "Why?"

"It was a bad idea. I don't know what came over me, we were walking back to the car after dinner, and he'd just put Chase in his place, and he's so sweet to my dad..." This was sounding more pathetic by the minute.

"And he's gorgeous, and he took care of you," Lilly added.

"Yes. That, too." Jordan took a long sip of her tea. "I completely lost my mind."

"Okay, but how was it?" Fiona, who was right next to her, bumped her shoulder.

Jordan sighed. "It was amazing. The guy is a bona fide panty-dropper. Which is why this is so bad."

Lilly was standing in the corner, grinning like a fool, while Mia and Fiona were puzzled as to why this was bad.

"I'm very confused," Fiona said flatly. "Again. I mean, I can see why you don't want to lie. But if he is all good things, and you're attracted to him, why is he a bad idea?"

Mia was now lying on her back with the dog draped across her stomach, shaking her head. "I tried the avoidance thing with Adam. Didn't go as planned." She wiggled her left hand, which was sporting a very sparkly diamond ring. "Sometimes you have to go with it. How did it feel? The kiss?" Mia sat up, adjusting Gertie. "And I don't mean physically. I mean here."

She clasped her hands over her heart.

Jordan didn't want to think about it because the feelings—the deep down, this-could-be-about-forever feelings—were the scariest part. She could handle attraction, she could handle sex. But when her heart was involved, that was the danger zone.

Still, she couldn't lie to her friend. "The kiss was magic. Perfect. And it made part of me wish everything about us was true."

"So, why are you writing him off?" Lilly's question was the one she'd started asking herself. "I'm confused."

"Me too! I'm so confused. He's perfect, and I thought Chase was perfect, and we all know how that turned out."

"Well," Lilly began with a shrug, "that's just dumb."

"It's not dumb." Ever the romantic, Jordan should have known Lilly wouldn't understand. "I have no judgment with men. It's self-preservation."

Fiona burst out laughing. "No, it's not. You're chicken."

Here she thought her friends would be supportive; she should have known they were going to gang up on her. Suddenly, Gertie was up, barking at the door. Mia was on her feet. "What is it, honey? Is something there?"

Jordan heard the front door open and saw Mia step back. "Yep. There sure is."

Nick stepped into the room, carrying one of his grandmother's thermal bags. She'd sent food. Hopefully she'd also sent alcohol.

"Wow, this party came together quickly." He flashed that perfect grin and made eye contact with all of them. No one was immune to Nick's ovary-popping charms, including Mia, who even though was engaged to a big, gorgeous jock was gazing at him like a smitten thirteen-year-old.

Even her dog was in love with him. As if she was staking her claim, Gertie laid at his feet and rolled over with a moan. The slut.

"Hi, what brings you over?"

"Nona cooked, so I was dispatched. Should I put this in your fridge?" Why did he have to be so nice?

"Oh, yeah. Sure. You didn't have to bring it over."

"No problem. Oh." He fished in his pocket and pulled out a blue case. "You left your glasses in my car."

Taking the embossed case when he offered it, she dropped it onto the table. "Thank you."

Nick made quick work of the cooler, all while the women sat quietly enjoying the sight of a gorgeous man in the kitchen. Jordan had to admit, she liked having him back in her space.

When he was done, he walked right to her and left a soft kiss on her cheek. The smooth, soft pressure of his lips against her skin muddled her brain. It was completely unexpected and left her weak at the knees. "I'll see you tomorrow," he whispered.

Nodding absently, Jordan bit her lip and tried to stop the

meltdown that was inevitably coming. "Thank you."

"You're welcome. Ladies, good night."

Before leaving, he crouched down and rubbed Gertie's belly. Then he was gone.

Mia nearly keeled over when the door shut. "Mother of God. What is your problem?"

Her recent romantic success had Mia pushing everyone to be open to falling in love. It was sweet, and wonderfully optimistic, but in Jordan's view it was also incredibly naïve.

Mia threw up her hands. "He cares about you, Jordan. There was nothing *fake* about that."

"That may be true, for now, but I don't believe there's staying power in a relationship that starts as a lie. I know he meant well, but it's still a lie. And none of you can breathe a word about our...arrangement."

"What happened, exactly?" Fiona asked. "I'm confused how he went from personal physician and boy next door to fiancé."

Jordan curled into the couch and rubbed her temples. She was growing more exhausted by the minute. Just thinking about everything that had transpired that day was taxing her strength, but it was the reality of her father's illness that weighed most heavily "My father doesn't have long. Nick knows this, and he also knows that Dad is worried about me. He sees the engagement as a way to give my father comfort."

"So, this whole charade is for your dad?" Fiona's expression softened. "Wow. What kind of guy takes himself off the market like that for someone he barely knows?"

"Right?" Jordan squeaked. "Don't you find that odd?"

Fiona moved next to her. "I find it sweet. Kind. Sexy." Fanning herself, Fiona blew out a breath. "Should I go on?"

"No. I get your point. And I don't disagree, but…"

"Nana told me you never know who is going to be your love story. It might be Nick, it might not, but you'll never know unless you try."

Fiona nodded, her head bopping up and down like it was on springs. "Yes. *That.* I'm no romantic, but she's right. You guys have chemistry to spare, you should see what happens. I mean, none of us are getting any younger."

Now she was over the hill. Perfect. "I'm thirty-one, Fiona."

"Exactly, and every year there's less of a chance you'll find someone. Statistics don't lie."

"You're just a ray of sunshine." Like Jordan, Lilly was also thirty-one, and had no romantic prospects on the horizon either.

"Hey, I deal in facts, not fairy tales. Plus, he has the advantage of being a real gentleman, a war hero, and he's hot as hell. My question is: what are you waiting for?"

Jordan slumped back against the couch cushions. "I have so many issues, and we went into this knowing it wasn't forever."

"Issues? I have a kid. I did okay." Mia rose from her spot and circled the room like she was looking for something.

"Everyone is dealing with something."

Jordan thought about the first time she met Mia, and how much had changed since that night at Dock's End when they shared a table, and their friendship bloomed. She adored her new friend, but there were times she was jealous of the way Adam Miller fell at Mia's feet. She had no idea what it felt like to have someone so totally devoted to her. She wouldn't know what to do. That realization brought her back to her previous epiphany.

"He scares the crap out of me," she finally confessed. "And his experiences in the war haunt him. He won't talk about it. There's this big unknown piece..."

"He went through hell to recover, but yeah, my brother told me he's not talking about what went down in that clinic. People can only guess."

Mia sat on the arm of the sofa. "Putting your heart on the line is a risk. Anything risky is scary. And there is an unknown piece."

"So maybe I should find a nice, safe, boring guy. Someone who doesn't generate so much electricity."

Lilly laughed. "You mean stable, like Chase? That's what you said about him. He'd be steady and predictable."

Lilly's memory was way too good.

"Obviously," Jordan conceded, "I was mistaken."

"No kidding. *Safe* didn't work out for you. Safe turned out to be a nightmare." Lilly looped her arm around Jordan's shoulder. "Maybe you need to consider taking a little risk.

Try to get through to him. I think he's worth it, and so are you."

AS SOON AS he stepped in the house, Nick felt the charge from being near her slice through him. Raw, primal, her scent, her skin teased out every bit of hot lust. A kiss on the cheek drove him crazy.

He ignored his grandmother's calls and focused instead on clearing the woman out of his head. Heading up to his room, he figured he needed to beat up on something. The heavy bag in the basement would be perfect.

He kicked the door shut with one foot and somehow managed to hold back the urge to punch a hole in the drywall.

He wasn't angry at Jordan. He was angry at himself. He'd jumped to conclusions, pushed her in a direction she wasn't ready to go. Yeah, he was a fucking prince.

His whole life, Nick did the right thing. So why had he made such a huge miscalculation with her?

Heading back down the stairs and right into the basement, he once again ignored his grandmother. He knew some of his reaction was buried in the PTSD he never talked about. He'd let so many people down, and he didn't want Jordan to be added to that list. It was the same with the nightmares. Sometimes control was beyond him, and that's when he had to find a way to work it out. A way to push past his doubts.

Taping his hands, he pulled on his handwraps. The thick padding over his knuckles would keep him from getting too banged up.

Stepping onto the rubber mat he'd laid out in the basement, Nick got to work. He jabbed. He hooked. He crossed. He beat the shit out of that bag. Hitting it harder and harder, within five minutes he was breaking a good sweat. Ten minutes in, he was dripping. Still, he didn't feel any better, and that sucked.

By now the entire town knew they were engaged. He'd seen Chase eyeing her ring at the restaurant. A colleague from the elementary school where she teaches saw her and said everyone at school was happy she was getting better, and they were excited for her about the engagement. His shift at the pediatrics clinic tomorrow would bring more congratulations. And all of it, everything, was based on a lie.

Still hitting the bag like he was trying to knock it off its hook, Nick thought of all the ways gossip could spread in Compass Cove. Everyone knew everyone in town. The community was close-knit. It's what made the place special. It was also a freaking nightmare.

Breathing heavy, he dropped his hands to his knees and bent forward. He heard the basement door open and close, and footsteps on the stairs. Pops, more than likely. But when he looked up, it wasn't his grandfather. It was his dad.

"What the hell?"

"Jesus, I'm all for a good workout, Son, but do you want your head to explode?"

"Maybe. Why are you here?"

"Are you kidding? Your mother heard you were getting married and you didn't tell us? We were on the first plane we could catch to New York. Flights have been backed up since the storm."

"Yeah. Lots of people were stranded. I'd give you a hug, but I stink." Nick took a towel from a white plastic laundry basket on the far side of the room before making his way back where his father was standing. Realizing he was dripping with sweat, he mopped his face before running the towel over his neck and chest. "Mom's here too?"

His father raised an eyebrow. "Seriously?"

"Sorry, stupid question."

"Yeah, it is, but Nona has her corralled for now. I wanted to talk to you first."

Nick picked up a twenty-pound weight and sat on the edge of the bench. "Is this going to take long? I'm a little old to be lectured, Dad."

"I'm still your father, Nick."

"Yeah? Where were you when I was in the hospital for, oh, I don't know, forty-five fucking days?" Nick knew that was harsh. There wasn't anything Dad could have done while he was recovering. His father looked away and Nick scrubbed his face with his hands. "Sorry. I'm in a shit mood."

"I got that. Want to tell me what happened? You're engaged to George Velsor's daughter?"

"It's complicated."

"What's complicated, exactly? Are you engaged or not?" His father's face was stone. Absolute stone. No one would ever accuse Marco Rinaldi of being warm.

"He assumed. He's dying, and I wasn't going to argue with a terminal patient. Then it got caught in the gossip train and that's when it spiraled."

"You're telling me? Laura Earl called your mother to congratulate her. Imagine Mom's surprise. She came running into the bottling room to tell me. But she didn't know if she should be thrilled, or furious."

The last thing he wanted to do was upset his mother. For as tough as his dad was, his mom was soft as goo. She was hurt.

"How is the girl handling it?" Leave it to his father to reduce Jordan to *the girl.*

"Her name is Jordan. And she's having a hard time right now." That was an understatement. "Let's keep this between us, Dad. At the core of all this is George, and until Jordan makes a decision about telling him the truth, we need to keep the story going."

"Understood. But about Jordan, do you love her? I mean, that's a big lie to tell." Dad got right to the point. He had to give him credit for not beating around the bush.

"It's all so new." He put the weight on the floor, and faced the truth that had been swirling around for days. "I don't know. I'd like to find out."

"Fair enough. Then find out."

"She's resistant to the idea. Had a bad experience. Cheating fiancé. Broken engagement."

"Ah. A history." His father made a small circle around the room, finding a stool and bringing it over. "I wish I had a bottle of scotch. You sound like you need a shot."

Nick chuckled. A shot sounded good. "She's gun-shy. Independent. In short, she's a lot of work."

"Son, a good woman will always make you work for it."

"Great."

"To tell you the truth, it *is* great when you finally get there, but it's not going to be easy. And, you know what? It shouldn't be."

Nick thought about that. It resonated. Made sense. The question that lingered was, did he want her badly enough to work for it? Was he ready? Was she? They were both so conflicted, there was no right answer.

Figuring all that out was the challenge. For Nick, it meant moving past his own history to make something new with her.

Chapter Eleven

H ER CLASSROOM WAS exactly how she left it, except for one little thing. There were twenty-two pictures taped to the whiteboard behind her desk—one from each of her students, welcoming her back to school.

Jordan had never been so happy to get up in the dark as she had been that morning. Not only had she missed her kids, but she felt well enough to go to work. That was a huge improvement from the soul-sucking tiredness she'd been feeling for almost two weeks.

How she would be by that afternoon was anyone's guess, but she was anxious to get back to her work.

Jordan was a born teacher. She knew the very first time she went to school with her parents to help set up their classrooms for the school year that she would be a teacher someday. And no matter how many people—from guidance counselors, to advisors to friends—had tried to wave her off, Jordan knew it was the only place she wanted to be.

Teaching was in her family. Her parents, her grandparents, had all been teachers. Jordan never thought twice about her career choice.

"Yay! You're back!" Jordan barely had time to turn around when she was tackle hugged by her good friend Shannon O'Neill. Shannon was a social worker in the school, and she and Jordan had started together. They were the same age, both single, and both cynical about men.

"I'm glad to be back. It was pure hell. Between the storm and being so sick, I feel like I lost two weeks. At one point, I slept twenty-two hours straight."

"Wow!" Shannon walked with Jordan to her desk. "I did hear you had your handsome doctor to care for you, though."

Dr. Rinaldi was gaining quite the reputation. More than a few people had heard about the way he'd come to her rescue. No doubt, Lina liked to brag about her grandson. "He was great."

"Uh huh. How great? Like you're in love with him and you're going to marry him?"

"You heard?"

"Yes, but I should have heard it from you." Suddenly, her friend looked a little hurt. "I've known you for eight years, Jordan. You don't do things on a whim. What's been going on and why didn't you tell me?"

"It was very spur of the moment."

Grabbing her left hand, Shannon held it up. "This ring looks like the real thing, though. It's gorgeous."

A diamond ring would give that impression.

As many times as Jordan thought about taking it off, she

YOU SEND ME

hesitated, loving how it made her feel connected to something for the first time in her life. She and her dad had always had a strong love for the town, but they lived on the fringes. Not being as involved as some families, and not being as wealthy as others. Her father never thought much about it, but Jordan did.

"This ring is a family heirloom."

"It's beautiful." Shannon was hurt. Jordan could hear it in her voice. This was how lies could hurt people. "I guess we'll talk later."

Just then, she heard the sound of little voices and charging footsteps. Squeals coupled with laughter bore down until a sea of small bodies clad in winter coats and boots flooded the room. It was chaos.

But it couldn't have been timed better.

"You're back!" "We missed you!" "What's *pumomia?*" The questions, the love that gushed out of them, were like medicine. Yeah, she was really glad she was back.

Then she noticed the teddy bears. Every single one of her students had bears tucked under their arms or popping out of their backpacks.

Today was teddy bear clinic and she'd forgotten.

Poking her head through the connecting door between the classrooms, Jordan waved to her first-grade partner, Lisa Marino. A little bit older, and a lot more seasoned, she was one of the best teachers Jordan had ever seen work.

"Teddy bear clinic today? I totally forgot. Is there anything I need to do?"

Lisa shook her head. "No, we got everything pulled together last week when you were out. The two days we had for the storm actually helped with the planning. All the graphics and worksheets you need are on the shelf under the window."

"You have saved my life."

With a wink and a grin, Lisa shook her head. "Nah, I think your doctor did that."

"Cute," Jordan said. "And he's not my doctor."

"Yeah?" Lisa replied. "That ring says otherwise."

Jordan wasn't going to get into it with Lisa, but she had to accept the fact she was going to get a lot of questions. Word of the engagement had spread quickly. It didn't help that for the last six months, Nick had become sort of an enigmatic romantic fantasy in Compass Cove. He was 6'2" of hot, brooding, gorgeousness. No one knew anything about him, and that made him very attractive, and very interesting gossip fodder.

As close as they'd gotten, she still had plenty of questions of her own, but at that moment she thought about his hands and his mouth. His strong arms and his sexy grin.

The heat curled in her belly.

Watching her little munchkins find special spots for their bears at the tables, Jordan's mind drifted to how much she missed him. He'd been working the past few days, happy to get back to medicine, and he'd only checked in on her once or twice. There was also a lot of activity at the house, with people coming and going. Family, most likely, and she wondered when she was going to be pulled back into the cyclone.

Never in her life had Jordan been so torn. It seemed the right thing to do, to come clean about their lie...wasn't what she wanted. Everything about him told her to throw her caution out the window. He was sweet, he was sexy, he was smart, and a little bit dangerous. In short, he was perfect, and she was falling for him.

"Ms. Velsor, this is my bear, JoJo. He wants to be your friend." When Jordan looked down, she was captured by the puckish face and big brown eyes of Rachel Miller. The little girl was Adam Miller's niece, and she couldn't have been any sweeter.

"Well, hello JoJo. It's nice to meet you." Jordan shook the bear's fuzzy paw. "Are you ready to have a checkup today?"

"JoJo isn't so sure," Rachel said. "She doesn't like getting shots."

"I'm sure our guest doctors and nurses will be very careful and will explain everything first. Okay?"

Rachel nodded, albeit skeptically. "You're sure? I don't want JoJo to be scared."

"I'm sure. Now go have a seat so we can get our day started."

Returning to work was very good for her ego. The kids

had cheered, showered her with hugs, and told her she was pretty more times than she could count. Leave it to the innocent face of a six-year-old boy to make a woman feel like a million bucks. Once the kids had all settled, they said the pledge, and got through their morning routine.

They did the weather, talked about people who were born on that day, recognized class birthdays if there were any, and then talked about the subject of the day.

Today's discussion, however, wasn't about being healthy; it ended up being about pneumonia. All the kids wanted to know what it was, how they might get it, if they would die, if they would have to get shots, and if their dogs could get it. The problem was, Jordan hadn't done all her homework about the lungs. She knew they took air in and sent air out. That they kept blood oxygenated, which kept the brain and all the other organs functioning properly, but she didn't exactly know how the lungs worked. And of course, her kidlets wanted to know. That's when she had an idea. Going to the phone on the wall that connected to the main office, Jordan called the head secretary.

"Hey Betty!"

"Jordan, good to have you back. What can I do for you?"

"If any of the doctors or nurses arrive early for the clinic, can you send one of them down here? The kids all want to know about the lungs and pneumonia. Having not gone to medical school or nursing school, I'm at a disadvantage."

Betty chuckled. She'd been the principal's secretary at

Cove Elementary for almost thirty years; she knew everyone, and pretty much everything about the town.

"Teachable moment?"

"The best kind," Jordan responded.

It was good to feel like she was back in control of something. For a week, she'd been dependent on others for everything. Granted, if one of those people in particular hadn't stepped up, she could've died. Jordan thought about that for a second. Sure, it was unlikely. But there was no denying how sick she could have gotten.

Saturday, she'd spent the day by herself. The solitude gave Jordan a chance to get used to her cottage again. It wasn't that she was gone long, but the week prior to the power loss, and the broken pipe, had been chaotic. She was happy to have a relatively nice spring day, when the sun shone, and she could get some chores done.

She was still getting used to her new car that Mr. and Mrs. Rinaldi had dropped off to her Friday night. It was the same make and model as her old little SUV, but it was equipped with some very high-end options. They really were lovely people to take care of it for her, and she'd been very lucky.

The weekend was also when she found out visitors had arrived at the Rinaldis'. Nick's parents. According to Lilly, the gossip reached his mother in California and sent the woman into a tizzy. If it was her, Jordan knew that if she found out one of her offspring had gotten engaged without a word, she would have flown into more than just a tizzy.

She'd spent the better part of two days with her father and was waiting for him to question her engagement to Nick, to ask her why she was lying. It didn't happen. No, he was content and didn't suspect anything. He did talk about the two friends who had recently passed and filled her in on what he had for breakfast.

Bringing her attention back to her class, Jordan decided she had to stop thinking about Nick, their fake engagement, the fake wedding they were planning, pretty much everything. Because none of it was going to happen. Attraction or not, they weren't going to be together forever.

Just as she was about to start her math lesson, there was a gentle rap at the classroom door. Miranda, who was the helper of the day, rose from her seat, and opened the door.

Jordan's heart stopped. It was just her luck that the doctor who arrived early for the teddy bear clinic was the very gorgeous Dr. Rinaldi. Dammit.

And based on the self-assured grin he had on his face, the man was quite pleased with himself.

"Ms. Velsor," Miranda yelled. "There's a man here."

"I see that, Miranda, please have a seat."

Jordan went to where Nick was standing with his shoulder pressed into the doorframe. He had his white coat slung over his shoulder in a pose that would rival any male model. It was sinful how attractive he was in a pair of simple khakis and a button-down shirt with the sleeves rolled up. And delicious.

"You're the first one here?"

Nick narrowed his eyes. "Is that a problem?"

"No," Jordan replied sharply. "I just didn't know you were going to be here."

When he leaned in, his whispered words caressed her skin like a breeze, and Jordan's knees nearly buckled. "Maybe if you talked to me, Jordan, you'd know what was going on." Holding a black medical pack, he stepped into the room. "Nice ring."

Nice ring. She should have been annoyed with him for the sarcasm, but she had to smile. His comment was a little reminder that the rest of town believed they were engaged.

There was nothing she wanted more than for this man to make love to her. And she was probably going to hell for thinking about this in a room full of six-year-olds, but he affected her that much. If it was only physical, it wouldn't be a problem. But already she knew that with Nick, it wouldn't be how her body responded to his, it would be how their souls connected, how his words would touch her heart, how she would never want anyone else.

Jordan went to the front of the room, clapped her hands three times, and waited for the students to mimic in response. In seconds, the entire room was quiet, and waiting for her to speak. People who didn't understand education, or classroom management, saw the way she controlled first graders as some kind of magic.

She could see Dr. Rinaldi was impressed. He stood to the side of the room, watching every move she made. Based on the look on his face, she was pretty sure he was going to hell with her.

Once everyone was silent, their hands folded on the desks, Jordan proceeded. "Boys and girls, this is Dr. Rinaldi. He's here to help with the teddy bear clinic, and since he arrived early, he volunteered to teach you about the lungs."

"Hey, guys. You can call me Dr. Nick," he said as he left his perch on the wall. "So why do you want to learn about the lungs?"

"Because Ms. Velsor had *pumomia*, and we want to know what it is."

"Right. She did have pneumonia. That's an infection in the lungs."

Miranda expanded on his answer. "It's very bad, right? What do the lungs do? And don't leave anything out."

Looking straight at him, Jordan could see he was out of his depth. And it had nothing to do with his knowledge. Nick was coming to realize he was facing a really tough room. Charm was not going to cut it.

"Well, let me tell you about the lungs." He picked up a marker that was on the whiteboard ledge and drew two big ovals on the board. He put one horizontal line through one oval, and two lines through the other. He'd made the lungs.

Realizing he had to break this down into the simplest terms, Jordan watched him work. "The lungs are squishy organs, they are a lot like sponges. But instead of soaking up water, they soak up air to send to the rest of the body."

Miranda's hand was up before he was three sentences into his presentation. Jordan was fighting back her laughter.

"Don't you mean oxygen? The body doesn't need air, it needs oxygen."

"That is true, Miranda, but the air we breathe isn't pure oxygen. It's made up of several gases."

"Gas!" Spencer, a little redheaded boy who enjoyed eating the classroom crayons, was notably alarmed. "My daddy says if there's gas we have to leave."

Nick laughed. "It's not that kind of gas. I'll try to explain it to you later. To answer your question, Miranda, the oxygen is what feeds the blood, but the other gases have jobs too. Now, the pneumonia that Ms. Velsor had is an infection in the lungs. The infection causes fluid to build up, and people cough a lot and have a hard time breathing. If it's not treated, it can be very dangerous."

"Ms. Velsor, it sounds like you were very sick."

"I was, Aaron. I was very lucky Dr. Nick was around to take care of me."

Rachel Miller stood up from her seat, and walked straight up to Nick. Instinctively, he squatted down so he could be at her level. Jordan's heart did a little skip as she watched him.

"Did you save our teacher? Did you help her when she was sick during the storm?"

"Ms. Velsor was very sick. I'm glad I was there to help."

The man was a natural with kids, even if he was out of his element. Deciding that he could talk to them better if he was at their level, he moved to the story carpet, and the whole class followed. Now it wasn't just her heart twitching; her biological clock was screaming. It was said that in nature, women would gravitate to the man who would provide them the strongest DNA. The man who would give her children and be a good provider.

Jordan knew she could take care of herself, but her heart melted watching the war hero talk biology with a bunch of six-year-olds. She couldn't let this moment pass, so grabbing her phone, she took a picture. And then she took another. And finally, Nick noticed and gathered the kids around him, so they could all mug for a photo. Then they made silly faces and she took a few more.

His smile was wide and his joy working with kids was so complete, it gave Jordan the chance to see the part of Nick that she guessed few people had ever seen. His whole heart was on display, and as a result, Jordan lost hers.

BETWEEN THE TWO classes, Nick and his nurse practitioner partner, Jimmy, examined about fifty teddy bears. It was all worth it, because the kids left with the feeling that going to the doctor didn't have to be scary. The other team focused on healthy habits, like brushing your teeth and eating good food. Overall, a good day.

That he got to spend hours near Jordan was a bonus. The woman was tough and focused, but she also brought a gentleness to her class that any parent would want. She was going to make a great mother someday.

His father had asked him a straight-forward question the night he arrived from California: was Nick in love with Jordan? He still wasn't sure, but he knew given the time, he could.

As they packed the cases they brought from the office, Nick watched her chatting with several other teachers in the far corner of the gym. Happy and completely at ease, she was in her element. She probably had no idea how much he respected her. She loved her students, of that there was no doubt. And Nick could only imagine how much she would love her own children when she had them.

Jimmy stood next to him, loading the blood pressure cuffs and stethoscopes they let the kids try into a big blue tote. Still, Nick's eyes never left Jordan.

"Are you going to go talk to her?" Jimmy wondered. "Because you're looking at her like you're starving, man, and she's your last meal."

"I don't remember you being so nosy." Nick shoved a pack of rubber gloves at Jimmy to put in the tote. "I am going to go talk to her, but she's busy. And I don't want to be rude. You do understand the concept of rude?"

"Excuse me, Miss Manners. What crawled up your ass?"

Nick didn't respond, he just growled. Seeing the group of teachers starting to break up, he didn't want to lose the chance to talk to her, so he dropped what he was doing and took a walk across the gym. Jordan was still standing with the principal, Emily Rogers, and one other teacher.

This was living dangerously.

When she saw him coming, Jordan's eyes flashed and he saw the pink tip of her tongue touch her lower lip. Yeah, Nick wasn't the only one affected. He'd take it. He'd take whatever advantage he could get.

"Hello, ladies, would it be all right if I stole Jordan for a second?"

The principal smiled broadly. A tall slender woman with dark hair, and large gray eyes, extended her hand to Nick. "Of course, you can! Congratulations on your engagement. We're very happy for Jordan, and you are a lucky man."

"Thank you. I am." Jordan was right about feeling awkward. Lying wasn't in his nature either.

"And thank you so much for coming in to talk to the children. They really got a lot out of the program."

"Glad to do it, ma'am."

"We'll get out of your way," the principal said, gently directing the other teacher away to give Nick and Jordan a little privacy. Well, as much as you could have in a busy elementary school gym.

"How are you feeling?" he asked. "I've been worried

about you, especially knowing you were coming back to work."

"I feel okay, but I am tired. I wanted to believe you were exaggerating about that."

"I wish I had been. But no, I didn't lie about it." He meant that as sure as he was breathing.

"I'm sorry I haven't been around. I needed some time to myself. I hear your parents are in town?"

Nick acknowledged it. "They arrived late Thursday night. My mother heard about the engagement. To be honest, it's been a tough few days with them around. I'm considering moving into the Millers' boat house."

"Not a great relationship?" Jordan eased closer, allowing him to pick up the scent of her perfume.

"Not bad, but not great. Or close. My mother is very sweet, a little over the top, but my dad never approved of me making the military a career. He said I wasted my medical degree."

"Ouch. That's rough."

"It's not always fun. He's a good man, but he doesn't hand out praise when he doesn't feel it's warranted." Nick noticed a little boy streak back into the gym. Cute kid. Very verbal for his age. "That little guy over there." He pointed. "He's one of yours?"

"Eric. Yes. Super smart. Tough home life, though. We've brought him up at team a couple of times now. Why do you ask?"

Nick was glad to hear that, not because of anything specific, but a feeling he had about the kid that things weren't right. "I don't know. He asked a lot of questions. Not typical ones, either. Nice kid."

Lowering her eyes and biting those gorgeous lips, Jordan didn't respond immediately. Instead, she took his hand gently in hers, quietly turning it over, looking at his fingers and his palm. "He is."

Nick didn't quite know what it meant, but there was a change, a shift in the vibe between them. What was on her mind?

"Are you free for dinner?" she whispered, her gaze traveling up.

The fates were shining down on him today. "For you, I can be. What do you have in mind?"

Still holding his hand, she rubbed her thumb over his knuckle. "I could make you dinner. Whatever you want."

"I'm fine with anything, and thank you for asking." *Thank you for letting me back in.*

"I'm glad you were here today. You are wonderful with children." At this point, she was staring straight up at him, her eyes shining, bright and blue like a perfect summer sky.

"I'm glad I was here too. It was fun," he commented. "So what time for dinner?"

"Is seven good for you?"

Knowing it was probably a bad idea, Nick couldn't resist. He leaned in and left a gentle kiss on Jordan's cheek. Immediately she flushed, glowing the most gorgeous shade of pink.

"I'll be there."

Chapter Twelve

I T TURNED OUT to be a beautiful early spring day, with lots of sun and mild temperatures. A far cry from ten days ago, when two feet of snow fell on Compass Cove. When Jordan got home from work, she saw Lina and Angelo sitting with Nick's parents at a table set into the corner of the wraparound porch.

Of all the people in Compass Cove who had been asking questions, his parents were the two people Jordan wanted to avoid. Unfortunately, with Lina waving her over as she got out of the car, there was no way to dodge it. She had no idea what she was going to say, or, for that matter, what Nick had told them.

Interestingly, she found out in the faculty room that day that there were three different stories floating around town. One was about Jordan being a gold digger, and that she figured Nick, who everybody in town admitted was a catch, was better husband material than Chase. And since the Rinaldi family had money, she'd set her sights on him. The second bit of speculation had her pregnant. She'd fallen into his arms after her heart had been broken, and now she was knocked up. The third version was the closest to the truth: that they had made the leap to give her father some peace of mind.

After seeing Nick today, she wanted to talk this out with him. She wanted to know what he had heard, and she supposed, what would—or could—happen next. It was the first time Jordan admitted to herself that she might not want this thing between them to be a dead end.

A lot would depend on whether Nick was ready to put up with her special brand of crazy. Jordan loved her life, she loved so much about it, but if she'd come to understand anything since the storm, it was that she did miss being with someone. It wasn't necessarily about sex; it was about the closeness, the caring. About having someone to talk to.

It might have taken a few days, and a lot of thinking, but she liked that someone cared about her. If she had any reservations about Nick, it was about his inability to confide in her. He'd been through a lot, and the injuries he'd sustained in the little Afghan village; but few people knew the details, or how it had affected him. Based on what she could see, it haunted him.

She loved her dad with all her heart, and he was an amazing father, even under the most difficult circumstances. If he could move on from the loss of her mother, who was to say Jordan couldn't move on from escaping marriage to a total jerk?

Grabbing her tote bag from the back seat of the car, Jordan looked at the large porch and saw four pairs of eyes staring at her. She'd never met Marco Rinaldi or his wife, but seeing him, she could see where Nick got his good looks. The man had to be in his early sixties, but he'd most definitely aged gracefully. His wife, Nick's mother, stood next to him wringing her hands. Bella Rinaldi was petite and dark haired, her eyes were hidden by a pair of designer sunglasses. But even with her eyes covered, Jordan could tell she was staring at the woman who stole her son.

Making her way up the steps, Jordan braced herself. "You'd never know we had over two feet of snow ten days ago. The weather is gorgeous," Jordan said. "It's hard to believe it ever happened." Reaching out her hand, she smiled. "Hi, I'm Jordan Velsor."

"It's a pleasure, Jordan," Nick's father said. "I'm Marco, and this is my wife, Bella."

"It's lovely to meet you, Jordan."

Bella took off her sunglasses to reveal striking gray eyes. They were almost like Nick's, but not quite. "We got here a few days ago and the town was still cleaning up."

"They did an excellent job. It was a mess, there are still a few big snowbanks over near the cove."

Bella reached out and grasped Jordan's hand. "We heard you were ill. You're better?"

"Much better, thank you, but I do get very tired. Your family has taken very good care of me, but if you'll excuse me I think I'm going to—"

Lina, who was standing at Jordan's shoulder, gave her a little shove into a chair. "You'll have some tea, and biscotti. I made them today. They're fresh."

So much for a clean getaway.

Knowing she was out of her league, and that refusing food was an insult, Jordan acquiesced. She graciously accepted a cup of tea and one of Lina's homemade biscotti. Taking a bite of the crisp cookie, Jordan rolled her eyes in delight. Chocolate, a hint of almond, it was perfect, but it was also going to keep her on the porch for way too long.

"So, you're a teacher? What do you teach?" Bella had questions, no doubt about it.

"I teach first grade at Cove Elementary. I've been there eight years."

"It's a good profession. You like your work?" his mother continued.

Jordan nodded. If they were only going to talk about her job, she could live with that, but in her heart she knew this wasn't going to be limited to chitchat.

"I love my job. The kids are wonderful, and we have such a nice group of families. I'm very lucky."

"That's nice. Good. You like children."

"I do. Very much." Before Jordan could say anything else, Bella pounced.

"So, what's going on with you and my son? I came on a plane to see him as soon as I heard the two of you are engaged. Engaged? How could you be engaged without family knowing?" Bella's words came out in one great rush. And she just kept babbling faster and faster. "Why the secret? Are you pregnant?"

Jordan's heart stopped at the suggestion.

Bella drew her hand to her mouth. "Ohhh… if that's it, I might, *might* forgive you if I'm finally going to be a grandmother. Is that it? Please tell me that's it."

Holy crap. The woman could talk. Jordan was happy she took a breath before she passed out.

Still, Jordan waited a second before answering. There was a lot to process in that stream of consciousness, and while she did, she saw Angelo sitting in a chair in the corner, chuckling to himself. He was enjoying this way too much, the stinker.

Marco was more taken aback by his wife's word salad than Jordan expected. "I'm sorry about that," he offered. "Bella, come on."

"No, don't apologize." Jordan waved off her outburst. "But I am sorry to disappoint you, Mrs. Rinaldi, I am not pregnant."

Her face dropped. "You must think I'm crazy," she said.

Jordan reached out and rested her hand on Bella's forearm. "It's fine. I know you must be concerned, especially since you haven't seen him for a while."

"Don't get me wrong," Bella said. "If Nicky cares about you, I'm happy, but we didn't know anything. Marco thought coming here was silly."

"Did you?" Lina's brows pinched together, and Marco

looked away. "Silly. Your family is silly? You could come here any time, you know. Planes fly in both directions, Marco."

"Ma, my work..."

"This is about family. *Your family.* You're always so thick."

Jordan felt like she'd started trouble, and she didn't like being in the middle of a family argument. "I am going to go. I have to take a nap or my doctor will give me a hard time."

"He's a good doctor," Bella said, smiling. "A good man. I miss him."

"Yes, he is. I was very lucky to have him in my corner."

"Is Nick working all day?" Lina wondered. "He left early this morning?"

"He did the teddy bear clinic at school today." Jordan smiled. "He was wonderful with the kids."

"You saw him today, then." Lina was almost as bad as her daughter-in-law. The two were crazy for new information.

Jordan nodded. "I did. At school." With eye contact made between Lina and Bella, Jordan decided to make a move and get out of there while she had the chance. "Nice to see you all! Thanks for the biscotti, Lina."

Jordan was already on the path back to her cottage when Lina called after her, but there was no way she was going back. Nope. She waved and smiled, happy to let the two Rinaldi women talk amongst themselves.

She had no idea how Nick was going to get out of the house later, but that was his problem.

IT HAD BEEN a long day, and if he hadn't been looking forward to spending time with Jordan, Nick would have grabbed a sandwich and gone to sleep. After the clinic at the school, he saw fifteen patients. Fifteen, and none of them had been routine. Still, a bad day with a bunch of sick kids and worried parents was better than a day with a sniper.

Lights were on in the cottage, and he wondered what Jordan was up to. Was she thinking about seeing him as much as he was thinking about her? Was she cooking? Reading? His mind was running amok. She was everywhere.

God, he wondered when he lost his man card?

It was only a short time ago that he barely knew her. Now, he wondered how he'd feel if she wasn't in his life.

Walking in the door by the mudroom, he rolled his eyes when he heard the voices. Not surprisingly, everyone was talking at once. Normally, it didn't bother him, he loved the chaos that centered around the kitchen, but he'd had a long day, and now he just wanted some quiet.

It was time to find his own place. He'd hidden out with his grandparents long enough, but now that he'd been cleared to return to a full schedule at work, his life could get back on track—and with luck, that life might include one very beautiful teacher.

Naturally, he saw a house he liked a few doors down. It was on the water, had a nice yard, and looked to be in pretty good shape. He liked that it was only a short walk to town, and to his grandparents, especially as they got older.

It was big for him alone, but for the first time in his life, Nick wasn't thinking about a solitary existence. He was thinking about getting married and raising a family.

And he wanted to find out if Jordan fit into that plan. Her presence in his life had changed his outlook, and how he saw himself moving forward.

But right then, he was watching the scene in front of him. Nona and his mother were cooking. Nona's good friend, and his former history teacher, Janet Lang, had joined the group and was making a salad. His father and grandfather were arguing over wine. Pops had recently invested in a winery on the east end of Long Island, and now he was telling Nick's father that a Napa wine couldn't hold a candle to his reserve Pinot Noir.

They were his family. And as much as they got on his nerves, just like the town and the gossips, he was lucky to have them.

"Nick!" Mrs. Lang spotted him first, and came rushing from the other side of the island to give him a hug. "It's so good to see you. How is everything?"

"Hi, Mrs. Lang. I'm doing well, thanks. You look great."

"You're a dirty liar, but thank you. Lina said you were

helping out at Cove today?"

"I was. I helped out with a first-grade health project. It was fun. The kids were great."

"I bet *you* were great. That's so nice. Lina didn't know if you would be home or not. I'm so glad we will be able to catch up."

"Right, about that…"

His mother walked over and gave him a kiss on the cheek. "You need a shave, handsome."

"Thanks, Mom. Look, uh," he rubbed his hand across the back of his neck. "I have plans for dinner."

Nona's eyebrows shot up beyond the rims of her glasses. "Plans? What kind of plans?"

He leveled his gaze right back at her. She thought she was going to intimidate him. "*Dinner* plans."

"Nicky?" His mother was a little more persuasive. A little softer in her approach, she always was.

"I have a date. Now if you'll excuse me, I'm going to shower so I'm not late. You guys can talk about it all you want when I'm out of earshot."

"Nicholas Rinaldi, you come back here."

They were like a bunch of clucking hens, including his father and Pops. He had forty-five minutes to get his act together. Stripping off his shirt and tossing it in the hamper, Nick looked at the scars on his body. The one on his shoulder had faded some, but the one that ran from the top of his hip down to his thigh still screamed. He still felt it every time he moved, every time he stood up, every time he rolled over in bed. It was possible he'd be in pain for the rest of his life.

He wondered what was going through Jordan's head when she asked him for dinner. He loved that she didn't shrink away from challenges, and he guessed she saw their relationship, whatever it was, as a challenge.

Taking off the rest of his clothes, Nick stepped into a steamy shower and let the water run over his body. It felt good, helped him feel loose. Then, without any warning, he pictured Jordan in there with him. He was holding her, back against the wall, steamy water streaming over them while her mile-long legs were snaked around him. He could imagine how it would feel buried deep inside her. It was an image that had flashed in his mind since their games of twenty questions last week. They'd come so close to losing it with each other, Nick got hard just thinking about it.

What had he gotten into with her? On one hand, Jordan made him feel like his life could be normal again. On the other, she could force him to confront parts of himself he wanted to keep buried.

After he soaped up and rinsed off, he walked out into his room, stark naked, and ran right into his father. "What the hell, Dad?"

Grabbing a towel from the hook right inside the bathroom door, he covered himself up, but he was still annoyed. "Do you guys understand boundaries?"

"Be thankful it was me, your mother was ready to march

in here."

"This is a nightmare. You've all got to stop this. I'm not fifteen, I'm not even twenty-five. I don't need help with my decisions, or my social life."

"You're right," Dad said. "But we spent over a year worrying about you, give us a break."

Nick never pegged his father as someone who would use guilt. He was wrong. "I get that, but I'm okay. Getting better all the time, and I'm trying to get my life back. Which is why I have a job. Why I'm going on a date. But if you wanted to play the worry card, you could have called me once in a while when I was in rehab, you know?"

His father ignored the dig and plowed forward. "Dinner with Jordan?"

Nick nodded as he dried himself. "Yes."

"She's a gorgeous girl. Nice too. Smart."

"She is all those things."

"But you're still trying to figure out what you should do."

He knew what he wanted to do. Nick believed there might be a future if they really worked at it. But they had to be willing to take the step.

"Right now, I'm going to have dinner with her. We'll see how it goes." Nick zipped his jeans and pulled his favorite gray V-neck sweater over his head. "Have a wine recommendation?"

"Nick, is it possible you've jumped into this too fast?"

"For fuck's sake. Seriously?"

"Watch your mouth."

Nick grabbed his wallet and keys. "Are we done here?"

His father started to come back with a comment, but stopped, defeated.

"Wine?" Nick wasn't going to leave without a bottle. His dad was the expert.

Marco chuckled. "Yeah, take a bottle of your grandfather's Pinot Noir. It's excellent."

Nick shook his head.

"Good luck," his dad said.

Nick hoped he wouldn't need luck.

WITH A BOTTLE in his hand, Nick made his way to her cottage, just as he'd done during the storm. But now, they were upping the stakes. Before his feet even hit the porch, he heard Gertie's howling little bark. Just as he was about to knock, Jordan opened the door.

He took her in, top to bottom. Her blonde hair was loose and wavy over her shoulders, and the way her eyes flashed when she smiled set his heart pounding. She wore a loose flowy top in a shade of bright pink, and she'd paired it with black leggings. She was relaxed and comfortable, wore no makeup, but he smelled mint when he leaned in to kiss her on the cheek.

Passing the bottle of wine, he finally spoke. "Thanks for having me over."

"Thanks for coming," she said softly.

Looking down, he saw Gertie was on the floor, on her back waiting for attention. "She's predictable. I'll give her that."

Closing the door, Jordan nodded. "She really loves you."

"That's because I fed her and took her out in the rain. We bonded."

They'd moved to the living room and Jordan set the bottle in the middle of a warmly set table. "I'm glad you came over."

Suddenly, she looked nervous.

"Did you think I wouldn't?"

"I don't know. We've had a few little stops and starts. And last week was so intense…"

Taking a chance, Nick leaned in and kissed her. Her lips softened under his as his mouth moved ever so slightly. And for a second, it felt like he didn't know where he stopped and she began. It didn't have the fire of the kiss they'd shared after dinner last week, but he hoped she would get the message that he wanted to be there.

"What were you saying?"

Passing him a shy smile, Jordan touched the tips of her fingers to her lips. "Oh," she said softly. "That was nice."

Nick didn't respond, but he felt like he'd won a small victory with her. Jordan was the definition of the word *guarded.* He knew she'd been burned badly, and she'd been faced with incredible loss in her life. He could understand why she wouldn't want to put herself in jeopardy again.

Hell, he had issues of his own that could be scaring her off.

But he wasn't Chase Stanley, and dying wasn't in his plans. He just wanted to be with her, to see if they had anything going for them. He thought they did; it was Jordan who needed convincing.

The kiss was a step.

The cottage had a different feel when it wasn't doubling as a hospital room. Throws were folded neatly on the couch and chairs. Pillows were scattered on the furniture. Her desk on the far wall was arranged with books and a computer. It was as pulled together as she was.

And then the smell from the kitchen circled around him. "Whatever you're making, it smells amazing."

"Gosh, I hope you like everything. I made a garlic soup, and a balsamic glazed pork tenderloin."

"Garlic soup? I've never heard of it."

"Apparently, it's a recipe passed down through the Velsor family. They also passed down a recipe for eel soup, but I haven't tried that."

"I'm glad you didn't decide to try it on me." Nick followed her into the kitchen, where the aromas were even more delicious.

"Next time. If I can find the eel." She winked. "The Velsors were seafarers, and traveled all over the world, bringing the food back to Holland with them. But the story with the soup is that one of my grandmother's cousins was in Indonesia during World War II, and he shared the recipe on a stopover in the States."

"Interesting. I'm learning something new about you every day." And Nick loved it.

"That's about as interesting as it gets."

Putting the bottle of wine on the counter, Nick shook his head. "I doubt that."

Without him having to ask, she handed him a corkscrew so he could open the wine. It was easy to be with her. It felt very normal.

The cork came out with a pop and he took his time watching as she stirred and then tasted the soup. "Mmm. It is so good. Do you want a taste?" Holding out the wooden spoon, with her other hand to catch any drips, she brought it to his lips. "Be careful, it's hot."

Nick blew on the spoon and once he had the soup in his mouth, the explosion of flavors – butter, cream, garlic – caught him off guard. "Wow. That's amazing."

"Right? Come on. Let's dig in." She filled two bowls and carried them to the table. Everything she did was graceful; her movements were easy and fluid.

Once she sat in a chair, he offered her some wine. "It's from my grandfather's vineyard."

"Oh, then yes please." She watched as he poured, and

when he sat and faced her, Jordan took two pieces of crusty bread from the basket on the table and dropped them in her soup.

"Okay. When in Rome…"

Jordan smiled wide and Nick just about fell out of his chair. "Let the bread soak up the soup, and then spoon it all out together."

Nick was enjoying watching her. She was happy. And for a while there, Jordan had been anything but. "How's your dad doing?"

"Oh, you know. The same. He was tired today. He barely got up when I was there."

"Jesus. Really?"

"I know. He asked for you. The nurses say he can't stop talking about the wedding."

Putting his spoon down, Nick leaned back in his chair. "We can tell him the truth if you want, Jordan. I meant it when I said it. I know you hate lying."

She looked up from her soup and dabbed the corners of her mouth with a napkin. "I do, but…" She hesitated. "It could make it worse. I could lose him sooner."

"I don't think one has to do with the other."

"I think everything is connected." She dipped her spoon in her soup and then dropped it. "When I broke my engagement, he… I think that's when he started to get worse."

"I can't believe for one second your father would want you married to that snake." George adored Jordan, and he wanted her to be happy.

"I just wish we hadn't gotten his hopes up."

"I feel responsible. I'm sorry." He'd never meant to make it harder for her.

"It will all work out, somehow. How is the soup?" she asked, trying to hang onto her composure. Something else had happened.

"Are you sure you're telling me everything?"

Jordan took a deep breath. "Why would you ask that?"

Rising and going to the other side of the table, Nick squatted in front of her, taking her hands. "Tell me."

She dropped her head, her hair falling like a curtain around her face. "After I left, he got aggressive. Delusional. He didn't know where he was, he screamed at everyone, threw his dinner tray. They got him calmed down, sedated, but it sounded awful."

Delirium and exhaustion were signs the disease was progressing. He squeezed her hands. "Why did you keep this to yourself?"

She still wasn't looking at him, but he could hear her sniffling. "It's not like we can do anything. And I wanted tonight to be nice, you know? A fresh start."

Reaching down, he found her chin in the mane of hair and lifted her face to his. "It is. But you don't have to go through this alone."

Jordan's lip quivered, and then a lone tear tracked down her cheek. Her arms reached for him, and Nick didn't hesitate. Doing exactly what she wanted, he wrapped her securely in his arms, feeling her rest against him. There was no drama behind her tears. Leaning on him like this was soft, personal, and it fully expressed the frustration she must be feeling.

Like him, Jordan always wanted to help. She was a teacher, and the need to provide comfort and care was part of her. But she was also one who wanted answers. The disease was unpredictable. And that was another factor that was making this so hard for her. There was no way to know when the next stage was going to hit, when her dad would have a good day or a bad day, or when her father would say he'd had enough.

"Do you want to go see him after dinner?" Nick said into her hair.

Jordan looked up, her eyes bright, but hopeful. "You don't mind?"

"Not at all. If you want, we can talk to the nurses together, and find out what happened." Nick knew she was perfectly capable of standing up for her father, but right now he might be able to provide some extra support because of the MD after his name. "What do you think?"

Nodding, he could see relief on her face. "Thank you, Nick. Sometimes it's overwhelming. It's nice to have the moral support."

Tucking a loose strand of hair behind her ear, Nick marveled at not only her strength, but her ability to keep her focus off herself and on her dad. She was remarkable. "Let's enjoy this amazing meal, and then I'll drive you over."

Feeling her whole body relax in his arms, Nick received another gift when Jordan kissed him. She leaned forward, and pressed her lips to his. The heat kicked up immediately, because this wasn't a simple peck. Her soft mouth sipped at his lips like they were candy. There was a sweetness to the contact, and awareness that the two of them were more to each other than they'd ever planned. "I can't tell you how much I appreciate this." Her words sent her sweet breath over his cheek, and so he wouldn't lose that feeling, he held her even tighter.

Nick didn't have to think about this anymore. In a week's time, the woman had turned his life upside down. It might have been crazy, but at thirty-six he'd been around enough to know what he was feeling. And with Jordan, his heart was all in.

He just didn't know what to do about it.

Chapter Thirteen

T HERE WERE FEW things Nick missed about the military, but having close friends around would be counted among them. So, when Jack Miller called and told him he was going to be watching hockey at Dock's End with his brother, Nick didn't hesitate.

He and Jack went back to playground days at Cove Elementary. The two of them got into so much trouble together one year, their parents requested the two of them be placed in different classes.

It didn't do any good. They still managed to get in a shit load of trouble. So much trouble that his parents were ready to send him to private school. They didn't, which was good, because Nick would have just raised hell someplace else.

For a while, his family thought he was going to crash and burn, but around tenth grade, things started to click. He took a Classics class with Janet Lang, and AP Biology with Mr. House. Those teachers brought their subjects to life. His grades started to matter, and soon they shot through the roof. Nick grew—getting bigger and stronger, it didn't take long for him to land on varsity football and basketball before he even turned sixteen.

But his coaches were clear—if his grades started to slip, he was off. So, Nick made sure his grades didn't slip. He found he liked the grind. He had a tight schedule, slept and ate when he needed, and played on the weekend.

When he started college, he signed himself up for Navy ROTC to keep his ass busy. The last thing he needed was to get lazy, and screw up his future. Nick had never told anyone he wanted to be a doctor, so getting into medical school surprised pretty much everyone he knew, including his old friend, Jack Miller.

After college, Jack took a commission in the army, and then found his way to the FBI after a few too many tours overseas.

The Navy put Nick through medical school, and after two grueling residencies, he went wherever he was needed, whether it be on a ship, in a hospital, or a war zone.

The bullets that tore into his body threw his life into chaos. He had no plans other than to serve. It was only recently that he thought about staying in Compass Cove long term.

He leaned back in his chair and took a long pull on his beer, snapping out of his trance when a peanut hit him in the face.

"Need something, Miller?" Whenever Jack didn't know what to say, he turned into the pain in the ass he'd always been.

"Less thinking, more hockey. Our boys are losing." Jack nodded toward the big screen on the wall of the bar.

"Yeah." Nick acknowledged him, but his mind wasn't on the game. It was on a sweet teacher who had gotten under his skin. "Sorry."

Their server dropped off their plate of ribs and wings, just as Jack's brother Adam sat at the table. "How's that for timing?" Adam rubbed his hands together and ordered a beer.

Jack rolled his eyes. "Well, you're just in time to diagnose our favorite doctor. He's distracted, distant, and looking all moony-eyed."

Adam burst out laughing and Nick wasn't loving the attitude. It wasn't so long ago he was the one mooning over a certain librarian. "Bite me, both of you."

"Jordan?" Adam asked.

Jordan. It had been a week since her father's condition started to worsen, and Nick had been with her as often as possible. She was shouldering all the decisions regarding her dad's care, and the understanding that the end was closing in was breaking her heart. He was glad she was out with her girlfriends today. Nick hoped she could take her mind off her father's illness, even if it was only for a few hours.

Looking between the brothers, it occurred to Nick he was beaten. And if he was going to follow through on the fake engagement, he had to say something. "I didn't expect it. That's all."

Adam nodded. "You rarely do. But if she makes you happy, just go with it. Once I stopped fighting how I felt about Mia, I was much happier."

Jack shook his head. "You two crazy kids..."

"Fuck off," Adam snapped. "You've had it bad for Lilly Vasquez since you graduated from OCS. You just don't have the balls to do anything about it."

Jack looked down in his beer, and Nick had to admire the way Adam could put his younger brother in his place.

"We're not talking about me," Jack snapped. "I'm the one who isn't engaged."

Filling a plate with ribs, Nick raised an eyebrow. "Maybe you should be."

The bar wasn't as noisy as normal because their local team was getting slaughtered, but it was packed to the gills. Built on a pier on the far end of town near Roosevelt's Marina, Dock's End sold good food and great times. In warm weather, most people opted to eat outside catching some sun and a breeze from the water, but whatever the weather, the place was always hopping.

Nick liked coming here, but it was his first time since settling back in town. He needed to change that.

Without any warning, a tall blond man grabbed a chair, spun it around and dropped it by their table. Liam Jennings smiled as he straddled it and sat down. "Hey. Ribs." Taking one off the plate, Liam grinned. "The game is bullshit, so what's going on here?"

"Nothing," Adam took a sip of his beer as soon as it was set down. "Jack is jealous because he doesn't have a woman. He accused Nick of being moony-eyed."

"Did you really say that?" Liam was an artist. He ran the compass shop like a small gallery, but when it came to fitting in with the guys, even jocks and military types, he had no problem. He could trash talk with the best of them; he just tended to use bigger words. "Since when is that in your vernacular?" Then he turned to Nick. "He's right though, you are kind of moony. You've got it bad."

"I don't need this shit." Nick finished his beer and signaled for another one. "She's smart. She's funny. She's gorgeous. I'm not stupid."

"No argument here," Jack began. "But when did it all happen? You guys flew way below the radar."

Nick dropped his head as the question ran through his mind. This is what he and Jordan had prepped for. They'd spent hours refining and polishing their story, but all of it paled beside the truth. "She got to me the first time I saw her. She was coming in from a run. She was wearing an old tank top, some leggings. She was sweaty. But the way she moved when she walked up from the beach... the way she smiled... that's the moment I knew she was special. That I had to find out more about her."

Jack and Liam stared at him, their expressions blank. But Adam patted him on the shoulder. "I get it."

"You do? Because I don't get it." Nick didn't know what

made him digress from their planned script, but what he said was the truth. She had affected him from day one. Everything about her made him take notice, and that never happened. The raw chemical reaction was overpowering.

"Please. The second Mia entered my orbit, it was over. I'm no believer in love at first sight, but I knew she was different."

Jordan pretty much had him by the short and curlies. The woman owned him, and Nick knew it. Watching the way she handled the people she knew with care and compassion—from her students to her father—she was extraordinary. She was everything he never knew he wanted.

Liam raised his beer. "Power to you, man. She's awesome."

Nick clinked his bottle with Liam's. "She is."

With his chair tilted back on two legs, Jack folded his arms, looking every bit the G-man that he was. He didn't believe Nick for a minute. He was going to have to tell his friend everything at some point, but at least it wouldn't be a shock.

Jack knew him better than anyone. Possibly even better than his own parents. But Nick couldn't shake the fact that what he felt for Jordan went far beyond what he ever expected, and even though their plans weren't long term, he wished things could be different. For the first time in his life, he wanted more.

THE BRIDAL SHOP on Main was a relatively new establishment in Compass Cove, and in the year since the doors opened, brides had been coming from all over Long Island to find the perfect dress. The shop, which was run by a newcomer to town, had gained a big reputation in a very short time.

Madeline King, the shop's owner, was a California transplant who landed in Compass Cove purely by accident. When her wealthy ex-husband decided to leave her for a twenty-something actress, the thirty-nine-year-old costume designer picked out a name on her contact list and made a phone call. The name she chose was Lilly Vasquez, whom she'd worked with on several films. So, with a big fat settlement check, Maddy decided she was going to make dreams come true. If she couldn't have her own happily ever after, she'd make sure new brides looked spectacular on their special day.

Jordan liked Maddy. She put off a great vibe that was part down-to-earth, part sophisticate. Every dress she created was a work of art. The shop was filled with gorgeous one-of-a-kind gowns, and the custom designed gown she'd started to make for Mia was frothy perfection. As Jordan watched her friend walk out of the dressing room, with the tulle and chiffon skirt fluffed like a cloud, no one could have said otherwise.

"Adam is going to die," Fiona deadpanned. "The gown isn't even finished and you look gorgeous."

"She is the embodiment of a beautiful bride," Maddy said as she adjusted Mia's skirt. The group was seated around the elegant showroom on pale yellow upholstered chairs that made the room glow almost as much as the brides.

Jordan found herself a bit overcome. She watched Mia, who a year ago wasn't in her life, as she looked at herself in the mirror. "It's beautiful."

Lilly was near tears, and Mia's nana, Janet, was trying to keep herself together. It was emotional for everyone because Mia, who had endured so much, had managed to find her happy ever after with the most unlikely of princes.

Jordan was happy for Mia, and could only hope she'd be just as happy for herself someday. Playing with the ring on her left hand, she wondered if Nick had the nerve to open up to her. If he could, the fake engagement might just become real.

Maddy stepped back and smiled. "Girl, you are gorgeous. That is going to be my best work yet, if I do say so myself. At your next fitting we will start to talk about the detailing."

"I can't believe I'm getting married." Mia's eyes welled up.

"You are!" Lilly stepped behind her friend and pulled Mia's soft mane of curls off her shoulders. "Up or down?"

"I haven't even thought about it." Mia's eyes went wide. "What do you think?" She looked around the room, and like it was choreographed, everyone answered at once.

Fiona and Janet said *up* at the same time Jordan and Maddy said *down*.

Mia shook her head and Lilly laughed. "We can do both. Up and down. It will look beautiful, and you won't even need extensions."

Janet went to Mia and took her granddaughter's face in her hands. "You are beautiful, and you are going to have a wonderful marriage."

Mia was near tears, and so was Jordan. She didn't know who would be there for her if she ever got married. Her mother and her grandparents had died years before. Her dad was going to leave her soon. It was crushing, and all at once overwhelming. Feeling the air leave her lungs, Jordan had to get out. "Excuse me a second."

Not wanting to ruin Mia's moment, Jordan made her escape from the shop, and stepped into the gorgeous spring afternoon. The sun hit her face, and she took a deep breath, drawing in the scent of the water, and trying desperately to steady herself. "Get a grip. Get a grip," she whispered.

Walking up and down the sidewalk, she was sure she was a curiosity on a busy Saturday afternoon in town, but she didn't care. People glanced her way, said tentative hellos, but no one was willing to engage the crazy lady.

"Jesus." Closing her eyes, Jordan pulled herself together before setting off down Main. She loved how small business-es thrived in Compass Cove, when in other towns they struggled. In her mind, it was a testament to the way the town took care of their own. She passed the butcher shop, the bookstore, the stationary, and then instinctively turned into Rinaldi's Café.

The café was a wonder. On one side was the actual restaurant that served some of the best food on the North Shore. Simple comfort foods, creative specials, and the best pancakes anywhere. Of course, there were the onion rings. Lina should go to heaven just for the onion rings.

The other side was the original bakery, opened by Lina's father, which had morphed into a busy coffee shop that could rival any chain. They sold cappuccinos and lattes, frozen coffee drinks, along with all sorts of pastries and homemade gelato.

She approached the counter to see her former student, Krissy DeSano, flashing a megawatt smile. Krissy was in her class her first year at Cove Elementary, when she taught fourth grade.

"Hey, Miss Velsor!"

"Hey, Kris. How are you today?"

"I'm good. What can I get you?"

So far, so good. This was a simple enough exchange. "A vanilla latte and a chocolate tarte, please?" The chocolate tartes were the stuff of legend in town. The flaky mini crust held a hazelnut chocolate filling that melted when it hit your tongue. Jordan suspected it had to be 5000 calories.

Krissy put in her order and rang her up. When Jordan

handed her a ten-dollar bill, her former student grabbed her left hand and ogled her ring.

"Oh, my gosh! It's so pretty. It's old, isn't it?"

Jordan extracted her hand, cursing the fact that her mind was firmly back on weddings and engagements. So much for forgetting. "It is. The ring belonged to Lucy Velsor. She's one of my ancestors."

"Lucy? *Ohmigosh.* You mean compass Lucy? That Lucy?"

"Yes. That Lucy. The ring is a family heirloom."

"Miss Velsor, that is so cool."

"It's special. And a little intimidating to wear."

The initial shock having worn off, Krissy could think about the ring, and all it meant. "I bet! I mean, to be able to wear something that not only has so much history, but all that romance attached to it."

Krissy's hand drifted to her heart. *All that romance.* What exactly did that mean?

When the teen pulled herself together, she handed a cup and plate over the counter, but Jordan had to step back when a warm male body reached out to take her food.

"I've got that." Nick smiled at her, and she alternately wanted to smack his hand and fall into his arms. He was here for her. He knew.

He knew about her almost meltdown.

"What are you doing here?" All she wanted was five minutes to herself. That's all.

Walking her to a table, Nick pulled his chair extra close

to hers. His scent and his warmth surrounded her, and Jordan heard herself sigh. Leaning in, he whispered in her ear.

"A little bird told me you made a hasty retreat from the bridal shop. True or not?"

Jordan shook her head, her ponytail swishing back and forth. "No, no, of course not. I just..."

He raised an eyebrow. "No?"

"Okay, maybe I was a little affected by the whole family thing. I mean, I'm human."

"You are." His arm stretched behind her and he scooted a little closer. He was going all out on the couple thing, but that wasn't what Jordan needed at the moment.

"You want to talk about it?"

"No," she sipped her latte. "I don't think I do."

Krissy had arrived at their table with another coffee cup. "Manny said this is your usual, Dr. Rinaldi."

Nick reached up and smiled at the girl, and poor Krissy, totally unaware of the power of Nick's smile, nearly crumbled. "Thank you, darlin'."

"You, ah, you're welcome," she sputtered before beating a retreat.

"Jeez, have you always been that way?"

"What way?"

"Charming women with that grin of yours?"

"She's sixteen! Stop it. There's only one woman I'm interested in charming." Bringing his face so close to hers she could feel his breath on her cheek, Jordan's heart jumped. "You look pretty today."

Jordan shook her head and gave his shoulder a gentle shove. "Stop it."

"Why?" His eyes twinkled with life. This man had many sides, but he was starting to get on her last nerve. "You are pretty."

"Who told you?" In other words, which one of her friends ratted her out?

"That you're pretty? No one." He sipped his coffee. Games. He was playing games, and Jordan looked to the sky, wondering why she couldn't have a minute of peace.

"I think I'm going to take this to go." She grabbed her coffee and her tarte, realizing immediately she couldn't make a getaway with the café's mug and plate.

"Here. Enjoy," she said, setting her food down in front of him.

"What?"

Jordan didn't answer because she was out the door before he could finish. All she wanted was some downtime. She didn't want anyone to feel bad for her, or pity her, or send out anyone to rescue her. She hated being high maintenance.

She hated needing people, and she was starting to need Nick too much.

JORDAN WAS OBVIOUSLY feeling better, because she was moving pretty fast. Too fast for him, as Nick struggled to catch her as she raced down Main Street. He had to hook up with an athlete. He and his bum leg were totally overmatched.

He did his best, but her long, lean form was moving farther away. If he didn't do something, he was going to lose her. This was so fucking embarrassing.

"Jordan!" he called. She kept walking. The view was awesome. The woman rocked the jeans and high-heeled boots like a damn model. How the hell did she walk in those? "Focus, man," he grumbled. "Jordan!" Louder this time, she stopped and turned. He had chased after her for just about a block, and his muscles had cramped. Putting a hand on his hip for support, he hobbled to a bench.

Jesus. When was he ever going to get better? Maybe Jordan should keep walking. He was not worth her time. But when he looked up, she was standing next to him. A stray piece of hair had escaped her ponytail and was fluttering around her beautiful face. Lord, this woman was like an angel.

She sat next to him, and immediately he passed her the little bag he'd snagged on the way out that held her chocolate tarte. "You can't let this go to waste."

"Damn." Her hand came down to his hip, and immediately her touch filled him with more feeling than he knew what to do with. "How badly does it hurt?"

"Bad enough, but I think my pride is more wounded than my hip. I can't even chase after a woman anymore. It's going to kill my game."

"You know, this isn't funny, and you don't have to pretend on my account." Jordan's face was set, concerned.

"I'm not pretending. I'm serious." The last thing he wanted to do was spill his guts to her. Yes, his injury sucked. The war sucked, but there was nothing anyone could do about it.

"I can't even imagine how you feel." Her voice was barely more than a whisper.

"Yeah, well. I try not to think about it. It's pointless."

"I got that. But I doubt it's pointless."

"Jordan, I came here to help you. Let's not get wrapped up in my problems."

He realized how sharply he'd shut her down and rubbed her shoulder. "Sorry."

"I just needed to step away. That's all. I wasn't in crisis. I needed to clear my head."

"I'm sorry. I heard you were upset…"

Jordan nodded, then tilted her head. "By the way, how did you know where I was?"

Nick shrugged, letting the question sink in. "I don't know. I just did."

That realization hit him harder than he expected. How did he know? He homed in on her like she was microchipped.

Jordan's head dropped to his shoulder and she opened the white bag from the bakery. "Would you like a piece?"

"Sure. Thanks." Accepting the piece of pastry seemed like a small thing, but it was a truce. They were fine.

Jordan popped a piece of the tarte in her mouth, her eyes drifting closed as the taste surrounded her. "I'm sorry I made you chase me. I feel bad."

"You could always kiss it and make it better."

As soon as he said it, her eyes opened and narrowed. "Hmm." She lifted her head. "You're all right?"

He chuckled and kissed her on the forehead. "I'm fine. But my ego is bruised. I have to get running again."

"Anytime. I need to get back in shape. It's hell not running for almost a month."

"Damn doctor of yours is so bossy." He reached in the bag again, and watched her smile bloom.

"He is. So bossy."

"Are you going home?"

"I think so," she said. "I love them all, and I'm so happy for Mia, but I'm just not in the mood."

Nick took her hand. "Did something specific happen?"

"It's just... my dad always wanted this, you know? Seeing his daughter married. That's probably why I said yes when Chase proposed. Deep down, I knew it wasn't right, but I thought it was something I could give to my father." She shook her head. "I'm feeling it, that's all. I'm missing him already."

"You're human. And this is an awful time for you."

Taking a deep breath, Jordan squeezed his hand before letting go.

"I'm here for you," he reminded her. "However, you need me."

Leaning in, Jordan kissed him lightly on the lips. "I know you are. Thank you. But you need to remember I'm here for you, too."

"I know."

This woman was going to kill him. A simple kiss made him crazy. And when she mentioned how her dad wanted to see her married? He was ready to haul a judge into George's room at the hospice house and say 'I do.' He was out of his mind.

"I'll see you later," he said. "Movie tonight? If you're free?"

Jordan smiled. "Bring the popcorn."

More graceful in high heels than any woman he'd ever seen, Jordan started down the street, and Nick thanked God for his 20/20 vision, because he could watch her hips sway from 100 yards away.

Heading back to Dock's End, he wondered what being married to her would be like. It would never be boring. That was for sure.

He was such a goner.

And he didn't know how he'd tell her.

Chapter Fourteen

WHEN NICK GOT home from his afternoon in town, he found more family had descended on the big house. It seemed his mother had told his aunts about his engagement. Which meant his father's brothers, their wives, and a couple of his cousins had arrived in Compass Cove without him knowing it.

He thought about asking Jordan if she wanted to run away with him. He didn't care where they went—a warm island, a mountain retreat, a hotel on Fire Island.

A hotel anywhere would do it for him.

The kitchen was mobbed. Every seat at the table was filled, bodies surrounded the kitchen island, and Nona was cooking up a storm. He hadn't seen her this happy in years.

Didn't it figure?

If nothing else, it reminded Nick to get back on track with finding his own place. He'd called the Realtor about a couple of houses he'd seen in town, and a couple that were more off the beaten path. He spent so much time deployed when he was in the Navy, he'd socked away a lot of money. It was a good thing, because houses weren't cheap around here, but he did want to stay. As much as his family was a pain in the ass, and his friends harassed him to no end, Nick was home and he was going to set down some roots.

"Nicky!" His grandmother waved him into the room. "Everyone is home! Everyone! Isn't it wonderful?"

"It's unexpected, that's for sure."

His relatives crowded around him in a great swarm, smothering him in that special brand of Rinaldi love. All talking at once, he could only pick out pieces of what his aunts and uncles were saying, but the gist of it all was that they were congratulating him on his new job, on being home, and on finding a wife.

Shit.

Nona waved everybody off, and he noticed that a very large meal was being prepared. *Very* large.

"Pops, is there something I should know about?" His grandfather, sitting in his usual chair at the head of the table, was cutting a piece of cheese from a large wedge, and sipping red wine.

"Your mother called them all. She issued a summons like a judge, calling everyone in. They came. Everyone came, and now they are all stacked up around the house." His grandfather's eyes narrowed. "This is all your fault."

Nick had no response. His fault? How the hell was it his fault? All he wanted to do was find some snacks, a bottle of wine, and curl up with a girl-next-door.

Without another word, Nick made his way through the

house, up the stairs, and into his room. He closed the door and leaned his head into the hard slab of wood, the only thing separating him from the insanity downstairs.

There was a light tapping at the door, and he heard his mother's voice on the other side. That didn't take long. "Nick, can I come in?"

He opened the door to see his mother looking upset. Maybe even a little guilty.

Nick stepped back, but she didn't move. "Are you going to come in, Mom?"

"Oh, yes." Moving just over the threshold, Nick waited. "I'm sorry about the people. I know it must have caught you off guard. Honestly, that wasn't my intention, but they talked to your grandmother, and then everyone just showed up. They want to meet Jordan, and they want to see you."

How did he possibly respond to that? A better question would be: when did he become such an asshole that his own mother was apologizing to him? Reaching out, Nick pulled his mother into a hug, and as soon as he did she grabbed the front of his shirt and crumbled.

"I slept next to your bed the first week you were home. The nurses at the hospital in San Diego were so lovely to me. They kept telling me to talk to you, that you would hear me even though they were keeping you unconscious. I just wanted you to tell me to stop worrying. To get annoyed."

Nick sorted through the pieces of memories from his recovery, but from the time they brought him into the hospital in Kandahar to waking up in California, his mind was a series of broken images. He did have one or two of his mom. In both, she was crying. She was alone and crying.

"I knew you were there," he spoke into her hair. "And I didn't get annoyed, because I was scared, Mom. I was glad you were there because I was scared."

His mother looked up, eyes filled with tears, and she laid a hand on his cheek. "That makes two of us. I was so scared to lose you."

Giving his mother a kiss on the cheek, Nick smiled. "Did you have to call them all, though?"

His mom laughed, and Nick was now focused on how he was going to get Jordan to come over and have dinner with thirty people. All of them related to him.

"She might freak out at the sight of everyone, you know that?"

"I do," Mom shrugged. "But Lina said not to worry. Jordan could handle it."

If it had been a normal day, Nick was sure she would have charmed everyone. But it had been a hard day. A very hard day. "I was supposed to go over there later, just watch a movie. I guess that's not happening."

His mother patted his cheek. "You'll make it work. I have faith in you and your powers of persuasion."

Faith. Fan-fucking-tastic.

She left him in his room, and Nick had to think about what he was going to say to his fake fiancée to get her to meet his family. The act, in and of itself, that suggested a permanence they just didn't have. At least not yet.

Pulling his phone from his back pocket, Nick punched in a text.

Need to talk to you. Can I come over?

The response came quickly. *Sure. Is everything okay? There are ton of people in the house. Did someone die?*

She wasn't joking about that. *No. Nothing like that. I'll be there in a couple of minutes.*

Probably sooner than that. He made his way downstairs, through the house, and out the back door without stopping to talk to a single soul. He even waved off Nona, knowing he was going to catch crap for it later.

The walk to the cottage felt like an eternity. As he approached the front porch, he saw Gertie's head poke around the side of the house. "Hey, girl."

The dog turned and headed toward the side of the house that faced the water. That's where he found Jordan, sitting on the back deck, with Gertie keeping watch for birds and squirrels. The dog didn't even bark when he came over anymore.

"So," Jordan said. She was looking out at Jennings Bay, the blue water shimmering in the late afternoon sun. "What's going on over there?"

"It's complicated." Nick rubbed his jaw nervously. "But my whole family is here. Aunts, uncles, cousins—I think the only one missing is my sister, and she should be here right after dinner."

"Dinner? I guess you won't be coming over for a movie."

Nick was hesitating, and he shouldn't be. He just had to ask her. That was all. "No, but, ah, do you want to come have dinner with my family?"

Jordan locked eyes with him, and he was trying to read her expression, but he couldn't. She wasn't giving him anything to work with.

"I know it's more than you need right now, and I can make you excuses, but that just means they won't leave. They'll stay until they get what they came for."

"Uh huh." She grinned. "And that's me?"

"Yep. They're relentless." Stuffing his hands in his pockets, Nick rocked back on his heels. "So, what do you say? Dinner?"

"Hmmm…" In a move that shocked him, Jordan stood. He noticed under her wrap that she'd changed her top. Her hair was down and she'd put on a little makeup. "I thought you'd never ask."

This woman would never stop amazing him. "You're sure? It's a crazy that's like nothing else."

The corner of her mouth turned up ever so slightly. "It's okay. I like crazy. And I love big families. Always wanted one. The crowd will be good for me."

Stepping into her, Nick's hands settled on her waist, feeling the curve of her body beneath them. "My aunt Joy is going to ask how many kids we are going to have. So be prepared."

She didn't say anything as she let Gertie in the house, and closed the door. "You're the one that needs to be prepared, Doctor." Jordan took his hand, while she led him to the path back to the house.

"Why do I have to be prepared?"

"Because you're going to have to tell your family that I want six kids."

Nick stopped short. "Seriously? Six?"

"Yep. At least."

"All right,'" he said on a laugh. "Six it is." How about that? Nick didn't tell Jordan he'd give her those six kids whenever she wanted them. They could get started after dinner as far as he was concerned.

HER INTENTION WAS to help Nick relax. The look on his face when he talked about his family was complete dread. The poor guy was totally overwhelmed. Not that she wouldn't be; Jordan fully expected to feel like a fish out of water. But the Rinaldis, especially Nick, meant something to her, and she wouldn't let them down.

They were halfway to the house when she heard a roar come from inside. Great belly laughs, giggles, a slew of voices all talking at the same time. It was terrifying and thrilling all at once. Jordan envied big families, especially growing up the way she did. She loved the closeness; sure, she knew there was bickering, differences of opinion, but it was the one thing she always missed having just her dad.

Thankfully, Nick hadn't let go of her hand, not that she expected him to. They were holding onto each other for mutual moral support. Crazy as it was, the two of them were in this together, fake engagement and all.

Strangely, the fake engagement felt more real than the one that was going to send her down the aisle last summer, and Nick was more of a fiancé than Chase had ever been. Jordan pressed her free hand flat on her belly, hoping to steady her nerves.

"Just stick close to me," he said.

Jordan nodded and walked in the house, ready for anything. She wasn't disappointed. As soon as she stepped through the door, everyone stopped talking. *Everyone.*

Lifting her hand to wave, Jordan put on her best smile. "Hi."

That was all it took. At least a dozen people surrounded her. They shook her hand, patted her cheeks, gave her hugs, and most of all they welcomed her to the family.

"She's a looker, Nicky." A man who looked similar to Nick's father grabbed both her hands. "Hey there, beautiful. I'm Uncle Joey. So nice to meet you. Boy, you're a tall girl."

Jordan was a couple of inches taller than Uncle Joey without her boots on. "It's nice to meet you all, Nick has told me so much about you."

"Uh oh. Whatever he told you, it's not true. We're not

that bad." Another dark-haired man, presumably the third Rinaldi brother, gave her a kiss on the cheek. "I'm your uncle Mike, sweetheart. The youngest and most charming of the brothers."

"Uncle Mike is also the family flirt. Lay off, Uncle Mike. She's taken." Nick was lacing his comments with good humor, but that was definitely a shot across his uncle's bow.

"You are a very pretty girl," a woman said. She had neatly styled dark brown hair, and big dark eyes, with pleasant crinkles in the corners. "But you're so thin. Babies need nourishment."

Ah, Jordan thought. Babies. "You must be Aunt Joy."

The woman didn't know if she should be happy or offended that Jordan knew who she was. Her eyes darted around the room at different relatives, wondering if anyone gave her up. "I'm Joey's wife. The two boys stuffing their face with cheese are my sons, Dominic and Jimmy."

"There's so much going on," Jordan was desperate to change the subject. "Can I help with anything, Lina?"

"Honey, you go get acquainted with everybody. There will be plenty to do later."

Aunt Joy led Jordan into the living room, where Nick's mother was seated with another elderly woman.

"Hello, sweetie." Bella rose and kissed Jordan on the cheek. "Jordan, this is my mother, Antonia Lucchese. Nick's other grandma."

Nick entered the room and stopped short. "Grandma. I

had no idea you were here."

"I just got here, Nico. Came out from the city to meet your bride. I thought you would bring her to meet me, but when you didn't…"

Jordan jumped in. "That's my fault, Mrs. Lucchese. My father is very ill. I've been with him every minute, and Nick has been so supportive."

"That's true, Grandma, and I'm sure you heard that Jordan is recovering from pneumonia. It's been a difficult few weeks."

Hesitantly nodding, his grandmother gently patted the sofa cushion next to her. "Come sit. Tell me about your people."

"My people?" Jordan didn't know what to say. *Her people?* She didn't have a large family, and she couldn't make one up. "Uh, okay. I was raised by my father. My mother was killed in a car accident when I was six. I have an aunt who lives in Chicago."

With a wave of the older woman's hand, she realized that wasn't cutting it. "Your people. Where are you from? You're tall, blonde, and blue-eyed. You, young lady, are not Italian."

Nick closed his eyes, pained.

Jordan was getting the sense the old lady wanted to know if she was worthy of Nick. Fine. She wanted her people, Jordan would talk about her people.

"My mother was English. She and her family immigrated to the United States right after World War II. My grandfather found work here as an engineer. My father's family has been in Compass Cove since the 1600s. In fact, the compass legend—I'm sure you've heard it—centers on one of my ancestors, Lucy Velsor."

Nick's grandmother was unimpressed. Jordan didn't know what else to say. She didn't talk about her family much because the connection to the town legend always made her feel pretentious. Obviously, that wasn't the case with Mrs. Lucchese.

"That's very nice, dear. So, your people are from the north."

"Yes, my father's family is Dutch. There are still some distant relatives in Holland."

"I see. Well, my grandson apparently loves you." Nick's grandmother then turned her face straight ahead, and tapped her cheek. Jordan was confused. She looked at Nick, who looked stricken, but mouthed the words *kiss her cheek.* Jordan nodded, and did what he told her to do.

Satisfied, his grandma turned, and appeared to smile. At that point, everyone in the room exhaled. "Now, let me see your ring."

Jordan held up her hand, happy to show Nick's family the heirloom ring on her finger. "It's lovely, isn't it? It's an antique. It's been in my family for over two centuries."

"Your family? You're wearing your own ring?" Aunt Joy was shocked.

"I'm having a wedding band made to match it," Nick

said. Jordan had to give Nick credit, he was fast on his feet. "This ring has tremendous sentimental value to Jordan's family. I'm glad she's wearing it."

Nick's mother smiled. "It also has quite a connection to the town, Mom. This is the ring that was given to the woman who owned the compass. You know, the one from the story Jordan mentioned."

"The one in that little shop in town? The story about the widow and the compass maker?" She looked back at Jordan. "*That* ring?"

Now she understood.

"Yes. The same one."

Grandma picked up her hand and examined the ring again. "Well, it must be good luck."

There was more exhaling. Jordan considered it another victory, especially since everyone in the room was now breathing again.

"So," Grandma began. "You say your father is ill, and I'm not getting any younger, so when are you two getting married?"

Damn. It was the question neither she nor Nick knew how to answer. Obviously, they hadn't set a date because the engagement wasn't the real deal. They might have been testing the waters with each other, but there was no telling how all this was going to go.

"We're working that out, Grandma. But there are a lot of considerations." Nick answered as vaguely as possible. And

Jordan was thankful, even if she was a little sad.

"You two better not wait too long," Aunt Joy said. "Neither of you are getting any younger either. When are you gonna start having babies?"

Considering she and Nick hadn't even slept together, it could be a while. Not that she didn't think about going to bed with him. No, Jordan thought about it all the damn time.

Startled, Nick took Jordan's hand, and started pulling her toward the hallway that headed upstairs, shocking the three women in the room.

"Where are you going?" His mother finally found her voice. "Nick?"

"You three want babies? We need to get started. Is that what you want?"

"Nicholas Rinaldi, have you lost your mind?" His mother was horrified. And it was awesome. It took everything Jordan had not to burst out laughing.

"Making six kids could take a while." Jordan shrugged her shoulders. "And my biological clock is ticking."

"Do twins run in your family?" Nick wondered. "It could save some time."

"I'll find out."

That did it for his aunt Joy. She burst out laughing. "You two are wonderful." She came over to each of them and gave them loud smacking kisses. "That's the way to tell us to butt out of your business. Well done."

Still holding her hand like it was the most natural thing in the world, Nick smirked, and Jordan felt little popping sensations in her ovaries. Those damn ovaries. Jordan was starting to think they actually knew what they were talking about. The thought of having babies with Nick, of being with him, seemed like the most natural thing in the world.

It wasn't that they didn't care about each other, they did. But Nick was keeping part of himself locked up tight. And after what had happened with Chase, Jordan needed him to open up before she went all in.

THEY WEREN'T LEAVING. Nick sat on the back porch, listening to the creaking of the old swing, sipping a mug of hot coffee and wondering when the hell his relatives were going to go home. What made him smile was that Jordan was in there playing Monopoly like she was betting the family fortune. The woman was competitive, and watching her handle his uncles was so much fun.

He heard her laughing, big and bold, and it was coming closer. When the door opened behind him, she was trash talking his uncle Mike.

"You keep whining, Mikey. Just remember, I won, even though you were stealing from the bank."

The door closed, muffling the noise from inside. "Having fun?"

"Oh, my God. So much. This is exactly what I needed."

"And to think I was worried about you with them."

Jordan sat next to him on the swing, settling her body right against his.

"You're so lucky. I mean, I get how they could be overwhelming, but there's so much love in there."

"I know." He did, and seeing it through her eyes was a good reminder. "We're up to our neck in the engagement story now, though."

Resting her head on his shoulder, she sighed. "I know. But, everything just felt right. It will all work out."

He thought about that. It did feel right. Watching her help with dinner, teasing his cousins, having her cuddled next to him, all of it felt right.

"Let me walk you home. It's getting late."

"I'm not going to sleep. I'm too wound up. I'm probably going to watch the movie I'd picked out for us."

He glanced down. "You want company?"

Looking up, Jordan bit her lip and nodded. "I'd love some. There's a couch and a blanket all ready for us."

Seeing her eyes sparkle in the porch light, his heart crept into his throat. It was good to see her happy. Everything inside her came alive. Which was why Nick wanted to spend time with her. It might not have been the best idea, since both their hearts were on the line, but what was life if you couldn't live a little bit dangerously?

Chapter Fifteen

O N MONDAY MORNING, Lina was sitting at a table in the café, watching the breakfast crowd thin out and going over her inventory for the next few days. Rinaldi's Café was the hub in Compass Cove. There were regulars who came in every day, some who came in once a week, and others who stopped in sporadically. But the food was good, the prices fair, and Lina was proud of the business she and Angelo had built over the years.

It hadn't been easy. There were times when she was trying to raise a family, that she was up making pastries at 3:30 in the morning, but in the end, it had all come together. Family and friends pitched in, kids got raised, and she grew to appreciate the special place she'd chosen to live.

Oh sure, no place was perfect. Compass Cove had its snobs, its mean girls and boys, its social challenges—but none of that outweighed all the good people who were part of this community.

Nursing a second cup of coffee, Janet plopped in the booth across from her. Her long-time friend, no doubt, had heard about the family dinner and wanted to know what everyone thought about Nick and Jordan. Whereas Lina wanted to know what Nick and Jordan were thinking about the family dinner.

The truth was, there was nothing for Lina to tell. And if she listened to her son and husband, she would know it was none of her business. She'd mumbled, "Family was family and it was always her business."

She and Nick had crossed paths briefly when she left this morning. He was on his way back from Jordan's cottage, looking rumpled, and Lina was heading out to work. He didn't say much, and for once, she didn't ask.

"So?" Janet leaned forward waiting for Lina to dish. "How did it go?"

"All right. Everyone loves her. They went back to her place after dinner to watch a movie. He didn't come home until morning." Lina stopped talking when a server brought Janet a mug of herbal tea and the honeypot. "He said he fell asleep on the couch."

"Gosh, I hope that's not true." Janet slumped back. "What do you think about this?"

Lina shrugged. "I don't know. I just want them to be happy. They both deserve it."

"Anything we can do to help?" Janet was determined.

"Angelo and Marco have told me to stay out of it. Which means you have to stay out of it, too."

"Pfft. And you're going to listen to them?"

Her friend knew her well. "I'm going to try, but I agree,

they have to get out of their own way."

"Can I join you two?" Her daughter-in-law appeared without warning.

Lina scooted over in the booth, making room for Bella. "What do we really know about this Jordan? Is she a gold digger? Is she just trying to get her hooks into a doctor? I mean, she completely charmed everyone, even my mother, but I don't know much."

"He couldn't do better," Lina said. "And she's no gold digger. Really, Bella."

"Jordan is a prize, Bella," Janet said. "You don't have to worry."

"No? I heard she dumped her fiancé the night before her wedding," she whispered. "Didn't give back the ring."

Lina couldn't believe how fast the old gossip had circled around to Bella. "Oh, for Pete's sake. She dumped him because she found out he was cheating on her. Caught him red-handed. As far as the ring? The man wouldn't take her calls. After a while, she sold it, donated the money, and that's when the Stanleys started to make noise."

"Don't believe everything you hear," Janet warned. "Especially when Helen Stanley is involved."

Lina nodded. "Chase's mother. New around here. Not a nice person."

"They're not new, Lina," Janet said flatly. "They've lived here for twenty years."

"Hmm." Lina wasn't impressed. "A drop in the bucket."

Bella's eyes went wide. Standing right next to them, was Nick.

"Morning, ladies. Look at the three of you sitting here."

"Nicky, what brings you in?" Bella grinned nervously when Nick bent down and kissed her cheek.

"I'm on my way to work. Thought I'd pick up a sandwich for later since I won't be home until eight."

"Oh! What would you like? I'll get it for you. Bella, move." Lina gave her daughter-in-law a little push with her hip.

"No need, Nona. I already put in my order at the counter. So," he said, motioning for Janet to scoot over so he could sit. "What are we talking about?"

"Oh, nothing," Janet said. "The weather. Every day the sun is out is a relief after the two storms we had."

"Riiight." He leaned in conspiratorially. "Look, you busybodies will stay out of my affairs, okay? Jordan and I are dealing with a lot right now. We don't need any help—or hindrance—" he looked at his mother "—from any of you."

"Busybodies! Hmpf." Lina feigned offense, but she could see her grandson wasn't the least bit moved.

"Oh, come on. I heard you talking when I walked in. The whole café could hear you."

Amare Jenkins, the new attorney in town, turned around and nodded. "I heard the whole thing. These ladies have some strong opinions, Doc. You'd better watch out."

"You, hush, Amare. Eat your breakfast." Customer or

not, Lina treated everyone the same.

"Thanks," Nick growled.

"Nick," Bella said. "I just worry. You've been through so much, I want you to make a good choice. She's a bit of a mystery, that's all. I just want to know why you chose her."

"What kind of question is that?" he snapped.

A good one, if Lina thought about it. There were a lot of questions that needed answering, but Nick wasn't about to give anything away just yet.

Lina had to admire that. Her grandson knew what he wanted. And a group of old women weren't going to tell him what to do.

"I'll see you later." And that was it. Nick didn't let them respond or defend themselves.

"Well," Janet said with a grin. "He told us."

Lina agreed. "Yes, he did."

"He's a good man. He was always one of my favorite students."

Lina laughed at her old friend. "Janet, they were all your favorites."

Bella shook her head. "He's not thinking clearly. To talk to us like that? Something isn't right about this."

"He's fine," Lina assured her. "Nick is a man with a mission. We'd best stay out of his way."

NICK MADE THE right out of the café and walked two blocks down Main Street to Cove Pediatrics. Founded fifty years ago, the practice had changed hands a number of times, and now it was owned by two sisters. *Twins.* Thank God, they weren't identical.

No, Michelle and Christine Galetsky couldn't have been more different. Both were top doctors, both were wonderful with the kids and parents, but while Michelle was a peppy, pretty, pulled-together brunette, Christine was a fireball, with a sleeve tattoo, deep red hair, and a big personality. They drove each other a little crazy, but there was no doubt they adored each other. Add Jimmy, the nurse practitioner, and Betsy, the receptionist, into the mix and it was a fun place to work.

It was a fresh start for Nick, who had easily settled into the office routine. There was no adrenaline shot while checking swollen glands, or doing well-baby checks, but his patients and their parents provided him with a purpose and allowed him to be part of the community.

The practice was in an old Victorian house just off Main Street. It had a front porch where patients would sometimes wait when the weather was good, and a yard that faced out toward the town. The offices took up the entire first floor and Michelle lived in the apartment that claimed the upper two floors of the house.

Christine, who was engaged to a graphic designer, lived in Brooklyn, and made the trek east every day.

Still, it worked. Michelle was there for patients first thing in the morning, Chris came in a little later to avoid traffic and stayed later. Nick, since he also lived locally, could take whatever hours they needed him.

It was the perfect arrangement.

The waiting area was bright and welcoming, with the walls painted a sunny yellow. Red and blue accents peppered the room and a box of books and games sat in the corner. Nick set a cup of coffee on Betsy's desk and she smiled.

"You are a charmer, Dr. Rinaldi. You know a way to a girl's heart is through a large dark roast with just a little half and half."

He chuckled. "Right, I use that on all the ladies."

"Must have worked at least once." She winked and smiled.

"So, anything I need to know about?"

Betsy pointed to the corner of the waiting room closest to the door. There sat a dark-haired little boy with a girl who could have been an older sister. If his memory served, the kid was in Jordan's class. Nick remembered him. He'd asked a lot of questions.

"He only wants to talk to you. Asked for Dr. Nick, specifically."

"No parents?"

"Nope. Believe me, I tried. Michelle tried…"

"Hmm. Got it."

Setting his sandwich and drink on the shelf behind

Betsy's desk, he approached the two kids.

"It's going to be okay," the boy tried to soothe the girl with him. "He's nice. He'll help us."

"We should be home."

"Lacy, no…"

"He's going to be mad."

"Hey, guys. Mind if I sit down?" Nick didn't wait for an answer and scooted into a chair next to the girl, whose name, he now knew, was Lacy. She was nervous as a cat, her blue eyes darting around wildly, and not happy about him sitting next to her.

His Spidey senses told him to give her a little distance, so he moved over one chair. "So, I heard your name is Lacy, and I know you're in Ms. Velsor's class because I met you a couple of weeks ago. Eric, right?"

Nick stuck out his hand. The boy shook it like he meant it. He and the girl had the same bright blue eyes, but there was a spray of freckles across the boy's nose that made him look like a kid who knew how things went in this world. "Yes, sir."

"Eric, nice to see you again. What brings you in?"

The girl's eyes were open wide, and she was trying to signal her brother to stop talking.

"Lacy, I'm sitting right here, and I'm going to let your brother talk, so you need to relax. Okay?"

He wasn't going to be mean, but she needed to understand he wasn't clueless. "What's going on?"

Eric looked around, he was nervous. "My father hits my mother."

Boom. That was not what he expected. He knew there was something up with this kid when he met him a few weeks ago, but the bombshell was a shocker.

"Okay. Have you told anyone? Maybe your teacher?"

"I was going to, especially after last night, but Dad didn't get us out for school this morning. He said we didn't have to go."

"Where's your mother?" Nick wanted to get the woman help if she needed it.

"She's at work," Lacy finally spoke. Her voice was a shaky, but at least she found it. Drawing a watery breath, she went on. "She's hurt."

"I'm glad you're here. That was a smart thing to do."

Nick was making a mental checklist in his head. Mom was being abused, kids had a neglect situation. "Was your father home when you left?"

"No, he went out. We walked here," Lacy replied.

And he was going to be plenty pissed off when he found they'd gone missing. "Does he hit either of you?"

Please say no. They both shook their heads. *Thank God.*

"He yells a lot. *A lot.*" Eric was looking down now. Nick took the opportunity to signal Betsy to call the police. "I wish he'd hit me instead of my mom. He's a bully."

Nick had a few names for their father, and *bully* wasn't one of them. Personally, he'd like to hang him up and beat him like the heavy bag.

"It's going to be okay. I'm going to take you into a treatment room while we figure out what to do to help your mother. I'm going to ask Dr. Michelle to examine you, Lacy. And I'll have a look at you, Eric. We should make sure you're both okay."

Betsy returned to her desk and gave Nick an almost imperceptible nod.

"Do we have to?" Lacy's voice trembled with fear. Young as she was, the girl realized they'd gotten their father in trouble and it could come back to haunt them. No child should have to be afraid, ever.

"Yes, I think it's a good idea."

Michelle joined him in the waiting room. "Hi guys, I'm Doctor Michelle." She reached out to Lacy and waited for the girl to take her hand. When she did, Michelle smiled, but Nick could see the worry in her eyes.

"It's going to be okay," Michelle said. "You're safe here."

Abuse cases were the absolute worst, and Nick had to tamp down his own anger. The kids may not have been physically hurt, but emotionally, this would haunt them for the rest of their lives.

Like his sister, Eric was starting to show strain. Making this call had been a tall order for a little guy. "You called the police to come, didn't you?"

Nick nodded. "Yes. When you tell me, I have to report it to the police, and to the people who make sure kids are safe."

"Oh. Oh, I didn't know that." Eric's voice cracked, and Nick saw the bright little boy visibly start to shake.

Fear. He saw fear, just like he saw when the gunman shot up the clinic in Afghanistan. Nick's heart thudded in his chest as he thought through his response. He would not let these kids down. He couldn't.

Both kids were silent for a few seconds, processing what they'd done. They'd started something that was now out of their control. Finally, Lacy looked up. She nodded and stuck her hand out to her brother. "Okay. Come on, Eric. Let's get this over with. Mom always says to finish what we start."

The little boy stood and tentatively took his sister's outstretched hand.

Without another word, they went back into the treatment area. Nick anticipated a long day.

Michelle stopped at the desk and gave Betsy instructions. "Cancel all our patients this afternoon or reschedule them for tonight. I'll stay late. This is going to take a while."

AT TEN PAST nine, Nick pulled his car into the long driveway that sat between his grandparents' house and Jordan's cottage. Lights were on in the kitchen of the big house and he thought he saw his father move past the window.

Nick was so tired, he wasn't sure of anything anymore.

The living room light was on in Jordan's cottage, and he

imagined her reading, or watching TV. Looking at the clock again, he tried to convince himself it was too late to drop in. But he wanted to see how her father was doing. Yeah, that was a lie. He just wanted to see her. He hoped being close to her would help his mind settle. Those kids and their mother had been through hell.

He wanted to tell her what had happened. To unload the story and clear the pictures from his head. But he couldn't.

As the story unfolded through the afternoon, it became clear that given the chance, Eric and Lacy's father would have beaten their mother to death. It was just a matter of time.

Making a quick decision, he grabbed his jacket and instead of going to his grandparents, he went to Jordan's house, hoping that she wouldn't think he was a colossal pain in the ass.

Gertie must have been asleep because she didn't bark until he'd knocked on the door, but as soon as he did, she was at the window howling in greeting.

Jordan looked out as well, and immediately he heard her throw the dead bolt. When the door opened she looked worried. "Hi. Is everything okay?"

"Not really. Can I come in? I had a shit day."

She stepped back, and the way the light from the living room was backlighting her, she looked otherworldly. Her blonde hair was pulled to one side and braided. She was wearing the same pajamas he'd found her in when the tree had fallen on her car. Blue knit pajama pants and a long-sleeve T-shirt that outlined every curve. Her face was scrubbed clean, her skin pink and creamy, her eyes warm and welcoming.

The day had left him drained and exhausted, and as she led him through the house to the sofa, he felt the weight of what had happened to the kids bear down. He barely knew where to start, so he figured he'd ask her how she was doing first.

"How was your father today?"

"He had a good day today. He ate a little and didn't get sick. The pain is being managed."

"That's good. I'm glad. With all the different drugs on the market, there's no reason for him to be in pain."

"I know. For now, he's okay. He also asked me when he was going to get measured for his tux?"

Nick burst out laughing. "Did he? Holy crap."

"I know I did the same thing. Yesterday he was completely out of it. If I don't laugh, I'll cry."

Quiet settled around them, and it was begging for one of them to say something.

"You want to tell me what brought you here tonight?"

He nodded. "I do want to tell you, but I can't. More than anything. Privacy laws…" The corner of her mouth dropped, and he felt wrong keeping the information from her, especially since she was going to find out tomorrow. But the law was clear.

"Okay." Hooking her arm through his and leaning her head on his shoulder, Jordan's warmth seeped into him. It quieted him, and made him feel like everything would work out. One way or another, it would work out.

"Anything else you want to talk about?" she asked. "Crazy relatives, maybe?"

"You don't want to know. But you passed muster with my grandma Toni. That's not easy."

"Your mother, though... I have a feeling she's not convinced I'm a good bet." When he didn't answer, Jordan picked up her head and looked at him. "Distraction isn't working, is it?"

"I wish, but thanks for trying. And don't worry about my mother."

It was going to take him a while to unpack things, but just the images in his head of the kids' mother—her hand was bandaged, there was a bruise on her jaw she'd tried to hide with make-up, and a set of screaming bruises that were on her left side from her armpit to her waist. The woman had been pummeled. It turned out she had three cracked ribs, and any one of them could have punctured a lung.

"I'm trying to wrap my head around the way people treat each other. I don't understand. I just don't understand how someone could hurt a person he claimed to love." He was enraged, so angry he wanted to put a hole in something. "I don't understand."

Pressing the heels of his hands against his eyes, he knew he'd just said too much. He should have gone home and beat on the heavy bag, but Jordan was the only person he wanted to see.

What happened next was unexpected. Moving slowly, Jordan straddled his lap, setting her knees on each side of him, and took his face in her hands. With slow, steady movements, she applied gentle pressure and massaged his temples, allowing him to relax. Then she moved to his scalp, and then his neck.

The movement of her hands was steady, rhythmic. The gentle pressure lulled his senses, quieted his mind. For the first time since he arrived at work, his brain rested.

Nick's head slumped back, supported by the very soft sofa cushion, when he felt Jordan's lips touch his Adam's apple. Fire shot to his groin, and when she did it again, and again, Nick realized something between them was about to change. Not content to stay in one place, she nibbled on his neck, his ears... then she was unbuttoning his shirt and leaving soft, seductive kisses each time more skin was uncovered.

"Let me help you feel better. Let me make it all go away."

"Jordan..."

"Come to bed with me. I'll help you forget. I'll make it better, at least for a little while. Whatever it is, I want to help."

"I don't know what I did to deserve you," he whispered.

"Everything."

Chapter Sixteen

J ORDAN STOOD AND pulled Nick from the couch with both hands. He'd never seemed bigger or stronger than he did at that moment, but all she wanted was to take care of him, to love him, to tend to his needs.

Her desire, raw and scorching, had been balled in her belly for days, but this was something else. He was in pain, and Jordan wanted to ease his mind, help him forget whatever was weighing on him. This man was more important than she ever thought he'd be, and at that moment, his needs were all that mattered.

She led him to her room and turned down the bed. Seeming to be unsure of what to do, Jordan took his hands when he started to unbutton his shirt. "Let me."

He stilled and watched as she finished releasing the buttons. He was breathing hard already, a flush crept over his skin. When she pushed the shirt off his shoulders, she kissed the strip of hair at the center of his chest, and drew in his scent. Even after a long day, the essence that was so clearly him, like rain and the woods, pulled her in and made her crazy.

Moving to his belt, she unbuckled it and undid his pants. Lowering the zipper slowly, she finally slipped her hand inside and felt his erection. He was smooth and silky, a hard mass of flesh that was all hers. Easing his pants to the floor, Jordan got a good look at the man who was going to be in her bed. He was perfect, and she was sure she was in love with him.

Her hands ran up and down his sides and as she looked at him, she knew exactly what to do.

But first, Jordan stripped off her shirt and pajama bottoms, leaving her naked except for a tiny pair of pink panties. Reaching down with her hands, she stroked him and he arched back, hissing out a breath. She did it again, caressing him and making her way up the smooth shaft. He was big, not so much long but thick, and Jordan could already imagine how he would fill her.

She wasn't a virgin, far from it. And Jordan loved sex when it was with the right person. Nothing had ever felt so right as this moment with Nick. Dropping to her knees, she was eye level with his navel. But from here, she could also see the scar on his hip that was much bigger than she imagined. Moving her lips over it, she kissed it. And again, trailing kisses over his pelvic bones until there was only one thing left to do. She left a gentle kiss on the head of his erection, and Nick, who'd had his eyes closed, groaned.

"I want to be inside you," he said. "But I don't have a condom."

Jordan rose and kissed his lips. "That's okay. I do. Bottom drawer of my night table."

His eyebrows shot up. "I didn't see them when I was evacuating you during the storm."

"You wouldn't have, because I just bought them."

Pushing him on the bed, Nick fell back and settled himself against the pillows as Jordan climbed on top. He was letting her take the lead, and she loved it. Kissing his collarbone, she left another path of kisses down his body. Feeling his skin against hers was intoxicating. Her pulse leapt, her brain clouded. Everything about him made her body hum.

She was just one massive ache. From her breasts to her belly, she could feel everything inside her screaming. The desire pooled, then consumed her. Rising from the bed, she slid off her panties and took a condom from the drawer. As she was bent over, Nick's hand gently caressed her bottom.

Turning around, he was staring at her. "God, you're beautiful. The first time I saw you, I thought you were the most beautiful woman in the world, and now, now that you're mine..."

Mine. A single word with so much meaning. Jordan had fought giving herself to him, but now she craved it. She wanted him to own her, body and soul.

"Am I yours, Nick?"

Pulling her onto the bed, in a move as smooth as water, he turned her onto her back.

"Right now, you are most definitely mine," he growled.

Jordan almost came right then and there.

He shackled both wrists with one of his hands. "It's my turn."

His grin was wolfish, and she had no idea what to expect. They were discovering each other, and nothing was more exciting. He pulled a nipple into his mouth, tugging and nibbling. The sensations shot through her, lighting up every nerve ending. It was torture. It was bliss.

It was everything she'd been missing in her relationships. Sex and desire were one thing, but this chemistry—the compatibility—made her burn. It was beyond attraction. Jordan was consumed.

Releasing her hands, Nick moved down her body, giving attention to her breasts, then exploring the rest of her body with hot kisses. Just a little past her belly button, he looked up before pressing his lips to the soft mound.

"Open your legs for me, baby."

Planting her feet, anticipating what was to come next, she let her knees drop open.

"So beautiful." Nick ran a finger over her folds. "And so wet."

Rubbing his scruff along the inside of her thigh, Jordan's muscles quivered, betraying her nerves and her desire.

"Do your best to stay still, sweetheart. Hold onto the headboard and don't let go. I promise this isn't going to hurt a bit."

Wrapping her fingers around the rails of her wrought

iron headboard, Jordan readied herself for whatever he had in mind. His eyes flashed with mischief, and it was then that Jordan knew she'd done exactly the right thing. They'd been dancing around each other since the storms had thrown them together.

They needed each other. Emotions, deep and powerful drove the waves crashing between them. Every time they were together, the attraction bubbled under the surface. It overwhelmed her.

"I'm going to make you come, Jordan," he whispered. "I've been dying to watch you lose control. Are you ready?"

All she could do was nod. This man was a god, and Jordan fully expected to have her mind blown. But ready? She doubted it.

Running a finger over her, and then two, Nick sunk them inside her. The sudden invasion made her hips twitch. Inside of her, Nick's fingers teased, while his thumb circled and tormented her sex.

"Mmm. So good."

It was, too; then he added a third finger and Jordan loved the fullness she felt.

Gliding his fingers in and out, Jordan felt herself starting to unravel. He was not gentle, but she didn't mind—everything he was doing felt amazing, felt so good. She heard herself moan as her insides contracted, tightening around him before exploding. He kept moving his hand, his fingers caressing the walls of her vagina, staying until her orgasm calmed. Only then did Nick pull out, and his mouth covered her.

She could feel his tongue and his lips sucking and pulling. He was unrelenting, and she was slowly losing her mind. Her hips bucked, and he stopped her, holding her steady with his hands. He possessed her in every way there was. Feeling the build, feeling the pressure valve ready to blow again, Jordan arched and cried out his name. He didn't stop as she came, still sucking while her body convulsed. The man was relentless, as Jordan went over the edge again.

As she lay in a puddle on her bed, Nick rolled on the condom. "How are you feeling?"

"Like I've gone to heaven."

"God, Jordan, watching you come is like music. You're so responsive." Turning onto his back, he gave her a tug. "Come here. I want to see you."

Jordan kept her eyes on his as she settled her legs on each side of him.

Nick sat with his back straight against the pillows, and Jordan pressed against him. Running his hands down her sides, he took her hips and gently lowered her onto his erection.

Jordan drew a deep breath as she felt him at her entrance.

"Nice and slow," he said.

The expression on his face was taut, strained. She knew he wanted to bury himself, and Jordan could understand it, but the slow entry, feeling him slide inside her a little at a time, was perfection. Inch by inch, he filled her, taking his time to inflict the slow sensuous torture on both of them.

Finally, when she was fully seated, Nick bent down and pulled one of her nipples into his mouth, then the other. He sucked her, causing her body to move, to take him even deeper.

"You have all the control now," he ground out. "It's all about you."

Thrusting her hips, Jordan moved slowly, feeling him slide in and out. At the same time, Nick held her hips, giving her some leverage to truly torment them both.

Rising and falling, faster and faster, Jordan moved and Nick started pumping.

It was wild and intense, sex as it was in the early days. Mating. Claiming. She was his, and Jordan knew for all time, they would be bonded together.

Nick was her match in every way, and she'd been fighting it. But at that moment, they found bliss together, and the rest of the world could fade away.

Finally having enough, he banded his arms around her and flipped her onto her back. Jordan held on, digging her nails into his muscular shoulders. But it was then, when she felt him sinking with her into the soft mattress, that his hand came up and stroked her face.

She only heard him say one thing. "So beautiful."

She was lost.

His movements slowed; the heat inside her went from a

burn to a gentle warmth. The way his hips pressed against hers was so tender, so loving, Jordan felt her heart swell and her eyes fill with tears. He moved with purpose, kissing her sweetly, whispering in her ear.

Jordan felt the wave crest again, slow and steady, as Nick pushed himself, burying himself inside her, desperate and frantic for satisfaction. His shoulders and back bunched when his body finally released, and her name slipped from his lips. Jordan lost herself one last time, orgasming as his body ebbed. Then, finally exhausted, finally at peace, her hero slept.

IT WAS DARK in the house. But enough light came through the windows for Nick to watch Jordan, who was tucked in next to him, sound asleep. After they'd made love, they'd both passed right out, but she woke up long enough to pull on a T-shirt, give him a kiss, and fall right back to sleep.

She'd wanted to make him forget whatever had been on his mind, and she'd done that, at least for a little while. Nick was still thinking about Eric and Lacy's mother and the beatings she'd been taking from her husband. But being with Jordan also reminded him that there were people who cared for each other, and Jordan did that without a thought.

Not that sex was a measure of how good things were in a relationship, but if Nick had to judge, he and Jordan could be happy together. When he said he didn't know what he'd done to deserve her, he meant it.

He hadn't let people in. He'd seen too much, lost too much of himself on his last deployment, to risk hurting anyone. He always thought there was too much baggage to hope he'd have a normal life. But he knew he could work, he could help people, and that would be enough.

But she'd changed him. He wanted this woman in his life, and Nick had to figure out a way to break down the wall he'd built around himself.

With a barely audible coo escaping her throat, Jordan turned toward him and opened her eyes. She gazed up and smiled sweetly. "What time is it?"

Kissing her softly, he ran his hand down her side. "It's a little after midnight. Should I go?"

Snuggling against him, she shook her head and let her hands wander over his body. "Please stay." Tilting her face up, she kissed him. "Make love to me?"

Her request, so pure, so perfect, shook him to his very core. This woman gave all of herself. Whether it be her students, her father, her friends, or him, Jordan's heart knew no limits on what she offered others. In return, he wanted to give her everything she asked for, and more.

Gently easing her onto her back, Nick raised himself above her and examined her beautiful face. Content, happy, and so very seductive, her eyes gave him every reason to believe she loved him as much as he loved her. If she did, he'd consider himself one lucky bastard.

Grabbing the hem of her T-shirt, he pulled it over her head and tossed it on the floor. Their bodies touched, skin to skin, rough to soft, a contrast on every level.

Heart hammering in his chest, Nick ran his hand down her long, lean body. Every curve warmed at his touch as she arched to get closer, pressing against him and looping her arms around his neck. Dropping his head, his lips and teeth grazed her collarbone, giving him a taste of her sweetness.

"Tell me what you want," he murmured in her ear. "Anything."

Pulling his face down, Jordan kissed his lips. "Take me. Love me."

The request, so simple, so honest, moved him. His body hummed as she wrapped around him and caressed his body, kissing the scars near his ribs, lingering there.

"Does it hurt?" she asked.

"Sometimes."

"I wish I could take the pain away."

How did he tell her that in so many ways, she already had? The emptiness. The regret. The feeling that he'd never find his way back to medicine... she'd given him so much.

Without any more delay, he sunk into her. Unlike the last time, there was no urgency; they wanted this to linger. They knew each other now, their bodies melting together, awareness replacing nervousness.

The movements were slow, no rush to finish, but a desire

to keep it going. He filled her completely and her arms and legs wrapped around him, holding his body against hers as they moved.

"This is perfect. God, Nick... so perfect."

Pumping his hips a little harder, he moved in and out, the pace quickening only a little. Her wet heat teased him, consumed him, urged him further. Nick slowed, wanting to make it last, kissing her, his tongue invading her mouth. Jordan's thrusts matched his, thrust for thrust, until he felt a little tremor rush through her body.

She was getting close, he could feel the quaking of her muscles, and he wasn't far behind, but Nick wanted Jordan to come first, for her to shiver and convulse around him.

He didn't have to wait long. He could feel the build, the teasing heat coming off her. She pumped harder, pulled him deeper, and then as her back arched, Nick came, riding her wave, and watching her face settle into contented bliss.

Earlier, they'd taken each other with passion and heat, learning and discovering each other as they went.

This was a joining of hearts and bodies. It was so much more than he ever expected.

Dropping his head so he could kiss her soundly, Nick didn't know what he was going to do about her. Maybe coming here tonight was a mistake. Maybe they didn't have any business taking their relationship to the next step. But when he was with Jordan—talking with her, kissing her, or making love to her—Nick felt like he'd come home.

Chapter Seventeen

JORDAN KNEW SEX could cloud a person's thinking, but as she watched Nick get dressed at five o'clock in the morning, she thought it had to be the hottest thing she'd ever seen.

His back was to her, so she got to see all that wondrous muscle move from an entirely different angle. First, he pulled on his boxer briefs, and all that did was accentuate his fantastic ass. Then came the khakis. How did he make khakis look good? And when he slipped his arms through the sleeves of his checked button down, she thought she might cry a little at the way the shirt hid his body.

But Nick obliged her with one of his killer grins when he turned around and did up his buttons. "I'm sorry I woke you, but I want to try to get back in the house under the radar."

Jordan smiled and shook her head. "Silly man. They're up already."

Sitting on the edge of the bed, he leaned in for a kiss. "Did you call me silly?"

With her lips pressed to his, she nodded. "I did.

Whatcha gonna do about it?"

Pulling away, he took her hand. "You are so tempting. But I do have to go."

"I know. You can't tell me what was bothering you last night?"

With a furrowed brown, he blew out. "I would guess you're going to find out today. But I can't tell you."

"Okay," she said. "Can you tell me why you broke into a cold sweat and called out when you were asleep?"

When his face dropped, Jordan worried she might have crossed the line.

"How am I supposed to answer that?"

"Truthfully would be good. How long have you had nightmares?"

As he rose from the bed, Jordan got to watch Nick fully shut down. There was no discussing what she saw at two in the morning. She was supposed to forget how he called out, tossed and turned and then startled himself awake before drifting back to sleep.

"I don't talk about it," he muttered.

"Well, maybe you need to." Nick wasn't the only one who could get angry. Jordan hated to be shut out, especially when all she wanted to do was help. But if she was learning anything about Nick, he didn't take help. From anyone.

And it was going to kill the possibility of anything between them becoming more.

Nudging past him, she grabbed a pair of leggings and a

long-sleeved tee out of her drawer.

"What are you doing?" he asked.

"I'm going for a run."

Grabbing her clothes from her, he stared. "No, you're not. It's dark."

"You did *not* just tell me what to do, did you?"

A cold understanding appeared to wash through him, but that did nothing to change how she was feeling. Those few words, and Jordan was angry.

"I'm sorry. It's still too cold."

"It's been a month. I feel fine." Taking her clothes back, and refusing to respond, she walked to the bathroom and closed the door. "Jerk," she muttered. "Who does he think he is?"

"I'm your doctor," he called through the door.

"No, you're not." God, he was infuriating. Her doctor... Pfft. "I don't recall my doctor ever sleeping with me."

"Damn right about that," he said.

"Would you stop?" she yelled back. Not paying attention while she pulled on her sports bra, the elastic slipped and snapped Jordan on the chin. "Ouch! Dammit."

"You okay in there?"

"Yes," she lied, rubbing the red mark the bitch bra left on her face. Being extra careful, she wrestled the girls into place and settled the heavy elastic around her ribs.

The man was so aggravating. She'd been going out for early morning runs since she was in high school. There were times she couldn't sleep and getting up before the whole town gave her time to think.

Nick didn't seem to get that. Just like when she bolted from the bridal shop, sometimes Jordan needed the time inside her own head to sort out a problem. The rhythm of her stride allowed her to block out the confusion and the static that clouded her thinking. It was just her and her stride.

Brushing her teeth, Jordan didn't know what she was supposed to do. She was trying to be angry, but truthfully, she was hurt. Fake engagement aside, they cared about each other, but he had a wall up, and she couldn't get around it.

Taking a breath as she looked at her own reflection, Jordan liked that she saw a strong woman staring back. Six months ago, that wasn't the case.

When she opened the bathroom door, she jumped. Nick was right there, his shoulder braced against the wall. "You should not be going out. It's cold this morning. It could irritate your lungs."

"I need the exercise."

Without warning, Nick grabbed her hand and pulled her close. "Jordan, come on. Do you want to get sick again?"

Annoyed. She was so annoyed. And Jordan didn't know if she was more pissed at herself for allowing him to get inside her head, or him for turning this into a battle of wills. Jordan could forgo the run. She was trying to get away from him.

Because if she didn't, she was going to lose it. Why was he shutting her out?

Was it too much to want someone who was open, and honest? No, Nick didn't lie. But he didn't let her see what was inside his head. If he couldn't do that, how could she trust what was in his heart?

"Could you let me go?" she asked, her voice cracking.

"Is that what you want?"

Staring him down, Jordan knew she had no choice but to be careful around him. She loved being with him. He made her happy in so many ways. However, there was no way she wanted to give up that kind of emotional control ever again, especially if it was one-sided. Trusting people was hard for her, and as much as she wanted to, she was starting to believe the risk wasn't worth it.

"Yes. Let me go."

That wasn't the answer he wanted, and he waited a few seconds before scowling and then stepping back. "I still don't think you should go out."

"You're bossy."

Nick raised an eyebrow. "A few weeks ago, you were curled in that bed, really sick. I'm not saying you'll relapse, but you have to respect your recovery time."

Jordan looked away. She hated that he was right. There was no way she wanted to drag out her recovery. With everything going on with her father, she couldn't afford to. So, she nodded before looking back at him. His expression was softer now, sweet. "Take a walk later. Build up slowly."

"Okay." Agreeing was the easy thing to do.

Nick's thumb grazed over her cheek. "I'm just watching out for you."

"I know you are." That was the truth, but Jordan wished he'd let her take care of him too, at least a little bit. Last night she thought they'd made progress. Everything between them was close. Intimate.

They'd fallen asleep spooned together, so when the nightmare hit, Jordan knew immediately. His body lurched twice, jerking her against him suddenly, then he rolled onto his back. A sheen of sweat was visible across his skin, and his breathing was short and rapid, making his chest rise and fall at a frantic pace.

He was reliving a crisis situation; the shooting, she guessed. That was the only thing that made sense, but Jordan didn't know what to do. When she dropped her hand on his arm, he jerked it away. She wanted to hold him, soothe his panic, but she had no idea if anything would work. When he called out, the anguish broke her heart. He was a man in pain.

"Noooooo." It was agonizing, pleading. "They're just kids. NO. NO."

Kids. Children. He was begging for the children. He'd seen horrible things, sacrificed so much… if only he could trust her with his pain the way she'd trusted him with hers.

The memory chilled her to the bone. Eventually his

breathing settled, but Jordan couldn't sleep, not until she was sure he was okay. When he turned on his side, she pressed herself into his back and held on, hating that Nick had demons he was fighting all alone.

There was something brewing, something growing at too fast a pace. Never in her life had she met a man like Nick. Honorable, strong, smart, and good to the core. Just minutes ago, she was telling herself to stay away from him, but she couldn't. Her heart ached for him.

She didn't tell him. Instead, Jordan reached out and took his hand, pulling him into her. Nick needed her. He'd come to her when something had troubled him, sought out her comfort. That had to mean something. And as much as Jordan was scared, something told her not to let go. For now, she owed him the chance. For now.

"YOU WANT TO tell me what's wrong?"

Jordan had turned her back to him, and he saw her shoulders tense before she faced him. "I don't like to lose control. I hate it, and my whole life seems to be out of my control right now. Being so sick last month. My dad." She paused. "*You.* I'm not used to everything being so intense."

He got that, because he was feeling it himself. He was about to say something, but he let her keep going.

"I guess I realized this is more than a fake engagement, or

friends with benefits. I'm not naïve. This could be something and it's happening so fast…" Jordan plopped on her bed and folded her legs up in front of her. "I'm scared."

He sat next to her and resisted the urge to pull her into his arms.

"Of me?"

"Yes. Of everything I don't know about you."

He didn't expect that to come out of her mouth. Nick had to face the fact that going all in with Jordan would be a lot more complex than he ever thought. "I just…"

"I know, you don't talk about it. But I just went through something with you, Nick, and I'm worried for you. I hurt for you. But you won't let me help."

The nightmare.

She reached out and touched his cheek. Her eyes were overly bright, brimming with unshed tears. "Why did you come to me last night?"

"I just needed to be with you. I didn't think we'd end up in bed. I wasn't expecting it."

"Oh, I know that, but a booty call would make things less complicated, wouldn't it? Think about what you said. You wanted to be with me. Why did you want to be here? With me?"

Everything Jordan said was true. Last night was no booty call. He was looking for more. Sex could be written off as sex. What happened between the two of them was intensely personal. It meant something. "Because being with you settles me. It quiets my mind."

Admitting that was a kick in the ass.

Nick wasn't one to jump into something without thinking about it first. Whether it was a job, a situation at work, or a relationship. But with Jordan, he didn't just jump into the pool. His relationship with her felt like going over Niagara Falls in a barrel. Based on what she just said, he figured they were both in the same barrel. "How do you want to handle this?" he asked. "I hear everything you're saying, and I get it, but I don't want to stop seeing you."

"That's what's scaring me. No matter how much trepidation I feel, the thought of not seeing you is worse. What kind of magic is in your kisses, Nick Rinaldi? I feel like... I feel like there's something else at work between us."

Smiling, Nick clasped her hand and threaded his fingers with hers. "Maybe it's the compass magic," he said. "It could run in the family."

"I never bought into the compass woo-woo like everyone else," she said. "But I do believe in chemistry and attraction. We have both."

"You may not believe in the woo-woo, but I do believe in fate. Things happen for a reason, Jordan. What's going on with us may have started out as a lie, but it isn't now. Maybe we have to let this play out."

"Maybe." Jordan's thumb was making slow circles over the back of his hand. "But along with everything else, we need honesty. I won't budge on that."

Nick stilled at her words. "I've never lied to you, Jordan."

"No," she said softly. "But you haven't told me the whole truth, either."

Chapter Eighteen

WHEN NICK WALKED in the kitchen door at a little past 5:30 in the morning, the only one there was his grandfather. Pops was the earliest riser in the house, and he was always at least two cups of coffee into his day before anybody got up. He didn't say anything when Nick walked in. Instead, he rose from his spot at the kitchen table and poured Nick a cup of good strong coffee.

When he set the mug down on the table in the seat adjacent to his, Nick knew he had some explaining to do. Thirty-six years old, and he still had to answer to his grandfather. He really needed to move out.

"Long night?" Pops asked.

"You already know the answer, and I'm too old to have to tell you every move I make." Nick loved his family more than he could ever explain to anybody. But at times he wished he was still thousands of miles away. This thing with Jordan? It had the potential to change his entire life, and he didn't want his family doing anything to screw it up, no matter how well-meaning they were.

Pushing a basket of bread and a plate of cheese toward

Nick, Pops nodded. "Your nona baked your favorite bread, and we just had the cheese delivered from the city. Eat. Then we'll talk."

His grandfather waited while Nick took a plate, broke off a piece of the best crusty Italian bread in the Western Hemisphere, and took a chunk of creamy cheese. Saying no to food in his grandparents' house was just not done. Food meant love; if you rejected the food, you rejected their love.

With a piece of cheese sitting on top of the bread, Nick took a bite, and his grandfather started talking. It never failed.

"Let me tell you what I think, Nico. You and Jordan, you make each other nervous. Neither of you want the romance, but romance is what you got."

None of this was new to Nick. He was fully aware that he and Jordan walked on eggshells around each other. And it was stupid, really. They got along great, they had great chemistry, and he couldn't stop thinking about her. Every waking moment she was in the back of his mind. Her laughter, her smile, her flashing eyes—all of it. What Nick didn't know was how they were going to get out of their own way.

"Pops, I don't want to talk about this. I care about Jordan. A lot, if you want to know, but whatever's happening, has to stay between us. Promise me you'll stay out of it."

Angelo Rinaldi was a formidable man. He was decisive, intelligent, and blunt. He wasn't afraid of much. In fact,

Nick could only think of one thing that truly scared his grandfather.

His grandmother.

Pops shrugged. "Stay out of it. What does that mean, exactly? You're family, and families help each other, which means we know each other's business. It's not like where you slept last night is a big secret. Your car is right next to the girl's house."

Scrubbing his face with his hands, Nick looked up at the ceiling, wondering why he couldn't have a normal relationship. Then he thought about it. And he thought about that house he was going go to look at. And he realized it probably wasn't far enough away.

"What happens between me and Jordan is our business, not yours."

That seemed to do it. His grandfather stood and stretched, and then he shrugged. "Have it your way. You know where I am if you need to talk." Suddenly looking over his shoulder, after he turned to leave, Pops grinned. "Do you think you're gonna get very far with *mind your own business* to your nona?"

Nick locked his fingers behind his head and stretched. No, he wouldn't get very far with that at all. If he was lucky, his grandmother would give him a whack upside the head, and let it go. But he ran the risk of something far more serious than his grandmother, or his mother, or any other family member for that matter, being angry. He had to worry about hurting them. His family had been there for him when he was at his lowest point. He was the one who'd pushed them away.

"Pops…"

"Oh, don't worry. Nona won't say anything to Jordan, she's going to save it all for you. Your mother too."

Not that he was looking forward to it, but Nick was relieved the attention would be squarely on him.

"Nico, I have a question… this wedding thing. How long are you two going to keep it up?"

"What are you talking about?"

Pops chuckled.

"What's so funny?" Nick took another bite.

"This game is going to blow up in your face, Nick."

"What game?" Why was he even bothering?

"Oh, come on. The engagement. You think I was born yesterday?"

"What about it?" His grandfather had figured things out. He knew.

Pops gave him the side eye, followed by a nod, and a wry grin. "That's the way you want to play this, fine. You listen. You're not just pretending to be a couple. You are a couple. You confide in each other. You're supportive of each other. And then there's the sex…"

"Pops…"

His grandfather held up his hand. "You wanted an answer, you're getting it. The storm threw you two together.

You didn't have the months of going on dates like most people would have. You just fell into things. Then, you jumped right to 'commitment.' You and Jordan are a couple whether you like it or not. Which means if you aren't careful, someone is going to get hurt if it doesn't work out."

If it didn't work out. They'd just talked about this, about them, about where they were going. But his grandfather was right. It was already too late. His visceral reaction to being with her—proprietary, possessive—should have told him that.

"I don't know if I'm up for this, Pops."

His grandfather shrugged as he sipped his coffee. "Jordan is an intelligent, independent woman who is beautiful on the inside and the outside. I think you could do worse."

"I don't want to hurt her. And I could." Letting her see the darkness he lived with every day could do that. But not letting her in would hurt her too.

"It seems to me, you have a problem."

THE SECOND JORDAN arrived at school, she got word she was needed in the principal's office. Never one to be alarmed, the tone of the main office secretary got her back up. Something was off.

She dropped her bag and coat in her room, and went right to the office.

"Hey, Betty. Emily needed to see me?"

"Go right in. They're waiting for you."

"They?" Jordan didn't realize it was a group meeting.

Betty nodded and tilted her head toward the door.

When Jordan entered, Emily was sitting at the conference table with the school psychologist and Shannon, one of the social workers. Jordan immediately knew something had happened to one of her kids. "This is bad news, isn't it?"

"It's not good news." Shannon shook her head and picked up a piece of paper. "Eric Bell and his sister Lacy turned up at Cove Pediatrics yesterday looking for Nick Rinaldi. It seems Eric remembered where he worked and felt he could help them."

"They turned up? What happened?" Jordan was hearing Shannon, but the pieces weren't yet fitting together. "I'm confused. Eric wasn't in school yesterday."

Shannon nodded and continued. "Neither was Lacy. The children walked from home to the clinic when their father went out. It was almost a mile down a busy four-lane road."

"Why would they do that?"

"They wanted to tell Dr. Rinaldi that their father was beating their mother. Once Dad left their apartment yesterday morning, the kids took off. They were both examined and there were no problems, but when they caught up with Mom at her job, it was obvious she'd taken a pretty bad beating. She's being released from the hospital today. The kids have been placed with an aunt."

"Oh, my God. And their father?"

"Being arraigned this morning."

Jordan slumped back in her chair. That was why Nick was so shaken when he showed up at her door last night. After what he'd gone through in Afghanistan, she could only imagine how much this hurt him. And he'd looked to her for comfort.

That Eric sought him out said something powerful about the man. His compassion, his goodness, gave those children the confidence to trust him. Gazing at Lucy's ring on her left hand, Jordan's heart split open. Maybe it was time she did the same. Maybe this fake relationship could be real if she and Nick could find a way to push aside the past and look forward.

It had taken a while for Jordan to accept that her father was going to die. She knew when the time came, she'd be devastated, but she was no longer in denial about the progress of his disease.

In her heart, Jordan knew Nick would be there for her. He would catch her before she dropped into the dark well of grief. And for the first time since she'd broken her engagement, she wanted someone to be there for her. She wanted a man in her life and in her bed. She wanted the man to be Nick.

"Will I see Eric today?" she asked. "I'd like to know how to handle this."

Shannon, her friend, agreed. "I'll go over some strategies

while I walk back with you. I don't know if the children will be in today. I guess we will see."

ERIC HADN'T COME to school that day, which made Jordan worry, but his aunt called to explain they only had one car, and that the children would be in the rest of the week. Relieved, Jordan's attention immediately turned to the handsome doctor who was more of a hero than she'd ever imagined.

He'd been on her mind all day. So, it didn't surprise her when she found herself parked on the same block as the clinic after school had let out for the day. It probably wasn't her smartest move, but she didn't care. Jordan had to see him, to tell him she knew the story. That she knew what he'd done.

And that she wanted to kiss him senseless if he would let her.

Making the short walk to the clinic, Jordan couldn't believe how much the weather had turned this past week. It was early April, and a slew of daffodils were blooming in the gardens that lined the street. It was actually starting to feel like spring.

The clinic had been in town for years and occupied a pretty old house with a bright red front door. Upon walking inside, the walls were painted different colors, more than likely to impress the room full of young patients.

Lots and lots of young patients, some of whom were former students.

It wasn't going to deter Jordan, however. Nope. She wanted to kiss Nick and that's what she was going to do. Walking to the receptionist's desk, the dark-haired woman locked onto Jordan's face over the top of her rimless glasses.

"Can I help you?" she asked in a refined contralto voice.

"I'd like to see Dr. Rinaldi."

The woman, whose nameplate indicated she was called Elizabeth, raised an eyebrow. "I'm going to assume you're not a patient."

"That's an accurate assumption. No, I'm a teacher at the elementary school. My name is Jordan Velsor. I heard one of my students was here yesterday and I wanted to *thank* the doctor for taking good care of Eric and his sister."

"Ah. His fiancée." Elizabeth rose and nodded. "Come this way, please."

As soon as the word *fiancée* was said, Jordan's stomach lurched. It was a lie, but was it? Whatever they were to each other, there she was, jumping the line of parents and children and being directed into a small, wood paneled office. Elizabeth closed the door and Jordan breathed out for the first time since she walked into the clinic.

She examined the space and noticed the diplomas on the walls, the pictures of gorgeous seascapes, and as Jordan leaned her hip into the heavy cherry desk, she wondered what made her drive over here.

This morning, Nick had cut her off. He'd folded in on himself, refusing to share anything he was feeling. What if he did the same to her now?

Right then the door opened, and Nick walked in the room, stopping short when he almost smacked into Jordan.

"Oh. Hi," he said. Once the shock wore off, he stepped as close to her as he could without making contact.

"Hi," Jordan whispered closing the distance so their bodies just touched. "I'm sorry to bother you at work, but I... I just..."

Unable to control herself, Jordan placed her hands on his chest and stood on her toes to kiss him. "Thank you." She kissed him again. "Thank you for what you did for those children."

Taking her hands in his, Nick dropped his forehead to hers. "I'm sorry I didn't tell you, but..."

"It's okay. I understand. I had an early morning meeting and the psychologist and social worker told me what happened. Thank God you were able to help them."

"They really stepped up for their mom. I guess enough was enough."

Jordan marveled at the strength of those kids and at the compassion in the battle-hardened man standing in front of her. His warmth and his kindness penetrated deep. She could feel what he was feeling. It was intense and almost more intimate than spending the night with him.

Nick had a lot of scars from his time in Afghanistan, and they weren't all physical. Seeing how he reacted to the violence inflicted on this family told her he was wounded to his core.

"What's wrong?" Jordan asked, taking his face in her hands. "Tell me."

Shaking his head, Nick closed his eyes and drew a long breath. She watched as he crammed his feelings down, back where he kept them locked up tight.

"I'm glad they're all okay. Were the kids at school today?"

"Nick, please. You're deflecting. I can't imagine how hard yesterday was for you. Let me help."

His face drawn tight, told her the kind of strain he was under, but she never imagined he'd snap. "You're right, you can't imagine, so please don't push me." His words, clipped and final, slammed the door.

Jordan stepped back, creating the tiniest rift between them. "Push you?"

Turning his eyes away, he didn't respond, but went back to his original question. Cold and focused, he dismissed her concern. "How are the kids?"

Feeling like she'd had the wind knocked out of her, she answered. "I heard from their aunt. Lacy and Eric will be in tomorrow."

"That's good. They need to get back into their routine."

She could see he wasn't going to give her even the slightest glimpse into what was troubling him. The closeness and the intimacy had vanished, creating a tiny crack in Jordan's already fragile heart. "Are we ever going to talk about what's going on with you? I want to help if I can."

"You can't." Moving around some papers on his desk, Nick didn't look up. Once again, he'd shut her out. And it hurt.

"I should go," she said. "My father is expecting me."

"Any word on how he is?"

"The same, I'm assuming." She knew he was genuinely concerned about her father, but he was using it to change the subject. "I know you're busy. I just wanted to see how you were doing."

"I'm fine…" He folded his arms. "How are you? Really?"

Really? She wanted to cry—for him, for herself, for both of them.

"I'm fine," Jordan lied. Her stomach jittered with uneasiness and her body felt heavy. She wasn't fine. If she'd felt hopeful about their chances to make a relationship work, that hope was fading. He'd gone back inside himself.

"I'm done for the day," he said. "I can go with you to see your dad."

"You don't have to." Jordan had to put some distance between them.

"It's not a problem." He dropped a file on his desk, and picked up his jacket. "I can come back tonight and do my notes. I'm all yours."

"Nick, it's fine. I'll just go on my own." It was Jordan's turn to snap.

He froze. "I'm not following."

"Sorry," she said. "You stay here. I'm going to go see my father. I'll talk to you later." With a kiss on the cheek, she left, not giving him a chance to respond.

As she passed through the waiting room, she spied two of her students, and waved to them. The flu had been running rampant through the school, so it was no surprise to see at least a couple of kids snuggled against their parents.

Once she got outside, she exhaled, running her hand across her belly. The ache went to her core. How could he dismiss her that way? How could he reject her love?

Closing her eyes, images of him the night before, desperate and sad, filled her mind. He'd come to her for comfort, but now Nick was pushing her away, and Jordan felt the rejection as acutely as any other she'd experienced.

Vibrations from her purse had her digging out her phone, and she answered without looking. "Hello?"

"Jordan, it's Eileen. You need to come, it's almost time."

It felt like the ground dropped out from under her. "But I just saw him yesterday."

"I know. We often have no warning, but all the signs are there. You need to come."

"O…okay." The air left her chest, and Jordan struggled to stay focused on what she was being told. Her father was going to die. Probably within a few hours. Had she said enough? Done enough to help him?

"I know you weren't expecting this today," Eileen continued.

"No, ah… no, I just…" Swallowing her tears, she choked out a response. "I'll be there as quick as I can."

Jordan had thought about this day a thousand times, but never really processed what it would mean when her father died. Without any warning, she doubled over, trying to get her bearings. *Breathe*, she thought. *Just breathe*. Only when she felt a warm hand slide across her back did she inhale.

"Honey, what's wrong?" Nick grabbed her shoulders and turned her to face him. "I saw you from the window."

The words spilled out. "I just got off the phone with hospice. It's…" The words were caught in her throat.

"Okay, let me get my things, and we'll go."

She wanted to tell him he didn't have to go with her, but truthfully, she was so grateful not to be alone. "Thank you. I can't…" With a shudder and gulp, Jordan clasped her hand over her mouth. "Oh, my God, Nick. How am I going to do this? H-how am I going to stay strong for him?"

"You will because that's who you are. And I'll be there for backup."

Chapter Nineteen

ILEEN MET THEM in the hallway just outside George's room. She reached out and rubbed Jordan's shoulder. "He's still with us, but he took a bad turn a little while ago. I don't think it's going to be long."

"What happened?" she pleaded. "He was talking to me yesterday."

"Jordan, this disease is so awful. It's unpredictable."

"Is he awake, Eileen?" Nick was hoping Jordan could at least say goodbye, but often the medications to ease the pain rendered a patient unconscious.

"He's drifting in and out. He's waiting for you." Eileen pressed her hand between Jordan's shoulder blades while Nick slipped his arm around her waist. She was terrified.

"I'm not ready to say goodbye." Her voice, hoarse and choked with emotion, broke Nick's heart. "I can't."

"I'll be with you," he assured her. "I'll be right there with you. But he needs you, Jordan."

She bobbed her head quickly a few times, knowing she had to face this. Taking a deep breath, she swiped at both her eyes before entering the room. Nick watched her go to her father's bedside and sit down in the large armchair next to his bed.

The lights in the room were dim, and soft instrumental music played in the background, while the subtle scent of lavender filled the space. It was peaceful. Soothing.

Jordan reached out and took her father's hand. Examining it. From where he stood, Nick could see the mottling on George's skin, turning it shades of blue and gray. It was a matter of hours now.

Eileen's eyes were filled with tears. Nick had no idea how these hospice nurses did their jobs. Their strength and faith were astounding. It was probably the hardest job in medicine. "Can you stay with her for a minute? I have to make a call."

Eileen shook her head. "You have to stay with her. Give me a list, I'll call."

She brought him a piece of paper, and he wrote the names of the three people in Jordan's circle who would bring her the support she needed—the three "L's"—Lina, Liam and Lilly. "Liam and Lilly are probably at their shops. Nona is home by now."

"I'll take care of it. Any message?"

"No, just tell them where we are and what's happening. They know what to do."

They knew because Nick had spoken to the three of them a week ago, anticipating what Jordan might need when her father passed. She needed support from her people.

Including him.

Taking his place behind her chair, Nick placed his hands on her shoulders.

Glancing up for just a second, her gaze immediately returned to her father. "His hand is so cold." Her voice was weak, small.

"His circulation is slowing down."

She nodded. Nick figured she'd read a lot, trying to prepare herself, but now that it was happening, it was all surreal. Nick pulled her close and held her so tight, he didn't know where she ended and he began.

"Jordan?" Her father turned his head slightly.

"I'm here, Daddy." Turning to her dad, Jordan took his hand and leaned in. "Nick is here too."

"Good. I'm glad you're both here." He could barely speak, his breath rattled as he sucked in. Just a few words were sapping all his energy.

"George." Nick went to the bedside. "Don't talk. Just rest. We'll be here."

He motioned for Nick to come closer. "Just love her, son. Trust her. She'll bring you home."

Her father's words were like a knife, cutting clean to his heart. He hit Nick with the reality he'd been too scared to face. "I do love her. But I don't know if anything can bring me back."

George coughed; his breathing was labored, shallow. "Yes, she can. Her love is magic. It saved me. Trust her."

Jordan's head dipped forward as she wept quietly.

"Don't cry, baby girl. It's going to be okay. It will."

He drifted out again, his eyes closing, and Nick dropped to his knees to gather Jordan into his arms. He held her close, letting her cry and feeling his own eyes fill more than once.

He didn't know how long he held her, but he didn't let go, until Lilly charged in the room and went right to Jordan's side. Nona and Pops were next. Then Liam and his father, Edward. Each person sat with Jordan, telling her stories about her dad. Talking to George. Making her smile.

Nick, however, was staring at the man in the bed who had raised this exceptional woman who possessed his heart. She completely owned him. George was unconscious, but his spirit was in every person who'd shown up for his daughter.

Soon the room was filled with so many people he lost count. The crowd was a testament to a life well lived. No one could ask for more. Adam and Jack joined him by one of the windows. It was growing dark, and Nona had the café send over sandwiches and snacks.

"George would love this. Do you think he knows?" Adam wondered.

Nick nodded. "I think so. I think he's relieved that he's leaving her with so many good people."

"And with you," Jack added.

"Yeah. That goes without saying." He watched Jordan listen to Ed Jennings tell her how her father used Lucy's compass to woo her mother. She was smiling through her tears, laughing at the memory. Having her people around, feeling all the warmth, knowing she was never going to be alone, was exactly what Jordan needed. And for George, what a celebration of life. "I'm so gone, man. I never thought I'd fall this hard."

"I totally get that."

Mia came over and took Adam's hand. "It's late. We should go." Turning to Nick, she hugged him. "This was a wonderful thing you did, Nick. I'm so glad we could be here for her."

"Thanks, Mia."

One by one, people said goodbye and the room slowly started to empty. George was still hanging on, and by ten o'clock, only Jordan and Nick were left in the room. But this time, instead of sobs as she held her father's hand, Jordan's tears were accompanied by a smile. "So many people are going to miss you, Daddy. I heard wonderful stories about you, and could feel how much people love you." She sniffled and drew a shuddering breath. "I love you and I will miss you, but you can go be with Mommy now. It's okay. It's okay to go home."

Nick watched Jordan say goodbye to her father. Brave and sure of what she had to do, she rose onto her toes, and kissed him on the forehead. A tear dropped from Jordan's eye; it ran down George's face. He saw George's shoulders give a slight tremor, and then there was silence.

JORDAN WATCHED NICK rise from his place on the couch by the wall and approach the bed. He stood opposite her, and looking down at her father, he pressed his fingers to the side of her father's neck, checking for a pulse. He checked his wrist. Checked his breathing.

Jordan already knew her father was gone. She knew the minute he left.

Nick nodded, pressing the call button on the wall. The staff at the hospice had to make it official. When the night nurse came in, Nick came to Jordan, folding her in his arms.

The nurse did the same things Nick had just done—checked Dad's pulse, checked his breathing—but when she listened with her stethoscope, there was a slight nod.

"He's gone," she said, draping the stethoscope around her neck. Somehow hearing her say it made it more real. "I'm very sorry for your loss."

"Thank you. I..." The words stuck in Jordan's throat.

The nurse nodded as she started out of the room, but then stopped and turned back. "Your father was a remarkable man, and what I saw here tonight is exactly how I hope to go too. So much love. You have wonderful people, Jordan."

Jordan turned into Nick's chest and knew the outpouring from everyone in town was his doing. He showed her how many people were in her corner. She didn't have family in the traditional sense, but Jordan realized she had family in every way that counted.

Her people. Boy, would she like to answer Grandma Toni's question now.

Stepping away, she picked up her purse and locked eyes with Nick. "I think it's time to go."

"Do you need to make any calls?"

She shook her head. "No, they take care of calling the funeral home for me. I'll go there tomorrow morning."

He nodded. Taking her hand, they left the room, and surprisingly, Jordan didn't feel the crushing weight of loss like she thought she would. There was no doubt in her mind that grieving would be a long process, but at that moment, she understood that her father's time had come. He didn't have to suffer any more. And she was okay.

For now, she was okay.

Chapter Twenty

A WEEK AFTER her father had died, Jordan walked into the compass shop. It was the middle of a sunny Friday morning, and the weather was teasing them with glimpses of what summer would be like. It was warm with a soft wind coming off Compass Cove.

She'd spent a lot of time alone since Dad died, appreciating everyone who wanted to help, but needing the space to process what it meant. In some ways, she was on her own for the first time in her life. In other ways, she'd learned she was never going to be alone. It was confusing, and comforting.

Nick had come to her cottage last night, and they'd made love. She could still feel his large hands caressing her skin, and his strong body moving with hers. It was lazy and slow. Gentle and intimate, and Nick told her over and over that he loved her.

He loved her. And she believed him. But that morning, when she asked about his nightmare—the one that drove him from her bed, and out to the back porch—he wouldn't tell her. He wouldn't share what tore at him night after night. He was wounded, but he wouldn't tell her what was hurting him.

He was in pain, and Jordan wanted to help.

But Nick didn't trust her. And no matter how much love there was between them, that was the deal breaker. Without trust, they had nothing.

The bell tinkled overhead, bringing her back to the day just a little over a month ago that she came in here with Nick. Jordan looked around for Liam, but there was no sign of him. Unusual, since he was always in the shop.

There was so much history here. Sure, the merchandise had changed since the Jennings family first came to Compass Cove, but the family's heart was still in the shop, as well as the town. This place was an anchor to the past.

To Jordan's past in particular.

"Liam?" she called out. No answer. Wandering over to the polished wood case, she looked in at the compass that meant so much to so many people. The legend was at the root of a lot of romantic fantasies, and for a while, Jordan thought she'd found her true north with Nick.

"Jordan! What brings you here?" Turning when the booming voice traveled through the shop, Jordan was surprised to see Liam's father, Ed. Mostly retired, Ed had been a wonderful comfort to her dad, and her, over the last few months.

"Do I need a reason?"

Pulling her into a bear hug, Ed held tight. "Never. You belong here."

Once he finally released her, Jordan stepped back, resigned with what she had to do. Looking down at her left hand, she gave Lucy's ring a tug, and then held it out to Ed when it slipped off her finger. "I'd like you to put this back in the safe."

The ring sat in the palm of Ed's hand, and Jordan immediately felt its loss.

"I don't understand. It's your ring." Ed was baffled.

"I know, but I won't be needing it." She took an audible breath. "I might as well tell you, Nick and I pretended to be engaged to give my father some piece of mind. It wasn't real."

The older man tipped his head to the side, and his lips pinched together in a tight frown before heading to the glass case that doubled as the sales counter. He found a box to hold the ring, and slipped it inside, but not before examining it and snapping the clamshell shut. "I don't know what to say."

"He's a wonderful man, but there's a lot that has to go into a relationship."

"Well, best as I can see, you two are perfect for each other. That's why you were able to pull it off."

Jordan swallowed hard. "No, we're not."

With a wink and a sweet grin, Ed picked up the box and nodded toward the back room. "Give me a minute to put this away. I'll be right back. We'll talk."

Ed wasn't the only one who thought she and Nick were a

perfect match. So many people had said the same thing. At the wake, and funeral, later in the week when she was running errands in town, but there was no way to make anyone understand why they would never be a perfect match. Because in so many ways, they were.

Wandering around the shop, she plopped on a bench that was situated in the front window. From here, she could almost see the whole town. The view extended straight down Main Street toward the harbor.

If only they had told the truth from the beginning.

God, she felt foolish. Jordan should have gone with her gut and put a stop to the whole charade from the start. She did not need a man, and she certainly didn't need the entire town thinking she was weak and helpless.

Pressing her head against the cool glass of the window, Jordan shut her eyes and moaned. She'd been holding it together pretty well for the past week. Through her dad's wake, and funeral, she'd been okay. The comfort from family and friends had kept her going.

Now, she felt alone.

And betrayed.

And it hurt more than she ever imagined it could.

Pressing the heels of her hands into her eyes, Jordan willed back the tears she'd been fighting all week. She didn't cry, not in front of people, but that minute her determination was tested to its breaking point.

Nothing was like she thought. Nothing. How did this

happen?

She'd spent the last month and a half of her life living a lie.

And all at once as her heart fell to pieces, her resolve did the same. Her head, her body, ached with grief because she'd lost so much in so short a period of time.

"No. No... not now. I can't..."

Feeling her body shake from within, Jordan clenched her fists, clenched her jaw. She tightened her whole frame trying to maintain control, but it was no use.

She stood, thinking she'd get out of the shop, outrun the pain. But instead, her knees buckled and she crumbled to the floor, the antique bench being her only support.

Tears flooded from her eyes, but she couldn't speak. She was trembling, weak.

Terrified.

She heard the bell from the shop door, and within seconds someone was next to her.

"Oh, no. Jordan." It was Liam. His big hand clutched her shoulder, as he dropped to the floor and faced her. "Dad?"

"What... oh boy." Now Ed and Liam were there. Two men, staring at her, not knowing how they were supposed to react. Liam stayed close, his hand rubbing up and down her arm, behaving like a clueless big brother.

"Jordan, this was bound to happen. You've been so strong." Liam was totally out of his element. And she knew at some point she would break, but she didn't expect it to be in public, where everyone could see how much she was hurting.

When her father received the diagnosis a year and a half ago, Jordan didn't cry. She was hopeful, optimistic, and felt positivity was the best way to face any crisis. Losing her mind wouldn't do any good. Thinking about the future was pointless, because she didn't know what the future would be. It was strange, how the mind worked, how it dragged you through memories and emotions and could-have-beens. How one minute you could be fine, and the next minute you were laid out in grief.

That's what this was. Pure and simple. Her father was gone, and he wasn't coming back. All the emotions she'd been squashing came out in one massive rush. Everything she felt the day she found out her mother died swallowed her up. It was like she was dying herself. The pain was real, and it was everywhere.

Jordan remembered the day as clear as a bell. Mom was cooking dinner, realized she was out of the cheese she needed, and called out that she was going to run to the store. Her father offered to go, but he was helping Jordan with her homework and Mom said she would do it.

It was rainy, gray. But the market wasn't far. On a nice day, her mother would have walked. An hour passed, and her mom didn't come home. They didn't think too much about it. Dad said she was probably chatting with someone she met at the market. Then the phone call came and they went to the hospital.

Everything changed after that. Their family was in pieces. Her father was broken, and Jordan's world was turned upside down. The sadness that surrounded that time had drifted away and settled someplace in her mind where it was safe and couldn't bother her... until that moment.

Rage at her father's disease, sadness at his loss, anguish from her broken heart—they all swamped her at once, stealing her voice and her breath at the same time.

With her eyes focused down, she found herself examining the imperfections in the wood floor, wondering if this was the same floor that Lucy and Caleb have walked on all those years ago. If they knew that the legend of their love would push the whole town into believing in ridiculous romantic fantasies.

Ed was gone. Liam sat on the floor next to her, saying nothing, but with a reassuring hand resting on her knee. He was good people. She knew everyone in town cared about her, about her dad, about everything they'd gone through. But they didn't understand.

They couldn't.

And now she not only had to find a way to deal with her loss, but accept her own stupidity. Her broken heart was her own fault because she didn't face the truth. Because she didn't face her fear of being alone.

Talk about a hot mess.

"Can I get you anything?" Liam was sweet, and he was so confused. She had no idea what she should say. Nothing was comfortable, and as the tears streamed out of her eyes, she took cover in them, like the coward she was.

The bell jingled again, but this time sounded more urgent. That's when she heard him. "Where is she?"

Of all the people she didn't want to see, Nick was at the top of the list. Not because she was angry, but because she wasn't. She knew his arms would provide comfort. She knew he would make her feel safe, and loved. But the simple truth was Jordan didn't trust herself to stay on the course she'd just laid out.

"Oh, baby," she heard him say just before he sank to the floor behind her and pulled her against his chest. "Hold on to me. I'm not going anywhere."

He wouldn't. That much she knew, but Jordan also knew that when it came down to it, she didn't want to be an obligation. She wanted to be his partner, she wanted that more than anything. But she didn't feel like one.

There were no sobs. She didn't cry out or scream. She just sat with him. Shaking. Feeling empty and scared.

"I miss him," she whispered. "I can't believe he's gone."

"I know. I know you're hurting. Let me help."

She felt his kiss on the top of her head, so gentle and sweet. He wanted to make things better, but until they were on equal footing, that would never happen.

"I need to go home," she finally said.

"Where's your car? I'll drive you." Always the protector.

Jordan shook her head. "I walked."

Helping her stand, Nick stayed close. "I'll take you home."

"I'll be fine…"

With her hand securely in his, she knew his mind would be unchanged. "Let me take you."

She knew immediately when he noticed. His eyes locked with hers as his finger grazed over the place where her ring used to be. His question was wordless.

She was going to hurt him, and her reason wouldn't be enough for him. He wouldn't understand. In some ways, she didn't either.

NICK HAD A knot in his stomach the size of a basketball. When Ed Jennings called him at the clinic and told him about Jordan's meltdown, he surprised himself at how fast he could get someplace if he needed to.

It was just a matter of time before she crashed like she did. Her brave face wasn't going to last, and he knew how hard she'd been fighting to hang on. She'd had moments over the past few days when she'd shed tears with some of her dad's former colleagues, or with her friends, but for the most part, Jordan had been calm and composed.

Too composed.

Seeing her on the floor of the compass shop was almost a relief. Now she could begin to heal.

She was quiet on the walk to his car, and when he finally got her settled into the passenger seat, Nick could clearly see that there was no ring on her left hand. She hadn't said a word to him about it, but something told him the ring was back in the vault.

If he asked her why, Nick was sure he wouldn't like the answer.

Jordan's head was pressed to the window, her body turned away from him.

"Do you want to talk?" he asked.

"I don't know what to say. I fell apart."

"I want to help if I can."

Turning her head toward him, she nodded. "I know you do."

"Do you want to tell me about your ring?" He probably shouldn't have asked, but he wanted to know what he was up against.

"I gave it back to Ed. He'll keep it safe."

"I see."

Silence settled between them while Nick started the car and pulled away from the curb.

"That's what we agreed on. When my father died, we could stop pretending."

Slowing as he approached the one stoplight in town, Nick looked at her. "I'm not pretending. When I tell you that I love you, I mean it."

She nodded, gave him nothing more, and Nick didn't know what else he could say. Not wanting her to feel trapped in the car, he decided to back off until he got her home. Everything was on the line between them, and he couldn't help thinking their relationship was going to hell and there was nothing he could do about it.

It was a short ride to the house, and once they pulled up in front of the cottage, Jordan turned to him. "This is hard for me," she said, her voice weak and raspy. "You mean so much to me, but I can't... I can't be with you knowing there's part of you you'll never let me see."

"What the...?" His temples started to throb. "Jordan, let's talk this through. There's nothing we can't talk about."

"No? Nothing?" She shook her head in disbelief. "People are going to think I'm crazy, because you really are perfect in so many ways, but I don't need a savior, Nick. I need a partner."

"I don't understand. I've tried to help..."

"Yes, and you have. But you don't let anyone help you. What do *you* need, Nick?"

"What do I...? I don't need anything."

As soon as he said it, Nick wished he could take it back. That's what she was driving at. "That came out wrong. It's not what I meant."

"I think it's pretty accurate, though. You *don't* need anything. You don't let me in. I don't know what drives you to do what you do, to be who you are."

Nick clutched the steering wheel and looked straight ahead. He didn't know what to say, but he was going to lose her if he didn't say something. "I love you. I…"

Leaning in, Jordan kissed his cheek, her soft lips lingering for a moment against his skin. "I love you, too. But that's not always enough."

Jordan got out of the car and went into the cottage without looking back. Nick wanted to go after her, but didn't know what he would say. There was some truth in what she said. He didn't open up, especially about what happened when he was in country. He didn't think it mattered that much. Why relive it?

Nick backed out of the spot and headed down the driveway, his head spinning as her words played over and over in his mind. Other than slicing open a wound that was not really healed, he didn't know how he was going to get her to understand that she was everything to him.

He drove back to the office on autopilot, and when he walked in the back door, he nodded to Betsy, headed to his small office, and closed the door. Patients were light for the next hour until school let out, and then there would be a full load of kids and parents to be seen. Until then, he could think about what to do next.

A light rapping at the door had him groaning. "Come in."

The heavy wood door opened and Christine and

Michelle slipped into the closet-like space.

"Dude," Christine said. "We need to get you a bigger office."

He shrugged. "This is fine. What can I do for you ladies?"

Michelle pressed her hip into the desk. "It's more like what we can do for you. A bigger office is a start."

"I'm fine."

"Fine?" Michelle chuckled and waved her hand around in the windowless room. "No. Not fine."

"Nick, we want to offer you the opportunity to buy into the practice. We're obviously doing this badly." Christine had taken a seat on the opposite side of the desk. "You've been a great addition, and the families love you."

Michelle nodded. "We love you, you've made the workload much more manageable, and your experience is exactly what we're looking for."

Buy into the practice? Could they have picked a worse day? If he lost Jordan, he was ready to head west instead of staying in Compass Cove. Even the thought of being on the same coast as his parents wasn't as awful anymore. "Wow. I, ah, I don't know what to say."

"Say yes!" Michelle said. "It's a great fit, and you're happy here." She leaned in and drilled him with a stare. "You are happy here, right? And with the wedding coming…"

The knot in his stomach had moved to his chest. Settling right around his heart. "There won't be a wedding."

The sisters froze. "No wedding?" Christine's shoulders dropped, her disappointment clear. Nick knew how she felt.

"I'm confused. I've never seen two people better suited for each other than you and Jordan. What the hell?" Michelle was incredulous.

"I don't want to talk about it." Nick looked around at his desk for something, anything to busy himself. "We're not together. That's all you need to know."

The sisters glanced back and forth.

Michelle sat in the other chair and crossed her legs. "Come on, tell us. Maybe we can help."

Pressing his head to the back of his chair, a groan escaped. Why couldn't they just leave him alone? "I don't even know where to start."

"The beginning." Chris leaned forward. "Always start at the beginning."

"Aren't there patients to see?" How could he get these women out of his office?

"Jimmy is seeing them, but there were only two." Michelle wasn't letting up. The Galetsky sisters had him outmaneuvered.

"We're not getting married. I guess we... want different things."

"Different things?" Christine's eyebrows pinched. "Did you do something stupid?"

"No. No, I didn't. And I'm not talking about this. Thank you for the offer to join the practice permanently. I'll let you know in a couple of days."

"But…" Chris tried to draw him out, but he wasn't budging.

"I'm not talking about it." He growled more than spoke, but that finally seemed to do it. They both clamped their mouths shut. Christine rose, and Michelle nodded and followed her sister's lead.

Turning back, Michelle looked sad, and he got that, he was pretty upset himself. "Whatever happened, I hope it works out. And take all the time you need to decide. We're not offering the partnership to anyone else. You're the best fit."

He nodded. That was all Nick could do without losing his mind and completely giving up his man card. Jordan had him on his knees. If he let his emotions take hold, there was a good chance he wouldn't be able to breathe.

He couldn't tell her he was a coward. That he failed people. That he'd let children die. She'd hate him, and that was even worse than her walking away. Talk about a no-win situation. This was it.

Leaning back in his chair, he stared at a photograph on his wall of the beach right behind his grandparents' house. It was the beach where he first saw Jordan that night in the summer. It was where he'd seen her running. Where he'd kissed her only days before.

In just weeks, she'd become part of him. If they were truly over, he wouldn't be accepting Michelle and Christine's offer, because he was going to get the fuck out of town.

He wouldn't do that to her, he wouldn't stay. Too many people would be talking about the breakup; it would be better if it looked like he picked up and left.

Doing that would leave him shredded, but there was no other alternative.

Chapter Twenty-One

WHEN SHE WAS stressed, Jordan ran.

That's the way it had always been, and now, with her life falling apart around her, she needed it more than ever. She hadn't seen Nick since yesterday; in fact, she'd blown off everyone. She didn't pick up her phone, didn't call people back... she needed time to regroup. And she needed time to make some decisions.

She had to think about where she was going to live.

As much as she loved the Rinaldis and her little cottage, there was no way she could stay here since she and Nick were over. If they'd worked out, she could have stayed.

Now, there wasn't a chance. No one was telling her to leave. There was absolutely no pressure, but it didn't feel right. Nick was family, and family should stick together.

As she walked up from the beach, Jordan pulled out her earbuds and immediately heard barking. It was Gertie's bark. Certain she left the dog in the house, she jogged toward the cottage, to be greeted by her pup, as well as the displeased stares of her three friends. Fabulous. The inquisition was in town.

Lilly, Mia, and Fiona were sitting in the Adirondack chairs on her back porch, arms folded and staring. Cold and pissy, Jordan knew she was about to get crap from them about avoiding them for the past few days, and she was in no mood for it.

She loved her friends, but her brain was a jumbled mess, and she needed time to make sense of what she was feeling. And she didn't need help.

Gertie hopped at her legs and Jordan took a deep breath as she squatted down to scratch behind her ears. The dog loved it, but Jordan was stalling, trying to gather her thoughts before the questions hit.

She had no idea if they knew she'd broken it off with Nick. If they did, she was going to hear about it. If they didn't, she was going to have to tell them, and then she'd hear about it. Talk about a no-win scenario.

Jordan stood, and took the final steps toward the porch. Mia rose and wrapped her in a warm hug. The kindest person she knew, Mia always worried about others. "How are you doing?"

"Okay, I guess," Jordan responded as Mia held tight.

Easing away Mia's large brown eyes were full of compassion and understanding. "Yeah? Are you sure?"

Jordan nodded relieved that she wasn't going to have a confrontation.

"Really? Then what possessed you to dump Nick?" Mia's compassion turned to exasperation in nothing flat.

"Sweet Jesus." Jordan walked away from Mia only to be met by Lilly and Fiona.

"She's right," Lilly said. "What could possibly have made you do that? He loves you, Jor. And you love him. I know you do."

Lilly wasn't wrong. Jordan loved Nick so much she ached. She knew he also loved her. So how did she explain to her friends that stepping back hadn't been easy, that the decision still gutted her? "He may love me, but he doesn't need me. He doesn't trust me."

"What the hell are you babbling about?" Fiona snapped.

Jordan maneuvered around her and headed inside. She did not need this. Apparently, her friends didn't get the memo that she was capable of making her own decisions.

The back door opened into Jordan's bedroom, where she kicked off her shoes and grabbed her bathrobe. She had no intention of listening to anything they had to say. She was going to shower, and eat something, and she was going to get lost in junk TV. If they wanted to stay and be quiet, that was fine.

Of course, Lilly followed her right into the bathroom. Closing the door, her friend threw the lock, right before parking her butt on the closed toilet seat. "Talk to me."

"For Pete's sake, can't you just leave this alone?"

"Not when you're hurting. I don't believe you really want things to end this way. Tell me what's going on in your head?"

The problem with Lilly's request was that Jordan wasn't sure. Everything was a jumbled mess, from the feelings about her dad, to how she felt about Nick—nothing made sense. What she did know was that she wanted more from him. She wanted him to trust her the same way she trusted him.

If he couldn't open up when he was at his worst, or most vulnerable, how would they weather the storms that come in even the best marriages? In her mind, relationships, and marriages, were more than just two people falling in love. Falling in love was the easy part. The trust, opening the most secret part of yourself to another person, that's what marriages were based on. Nick wasn't willing to do that for her.

Lilly reached out and took her hand. "You said something about trust. I know that's a sticking point for you, but what makes Nick untrustworthy?"

"It's not that he's untrustworthy. I don't think he's going to cheat, but he doesn't trust me. He doesn't trust me, Lilly. He's hurting and he can't tell me why, and that just breaks my heart."

Jordan had cried herself silly for days, and she didn't think there were any tears left, but one managed to find its way free and track down her cheek. "We all know what happened when Nick was in Afghanistan, and I know it was horrible for him. But it haunts him. Something that happened, something he's feeling, is haunting him. And he won't tell me what it is. He won't trust me with his pain. I think… I think in his mind, it's enough to scare me off."

Lilly's eyes were focused straight ahead, she didn't blink, her face was frozen, motionless. "Wow. I never thought about it like that. Does he know that's how you feel?"

"He knows I feel shut out. I've asked him multiple times to tell me what's going on in his head. He says it's in the past, and we shouldn't dig it up."

"Okay, but did you tell him exactly what you just told me? About trust?"

"Not in those words, no."

"You know," Lilly began. "I don't have the best track record with men, so you can take what I say with a grain of salt, but it seems to me the male of the species doesn't excel at communication, and that means we are required to be direct. I'm guessing he's not wrapping his head around why you broke up with him."

"I'd spelled it out for him. How could he not know?"

Lilly laughed. "Seriously? He's a man, but I fully believe he wants to give you everything, he just doesn't know how to do it."

"I refuse to believe he's that obtuse."

Lilly shrugged. "I don't know, I wouldn't call it obtuse. My guess is, like you said, it scares him senseless. He may want to keep that part of himself buried forever. But if you don't ask him directly, tell him he has nothing to worry about from you, then he never has a chance to give you what you want."

"I don't know if I can face him again." Jordan was ready

to pack up and move, that's how badly she wanted to put distance between herself and her heartbreak. Seeing Nick again would crush her. "I'd be surprised if he even wants to talk to me."

Lilly leaned forward and dropped her hand on Jordan's knee. "I wish I had some advice for you, but I don't. All I know is the two of you are meant to be together. He loves you, Jordan. He loves you so much."

He did. He did love her. Which is what made the situation that much more tragic.

AT FOUR-THIRTY IN the morning, Nick didn't expect his parents to come clattering down the back stairs into the kitchen. But then he remembered they were flying home today. Over the past several months, he'd seen more of his folks than he had in ten years. He'd decided it wasn't a bad thing.

He'd just fixed himself a sub with Nona's leftover meatballs, topped with too much cheese, and he fully expected to get shit from his mother for eating like this in the middle of the night.

He was right.

"Nicky! What on earth are you doing?"

"Couldn't sleep."

"You're eating that? Let me…"

"Bella," his father said. "Leave him alone."

For once, his father's interference was welcome. His parents had flown home to California, only to fly back when Jordan's dad died. He was touched at how quickly they'd gotten back to town, but after a week and a half, it was time for them to go home. "I'm fine, Mom. I just want to eat this. Then I'm going back to bed."

"You're not going to sleep with that churning in your belly, you're going to have nightmares."

"That won't be anything new," he growled as he took a bite.

The room went completely still, as both his parents took seats on each side of him. His mother's head dropped to his shoulder, his father's hand settled on his back, and Nick felt their worry.

"Still having nightmares?" His mother clutched his hand.

He nodded. "Yeah. You knew about them?"

"Of course. I watched you suffer with them every time you slept. It wasn't like you ever wanted to talk about it."

He'd never allowed himself to entertain the possibility that his mother had seen his nightmares. He avoided talking about them to everyone, including Jordan, and she'd not only seen them, but felt them. "I still have a lot left to unpack, I guess."

"You guess?" His father sat back and glared.

"Dad, look..."

Throwing up his hands, his father stood and walked a

circle around the island. "I know. I'm not allowed to have an opinion because I wasn't there."

"Jesus." Nick ran his hand through his hair. All he wanted was to gorge himself in peace.

"You still haven't told him?" His mother was the one glaring now... right at his dad. "You promised me you'd tell him."

His dad waved her off, but Mom wasn't about to let this go. "Marco!"

"Tell me what?" Nick hated when people talked around him, especially when it obviously had something to do with him.

"It doesn't matter." His dad wouldn't look at him, and that was a strong break for the man who had the mettle to stare down a raging bull.

"Fine. You're not going to tell him, I will. Your father had bypass surgery the day we got word about you. I was in the hospital waiting room when I found out from the Navy what had happened."

"Bypass?" Nick felt like he'd been punched in the gut. "Why didn't anyone tell me?"

His father turned and faced him square. "Because you needed to focus on your own recovery. I could deal with you being angry with me, but not worrying. I made your mother promise not to tell you."

"Dad, I'm a doctor. I should have known!" He couldn't get his brain around his parents' thinking. Over a year.

They'd kept this from him for over a year.

"No. You're my son." His father approached and reclaimed the stool next to him. "Nothing is more important than that. I wanted you to get well. I managed okay. Your sister was around to keep me honest."

Nick ran a hand across his chest as he thought about the anger he'd been harboring against his father, all because he didn't know the truth. There was a hollow pang deep inside, and sadness—true deep sadness—because he wasn't the son he should have been.

"Are you okay now?"

"Good as new." His father's grin was sincere and solemn at the same time. "Now it's time for you, Nick. You have to deal with the scars. You can't hide from them."

"It's not the same." The guilt he felt couldn't be fixed with an operation.

"I know. But it's running your life," his mother said softly.

It was *ruining* his life.

There was a gentle rapping on the side door, letting them know the car to take his parents to the airport had arrived. For the first time in a long while, he was sorry to see them leave.

His father clasped his hand and pulled him into a great hug. "You have a good woman who loves you. Let her help. She has a heart of gold, that one. Let her in."

What had George said to him? *She'll bring you home.*

His mother clutched his face and kissed both his cheeks. "I love you, my boy. Please remember how many people love you."

Walking his parents to the door, he waved as they got into the black SUV sitting in the driveway. His mother, sweet as ever, blew him a kiss.

Once the car pulled away, Nick was left staring at the little cottage where Jordan slept. She'd saved his life, and the only way he was going to get her back was by letting her see the worst part of himself. The war had left him empty, and it was only because of her that he'd started to find his way home.

And it was only in facing his demons that he could finish the journey back.

NOTHING BEAT A chilly night near the bay. The air was clean, and now that the last bit of pneumonia was gone, taking a deep breath was even more glorious. Wrapped in a soft knitted throw, Jordan sank into the Adirondack chair, watching the moonlight make patterns on the rippling waves. She sipped her coffee, happy for the quiet.

She sure was going to miss the place, but considering how things had gone with Nick, and that she hadn't heard from him in almost a week, Jordan felt it was best for her to leave the cottage.

Lina still didn't know, and Jordan expected her landlady would tell her it was fine to stay. That her living there had nothing to do with her grandson, but that wouldn't be fair to any of the Rinaldis, especially Nick. He needed his family, and Jordan wasn't about to hijack them. Taking a long sip from the big china mug, she thought about where she might go.

There weren't a lot of places to rent in Compass Cove, which was why she'd started looking for a house. Her father had left her some money, and it was enough to buy something in town, close to her friends and her very extended family.

Liam and Ed had stopped by after her meltdown, had offered some advice and another small memento of Lucy's. The ring was going to stay safely in the vault, but instead Ed had found something equally as valuable if not more so: a bracelet, and hanging from it was a carefully crafted compass charm.

The gold ornament was detailed to look just like the compass Lucy brought to Caleb. Her new husband had made the miniature as a wedding gift, so she would always remember what brought them together. It was magic in its own way, and Jordan cherished the gift. She believed in love, and she hoped one day the kind of love she needed would find her.

It seemed no matter how many questions she asked—of others or herself—there weren't any answers. She'd sat up late with Lilly the night before, and she couldn't offer any advice or insight other than one thing: this was Nick's battle to fight. And until he faced his own demons, there wouldn't be any answers about what was holding him back.

She heard footsteps coming around the cottage and wondered who it was this time. People had been popping in and out all week to check on her. It wasn't unexpected, especially in a place like Compass Cove, where the town was like a big family. She was, however, surprised to see Nick. She heard he might be heading out west to see his parents, but apparently that wasn't the case. Her heart did a little skip when she saw him, and it started flip-flopping as he came closer and she could catch his scent on the breeze from the bay.

He turned and faced the water before sitting on the top step only a couple of feet away from her. They sat in silence for a long time, staring at the water and listening to the brand-new leaves rustle in the breeze.

"Six children died the day the clinic was attacked. Six. Including a baby who wasn't even six months old. Parents were all dead too."

She opened her mouth to speak, but he held up his hand. "Let me get through this, okay?"

"Okay," she whispered, but she joined him on the step and took his hand in hers. When Nick looked over, his eyes filled, but the tears didn't spill over.

"When I heard the shots, I looked out from the examining room, and my first instinct wasn't to help, but to run. I got the nurses and the patients out the back door, and I was about to follow when I caught sight of my side arm." He took a deep, shuddering breath. "Once they got out, I stopped, and thought probably three seconds too long before I grabbed my gun and went back in."

He paused, gazing at her for a long moment, but she didn't flinch. Squeezing his hand, she urged him to go on. "By the time I got to the waiting area, the last person was dying. A young mom, holding her child. She was bleeding out. I aimed at the shooter. We must have fired at almost the same time. I hit him in the head and he went down, spraying bullets. I'd already been hit once. I was caught twice more."

"It sounds like you did everything you could." She wanted to comfort him.

"She was still alive, the mother, clutching her dead baby, knowing that she was going to die. And she looked right in my eyes, wordlessly pleading with me to help, but I couldn't. I couldn't move. I couldn't help. All because I hesitated. I failed them all."

Nick's head fell forward, and she felt helpless. He was in such pain, all for something he didn't do. "I don't think you failed anyone. You did everything you could."

Pressing the heels of his hands into his eyes, he tried to pull himself together. "That hiccup, that fleeting thought I had to run out the back…"

"Was normal. You acted just like any other human being. Except for one thing."

"What's that?"

"You didn't run. You went back in, and kept that maniac from killing another day."

"I hesitated."

"You sacrificed yourself. You were fully prepared to die, weren't you?"

Pausing, he nodded. "Yes."

Jordan leaned her head on his shoulder. His strong shoulders that would hold the world up for the people he loved, but crumbled under his own guilt. "I'm glad you didn't," she whispered. "I don't know where I'd be without you."

"Better off." He shook his head, dismissing how much he meant to her.

"No. Not better off. How can you say that?" Jordan felt her own eyes fill. He had no idea that he'd saved her. In so many ways, he'd saved her from herself. "If I have to spend every day of my life convincing you that you're wrong, I will."

"You should run."

"No." Easing her way into his lap, she hugged him tight. "No, we'll get through it together. Whatever life throws at us, we'll get through. That's what love is all about. It means you stick together, no matter what. I love you and I believe in you."

"I won't let you down, Jordan. I promise. I will do everything I can to make you happy."

Jordan leaned in and kissed him gently on the lips. "I'm going to hold you to that, Doctor."

Nick held her close and then, to her surprise, eased her off his lap. "Hang on a second. I have to get something from the car."

Leaving her, he headed around the house, and that gave Jordan a few minutes to think about what had just happened. He'd trusted her. And for all the times he'd told her he loved her, opening his heart and laying himself out brought them closer than ever before. Jordan was relieved, because she didn't know how she would go on without him. Now, she didn't have to find out. Looking out at the water, Jordan noticed the wind had quieted and the water stilled— much like her heart. It was quiet, steady, calm.

Nick returned and handed her a gift bag.

"What did you do?" Jordan's eyes filled, while at the same time she smiled.

"Not what you think. Open it."

Jordan pulled a square black box from the gold gift bag. When she opened it, sitting on a field of red satin, was a Jennings compass. Her heart literally skipped a beat.

"Oh, my God. Oh, Nick…"

"Ed made it. It's a replica of Lucy's compass. I'm telling you, the man is an artist."

"It's perfect." Jordan turned it over in her hands, feeling the brass warm at her touch. Flipping open the protective cover, she saw the tiny sundial folded against the crystal protecting the face. Tilting it up, she watched the needle.

She had no idea if this compass was magic, but she felt like it could be, and her proof was that the needle, steady and sure, pointed north.

When she turned it over, she saw the engraving, and the message made her unshed tears track down her cheeks. Pressing her fingers to her lips, the message said all she needed to know.

Jordan, You are my true north. Always, Nick

True north.

"I want to marry you," he said. "And I don't want to do it because of a promise to your dad, or because people expect it. I want to do it for us. Selfishly, for me." His hand, warm and strong, cupped her cheek. "The other day you asked me what I needed. I need *you*, Jordan. I need you to be whole again."

As much as it sounded like a cliché, Jordan's heart grew, and it was time for her to give Nick the gift she had for him.

"Can you hold onto that thought?" Pushing herself up, Jordan handed him the compass and headed toward the back door, Gertie following on her heels.

"Wait. What is it?"

"You'll see," she said, dropping a soft kiss on his lips. "I have something for you, too."

Nick didn't know if he should hang on to just being confused, or if he should move to worry. Jordan didn't tell him to get lost, so that was a plus, but what could she possibly have to show him after he'd just proposed to her?

Whatever she went to retrieve, it didn't take her long.

In one smooth move, she sat next to him and held out a small folded towel.

"It's… it's a towel."

"There's something in there." She gave his hand a little push.

Nick carefully opened the towel and his heart leaped. In all his life, no one had given him a more valuable gift. Never had he felt so humbled. In his palm was a narrow, plastic stick. A pregnancy test. And the word in the window was clear: *pregnant.*

"Jesus." His breath caught as he thought about how everything had just turned upside down in a split second. They were going to be parents. A family. "You're having a baby? When did you find out?"

"Today. Just today. I wasn't feeling well, and the timing…" He took her hands. "Whatever happened, I wasn't going to keep this from you, but now…" Jordan sniffled, her eyes smiling through the tears. "Now all I can think about is being a family. I love you, Nick. And I want to marry you. I want us to share everything."

They reached for each other at the same time. Jordan's arms slid around his neck as he pulled her close, holding her body firmly against his. She fit. She was perfect for him, and never would he have expected when he woke up this morning that everything was going to change for them.

The nice thing about what was happening… it wasn't over. It wasn't going to end.

"I guess I should tell you about the house," he commented.

"Excuse me?" Jordan pulled back and gazed into his eyes. "What house?"

He couldn't peg the expression that slid across her face—shock, horror—but there was no turning back. "I was going to put in a bid on a house," he told her. "Two doors down from here. It's big. Five bedrooms."

Her eyes widened. "That is a big house. Lots of bedrooms."

"Yeah," he murmured into her ear. "Wanna fill them up?"

She giggled and nuzzled his neck. Nick felt her soft hair against his skin and his body knew it was home. She was his home.

"That's an excellent idea," Jordan responded. "Really excellent."

Nick knew there was one thing left to do.

Taking his phone out of his pocket, he slid his fingers over the screen and smiled at the woman who had given him his life back.

"Who are you calling?"

Nick held up his finger, putting her question on hold. "Hey, Liam, it's Nick. About Jordan's ring…" He watched her smile bloom. "We need it back."

The End

The Compass Cove series

Book 1: Then Came You

Book 2: You Send Me

Book 3: Waiting for You

Book 4: Coming soon

Available now at your favorite online retailer!

About the Author

Jeannie Moon has always been a romantic. When she's not spinning tales of her own, Jeannie works as a school librarian, thankful she has a job that allows her to immerse herself in books and call it work. Married to her high school sweetheart, Jeannie has three kids, three lovable dogs and a mischievous cat and lives in her hometown on Long Island, NY. If she's more than ten miles away from salt water for any longer than a week, she gets twitchy. Visit Jeannie's website at www.jeanniemoon.com

Thank you for reading

You Send Me

If you enjoyed this book, you can find more from all our great authors at TulePublishing.com, or from your favorite online retailer.

TULE
PUBLISHING

Made in the USA
Middletown, DE
21 December 2020

29295933R00222